BOOK 1:
Luna Le Fai &
The Witch Amulet

By Lil Black-Woods

FOR ALL THE MATRIARCHS

I will never be afraid to step into the shadows

So be it...

Follow Lil Black-Woods
on Instagram
@lilblackwoods

COVER ART BY
JULIET BRANDO AT
SLIDERULESART

CONTENTS

CHAPTER 1:
ARIELLA'S BOOKS

Luna Woods was not like anyone she knew. She did not recognise herself in others and struggled to connect with most of the kids she went to school with. Luna always felt like the odd ball. The quirky one. The outsider. The one who saw things differently from others and was drawn to the unusual – she found it captivating. Without ever really understanding why. Luna embraced her feelings of difference – '*Who wants to be a 'normal',*' she would tell herself. This – 'being a normal' - was how she described most of the people she knew, especially at school. It referred to those who Luna saw as a perfect fit for the world we live in - they wore the right clothes, had the right hair, hung out with the right people, and said the right things.

Luna had shoulder length thick, light brown, curly hair; hazel eyes; olive skin; and a heart-shaped face. She looked quite distinctive, but it was certainly not her looks that made her exceptional. She had a superpower, or so she liked to think. Luna sometimes felt like she had a sixth sense, as though she was able to see and feel things that others couldn't. Some people said she was over-imaginative, a day dreamer, and even 'away with the fairies' – the 'normals' did not accept her unique way of thinking, but that was of course fine with Luna.

Luna did her best to keep to herself, choosing her inner circle with care. Her inner circle comprised of her 'bestie' Alex. They had been best friends since nursery and did everything together; their mums had also been friends which meant Luna and Alex got to hang out a lot. Alex, like her, did not fit in with the others; it was their uniqueness that bound them together. But everything was different now.

Today was Luna's thirteenth birthday, but instead of celebrating with her bestie, she was miles away in a new town, in a new school, with new people - she didn't particularly want to get to know - listening to her maths teacher drone on. Luna did not really enjoy school. In fact, she hated it, finding every opportunity to zone out and drift off to somewhere, anywhere other than Willow Way High. Luna moved to Lindull less than a month earlier and was still finding her bearings. Lindull was a small market town in middle England: *'It may as well be in outer space'* she thought to herself. From her perspective there wasn't much to do in Lindull, compared to Leicester, where she originated from. So far, she had discovered there was a small shopping mall in the town centre, a cinema, a couple of quaint looking shops – one of which was a second-hand bookstore she intended to visit - and a semi-decent fish and chip shop.

Luna lived in a three-bedroom detached house located on Hubble Road, a quiet cul-de-sac backing onto an expanse of woodland, which her bedroom overlooked. At night when she couldn't sleep, she would get up and gaze out of the window. Staring into the darkness, into the quiet abyss of the night, somehow made her feel at peace. An escape from all the chatter that often filled her head on those sleepless nights. It was during those times that Luna remembered her mum's words: *'Without darkness, there wouldn't be light. There's nothing to be scared of. Darkness, like the light, is our friend.'* This was something her mum would tell Luna as she tucked her into bed at night. Those were precious moments she would never forget, she couldn't forget, because those memories were all she had. Luna's mum died suddenly one year before she moved to Lindull. Now it was just Luna and her dad, Neil. They lived only a few streets away from Luna's maternal grandmother, she lovingly referred to as 'nang'. When Luna was a small child, she couldn't quite say 'nan' so 'nang' it was, and 'nang' it remained. Her dad didn't have any family - his elderly mother-in-law was the closest person he had to a mum; being near to nang was a comfort to him and Luna.

Luna had been staring out of her classroom window for most of the maths lesson, when her teacher, Mr Porter, a friendly looking man with a thick jet-black beard, short black hair, and piercing blue eyes, snapped her out of the daydream. 'Are you with us today, Luna,' he joked as he approached her desk.

'Er, yes Sir, sorry,' she answered rubbing her eyes as they adjusted to the reality of the classroom.

Suddenly the bell rang; it was finally the end of the school day. She sloppily bundled up her belongings and left the classroom. As Luna exited the school grounds, she took a deep breath and sighed, relieved that it was Friday – a whole two days without school to look forward to. Her home was only a short walk from Willow Way High, but it always took her much longer than expected. Luna was usually delayed, regularly stopping to retie her shoelaces, which never stayed together, and then to adjust her school blazer which regularly bunched up uncomfortably underneath her backpack. It was at that very moment whilst entering the top of her street, mid re-adjustment of her bag and blazer, that a tall, fair-skinned boy, with ginger hair, walked towards her. 'Need some help?' he asked on approach, gesturing to her backpack.

'No. Thanks. I'm fine.' she said curtly, but suddenly realised how rude she sounded, and corrected herself: 'Thanks. I'm okay'. The boy was still standing there looking at her expectantly, waiting for her to say something else. There was a pause, then Luna asked, 'Have I seen you before? Do you live on this street?'

'No not here. I live nearby though. Just a couple of streets down. I'm Jack.'

'I'm Luna. I live down here,' she pointed towards the end of the cul-de-sac. Jack's eyes followed her finger, and he nodded knowingly.

'Yeah, I've seen you before. You overlook the woods at the back.'

'Oh. Have you been spying on me?' she laughed nervously,

genuinely thinking he might be a bit of a stalker. He paused for a moment to think about his response, conscious of her paranoid thinking.

'No, why would I do that? I saw you coming out your house when I was down here the other day.'

'Oh right. That's okay then,' she said sounding relieved. Luna felt like she had met Jack before, or maybe she had just seen him walking past her home. 'Come to think of it, I think I might've seen you before. You do seem familiar,' she confessed. Jack flashed her a big warm smile and said, 'What you doing now?'

'Going home. From school.' As she spoke, Luna looked Jack up and down, suddenly aware that he was not wearing a school uniform. 'Have you not been at school today?' she asked curiously.

'Nah. Not today.' And with that Jack walked away and left the street, shouting 'See ya later Luna!' Luna watched him disappear around the corner, shrugged, then carried on walking towards her house at the end of the cul-de-sac.

On approaching the bright red wooden door of her home, she noticed that her dad, Neil, had pinned a large banner across the bay window. It read: *Happy Birthday Luna*. As she eyed the celebratory message she flushed with excitement and quickly turned the front door handle in hope that perhaps a surprise party had been arranged. At any moment her friend Alex was going to jump out and say, 'Surprise!!' As she opened the door and walked into the hallway Luna expectantly called, 'I'm home. Dad? I'm home.' No one answered. Luna dumped her bag at the bottom of the stairs, dashed through to the back of the house and into a silent kitchen. Looking disheartened, she slumped down in the dining chair and leaned forward, positioned her elbows on the table, and rested her chin between her hands. As Luna stared into space, she felt two warm hands on her shoulders, 'You're back love. I was just outside. Didn't hear you come in.' Her dad affectionately squeezed her shoulders and said, 'Did you have a good day at school?' Luna rolled her eyes and turned to face him.

'No. I never have a good day at school. You know that.' Neil looked slightly hurt and apologetically changed the subject, 'Well it's your birthday, so I thought we could maybe go to the cinema or go for a pizza?'

'Yeah. Whatever.'

'Okay love. I'll just finish what I was doing. I won't be long.' As Neil walked away Luna became momentarily lost in self-pity. She felt a wave of disappointment wash over her and thought about how everything was different before; everything was easier, happier, and, well, perfect.

Luna stood up and walked back to the front door to leave, she thought about her brief encounter with Jack and wondered if she would see him again. He intrigued her, but she was not sure why. After heading out, Luna walked towards the exit of Hubble Road, retracing the steps Jack had taken as he disappeared onto the next street, Cedar Way. This road led to Holly Drive, then on to Main Road, which was the main route into the town centre. Luna continued in this direction and paused at a set of shops not too far from Hubble Road. There were four shops in total, which included: 'The Mermaid King' - the local fish and chip shop; 'R.J. Parkers' - a small newsagents and convenience store; 'Brenda's Bakes' - a rather quaint old-fashioned looking tea-room; and 'Ariella's Books' - a second-hand book shop. Luna tried the handle of the bookstore, but the door was locked. She peered through the glass in the door, then through the window, to see if there was anyone in the book shop. As she surveyed the shop, Luna could see shelves of books running through to the back, which formed four narrow aisles. Towards the back of the shop near an interior doorway there were several piles of haphazardly stacked books. Luna fixed her eyes on the doorway and spotted what looked like an elderly woman pacing back and forth, muttering to herself. 'How odd. Who is she talking to? I don't see anyone else.' Luna said quietly to herself, continuing to peer inquisitively into the shop.

'I knew I would see you again!' came a voice unexpectedly from behind, which startled Luna causing her to bang her head on the glass of the door, making a loud thud.

'Ouch. Did you have to scare me like that!' Luna complained swinging around to see Jack standing there grinning. His expression changed when he saw the muttering old woman march from the back of the shop. 'I think she heard you.' Jack warned.

'Oh no. Come on let's go!' Luna panicked, running away from 'Ariella's Books' back towards Holly Drive with Jack matching her speed. As they ran down Main Road and around the corner to safety, they steadied their pace, catching their breath.

'I thought she was going to tell us off.' Luna said, sounding puffed.

'What do you mean *us*? *I* wasn't doing anything. *You're* the one who nutted the glass.' Jack teased.

'It was an accident. Besides, *you* are the one who scared me!' Luna snapped back.

Jack shrugged and changed the subject, 'What were you doing at Ariella's anyway? Wouldn't have thought you'd be interested in that stuff.'

'What stuff? It's a book shop. I can read you know. I do like books.'

'Oh. For the books. Right.'

'Well what else would it be for?'

'It's not a normal book shop you know. It's never open. It's just a front.'

'A front for what?' Luna asked sceptically, furrowing her brow, thinking Jack was getting carried away with his imagination.

'She's a witch.' Jack warned, pulling a serious face.

Luna started laughing in disbelief. She shook her head and said, 'A witch. Are you scared she'll turn you into a frog.' Luna imitated a witch cackling and mimed thrusting an imaginary wand towards Jack. This did not seem to sit well with him, and he adopted a more sober tone.

'I'm serious. Everyone knows.' He paused, then leaned in closer, whispering, 'She meets other witches there. They sometimes go to the woods at the back of you and do all this weird stuff.' Luna couldn't keep a straight face despite Jack's sincerity.

'Jack. Surely you don't *really* believe it. It's probably just a nasty rumour because she's a bit batty?'

Jack looked Luna dead in the eyes. 'Next full moon. You go into those woods and have a look.'

'Now you're sounding like *you* have lost the plot.'

'You'll see. Anyway, I gotta go. See you later.' Jack turned and casually walked back the way they had both came.

'Where are you going? Okay, bye then.' Luna called back at him as he quickly disappeared out of view.

That evening Luna shared a take-away-pizza with her dad and watched some television. It was not exactly how she had envisioned spending her birthday. At 9pm Luna decided to go to bed. 'See you in the morning dad,' she said with a yawn. As Luna walked up the stairs, she thought about the conversation she'd had with Jack. The rational part of her considered it to be nothing more than a cruel rumour about a misunderstood, and probably quite eccentric, old woman. However, there was another part of her which was intrigued about Jack's claim that the owner of 'Ariella's Books' was a witch.

Luna walked into her bedroom and sat on the bed for some time thinking, looking distant, as though she was lost in a daydream. Something must have shifted in her thoughts, bringing her back into the room, as she suddenly got up, knelt next to the bed and reached underneath, blindly grasping for something. 'Aha, got it,' she triumphed, pulling out a small rectangular wooden box, emblazoned with the word 'goth'. Luna sat up on the floor with her back positioned against the side of the bed, her legs stretched out. She placed the box carefully on her legs and reached into her pocket to pull out a small padlock key and unlocked the container. The 'goth' box had belonged to her mum - it was a wooden box she had decorated when she was a young teenager, using it to keep her precious belongings in. The box had been given to Luna by her dad, Neil, when her mum died. It still contained items belonging to her inside, including: an old analogue watch, with a gold rimmed face, and brown leather straps; a few old rings - including a very ornate one encrusted with a large purple stone; a gold ring with a green stone; a heavy plain gold ring; an old rusty-looking key; and, finally, her mother's crystal pendant. The latter was Luna's favourite. Luna often took it out of the box and looked at it. When she held it and closed her eyes she felt as though her mum was in the room. Luna picked up the pendant, closed her eyes tightly, and then brought it to her lips to kiss it. She held it there for a few moments and quickly put it back in the box, firmly locking it and placing it in its original location under her bed. She put the key in the top drawer of her bedside table.

Luna looked at her bedside clock and decided she had better get ready for bed. She walked across her room to close the curtains, but as she began to draw them together, an indistinguishable babble of voices caught her attention. It sounded like it was coming from the bottom of her garden where it met with the boundary of the woodland. Luna quickly turned her light off and surreptitiously peeped out of the window to see if anyone was there. She waited for a few moments when the voices started up again; it sounded like there were quite a few people, but she could not see anyone. Luna kept on listening and watching the area at the back of her garden intently, when she caught flashes of what looked like several torches darting around the edge of the woods. Her eyes glanced up at the sky and she noticed there was a full moon now visible from a tear in the overcast sky; she gasped, remembering what Jack had told her about the woman from the book shop. Luna's eyes darted back to the bottom of her garden, where she saw more lights, as though several people were following one another along the same trail. Unexpectedly one of the torches flashed across her garden, with the beam directed toward her house, and, up to her bedroom window. Luna shot down onto the floor, her heart racing, panicking that one of them had spotted her spying. She was too scared to look up. Thoughts dashed through her head: '*What if that's the woman from the book shop? What if Jack's right and she is a witch? What if she can see me? What if...'*

Luna kept as quiet and still as she could, fearful of what she might see if she looked through her bedroom window. She remained on the floor thinking about what to do next. The light of the moon filled her room, as it became more visible from between the clouds, making it seem lighter than usual. As the voices stopped Luna wondered if it was safe to get up. She slowly lifted her head and peeped over the windowsill, glancing outside, quickly scanning her garden for any movement. All was clear. There were no lights. Just darkness. Luna sighed, pulled herself up onto her feet, quickly shutting her curtains in case the disembodied voices returned. As Luna got herself ready for bed, she reflected on what she had witnessed, wondering if there was something sinister happening in Lindull woods, or if there was a very rational, and innocent, explanation. But what Luna did not realise was that she was already part of an extraordinary and inexplicable adventure that would change her life forever.

CHAPTER 2:
NANG'S SECRET

The next morning Luna woke up early, her mind was full of questions about Lindull woods and 'Ariella's Books'. Luna laid in bed reflecting on it, wondering how she could get some answers, when her dad shouted up the stairs. 'Luna, I'm just popping to the shops, won't be long.' With a sense of urgency, she jumped out of bed and indiscriminately pulled out a top and pair of jeans from her wardrobe, she then hurriedly threw on her clothing and rushed out of her room. Her dad had just walked out of the front door when Luna came racing down the stairs shouting, 'Dad! Wait for me!' She snatched her jacket from the banister, pulled it on, and chased after her dad who was already making headway down Hubble Road.

'Dad! Wait up!' Luna bellowed. Neil stopped and turned around, surprised to see her chasing him down the road.

'Are you okay love? Something wrong?'

'No, I just fancied a walk with you,' she said casually, thinking it best not to share the real reason motivating her.

Neil looked somewhat puzzled, and smiled vaguely, 'Okay love. That would be nice. If everything *is* okay?' he looked at Luna searchingly but couldn't gauge anything from her neutral expression.

They continued to walk towards the shops on Main Road, and after a few minutes of total silence, Luna started to fire questions at her dad. 'Do you think there's something strange about the woods behind us?'

He looked at Luna frowning suspiciously, 'No. Why do you ask? Do you know something I don't?'

'I just wondered. No reason,' Luna lied, deciding it was better to keep quiet about what she had seen the night before.

Luna and her dad continued to walk together down Main Road. As they approached the row of four shops, where Luna had been the day before, she held back; her dad turned around to ask why she had slowed down, 'Are you not coming with me?' he enquired, looking puzzled.

'Yeah. I am,' she said hesitantly, pulling the hood of her jacket up over her head, and diverting her gaze towards the pavement.

'Are you okay Luna? What's with the hood up? Oh wait, don't tell me, it's cos you're a teenager' he said, delivering a bad dad joke.

His remark seemed to irritate Luna, causing her to scold him, 'Stop it. I just pulled my hood up! It's cold!' He smirked and rubbed the top of her head affectionately, causing Luna to grumble further. 'Stop! You know I hate that!' It was at that moment Luna spotted Jack across the road and started frantically waving at him.

'Who are you waving at love? her dad asked curiously, unable to make out who she had seen.

Luna turned back to face him and replied, 'Oh just Jack. He's, a friend, I guess. He lives near us. I met him yesterday.'

'That's nice. At least you've found a friend. You will have to invite him over,' Neil suggested trying to catch a glimpse of Jack, but to no avail. Her dad seemed genuinely pleased she had befriended someone – he had spent a lot of time worrying about how she was settling into Lindull, wondering if moving had been a bad idea.

'Yeah maybe. Suppose I could ask him to come round sometime,' Luna said considering his suggestion carefully.

'It's important to have friends Luna.'

'Yes,' she replied mindfully, which made her think of Alex, her bestie back in Leicester. Luna thought about how much she missed her. The last time they saw each other, before Luna moved to Lindull, they swore they would stay in touch. But it hadn't worked out like that. Luna hadn't spoken to Alex since leaving Leicester. As her thoughts continued to drift to happier times, her nostalgia came to a halt as she glimpsed the woman from the book shop. Luna watched her unlock the front door of the shop and walk in, then watched her quickly shutting and locking it behind her. The mysterious woman had long white hair tied back in a tight bun and wore a long purple woollen coat; she looked rather like her nang. This provoked a sobering thought, *'How can Jack be so mean about someone who looks like my nang. She's just a harmless old lady. Why was I even worrying. I'm so stupid.'* Then thinking aloud muttered, 'I'm so, so stupid.'

Luna pulled down her hood and followed her dad into the newsagents and waited in the confectionary aisle vaguely looking at the rows of chocolate bars. There were two people talking in the next aisle; Luna couldn't help but overhear their conversation, despite their hushed tones.

'They were at it again last night I hear. Lyn was out walking the dog when she saw them down the woods. Some strange folk living in Lindull,' the first voice said suspiciously.

'Seems to be a regular occurrence. Last month it was the same. What do they actually do in there?' the second voice sounded intrigued.

'Well, you know what people say,' the first voice replied, then quietly said, 'they're witches.' Luna couldn't believe what she was hearing, and for a second, questioned whether she had misheard the conversation. She leaned in towards the rows of chocolate bars, to listen more closely to the voices in the next aisle, eager to learn more. However, the two locals headed off to the back of the shop and their conversation drifted away. Luna decided to follow them, unfortunately her plan was interrupted by her dad.

'Okay love. I've got what I need,' her dad said walking over to her in the aisle, indicating it was time to leave.

They both exited the newsagents, and by now Luna's head was spinning from this new evidence about witches in Lindull. It not only confirmed what Jack had told her but also provided an explanation for the activity she witnessed out of her bedroom window the previous night. Although Luna's rational mind was urging her to be cautious and consider everything carefully, she couldn't help but get lost in a fantasy of witches and the possibility of magic. Luna thought she had to be brave and find out what was going on, which might involve going into the book shop, and possibly the woods – if she could find the courage of course. Luna quickly formulated a plan. 'Dad, shall we have breakfast out this morning?' she urged, sounding slightly frantic 'we could go here.' Luna pointed to the tearoom.

'If you like. I have to say it's nice you suddenly want to spend so much time with me. I...'

Her dad was abruptly cut off by Luna as she forcefully pushed him into the tearoom, commanding, 'Quickly!' Her dad fell into the tearoom but managed to steady himself, catching his fall on the table near the shop door.

He looked startled and snapped, 'Luna! Be careful. You nearly took me out!' After his initial irritation, he once again examined Luna's face for clues to help him understand what had brought about her erratic behaviour. Baffled, he asked, 'Is everything okay Luna?'

'Fine!' Luna barked, as she sat down. She then proceeded to aggressively snatch the menu from the table and pulled it up to cover her face.

'What *are* you doing? You're acting strange,' her dad said, and sat down opposite her, still wondering what had triggered her odd behaviour.

Luna temporarily pulled the menu down to show her face and asserted, 'I'm fine. I'm just hungry. Okay,' she gave him a stern look and then pulled the menu back up to hide her face again.

He shook his head, whilst taking a long sigh, and muttered under his breath, 'Teenagers.'

'Stop it. I heard that. God you're annoying.' She briefly peeped out from the menu and glared at her dad, narrowing her eyes.

Luna had strategically positioned herself, so she had a clear view out of the tearoom window, but kept the menu up to conceal her face, occasionally glancing over and darting her eyes around the space outside. Her dad had noticed her covert observations and questioned her, 'Are you looking for someone? You seem fixed on what's going on out there...' He kept talking; however, she was too engaged with her surveillance to hear him. As Luna continued to look out of the tearoom window, she spotted the woman from the bookstore leave the shop and head onto Main Road towards the town centre. As she disappeared out of view, Luna unexpectedly stood up, and without a word to her dad, quickly left the tearoom. She looked in the direction the woman had headed, until she felt it was safe to approach the book shop. Luna slowly and cautiously turned the door handle of the store – taking a chance. And to her surprise it was unlocked. She paused for a moment then walked in. As Luna moved away from the door and walked further into the shop, she was struck by that aromatic smell of books and burnt incense which lingered in the air. The scent was comforting and familiar – her mum used to regularly burn incense to 'clear the air' - although Luna was never quite sure how smoke could ever possibly cleanse the atmosphere. Luna looked at the rows of books, which all appeared to be in random order, and certainly not organised by genre. Distracted by this, her eyes scanned over the first four books on the row directly next to her – *Exploring Greece: A Traveller's Companion* by J. D Hughes; *The Adventures of Lacie Lou* by Sarah Smith; *Lose Belly Fat Quickly* by Danny Cook; and the most intriguing *The Cauldron's Calling* by Rowan Elderwood. As Luna proceeded to pull this title from the shelf, a gentle-sounding voice interrupted her, 'Do you need any help dear?' Luna looked up to see an elderly woman smiling at her.

'Er, no I'm just looking, thank you.'

The woman glanced at the book Luna was now gripping in her hand and said, 'It seems you have found what you were looking for.' She looked at Luna directly in the eyes, her expression warm and friendly. Despite her affable demeanour, Luna gulped, smiled nervously, and quickly put the title back on the shelf.

For a moment Luna did not know what to do with herself, and without really understanding why, she just stood there motionless and stared at the woman.

Unexpectedly, the door of the shop opened. Luna felt a sense of relief when she turned around to see her dad standing in the doorway. 'I didn't know where you had got to!' he fretted juggling his newspaper, two cups of take-out tea, and a small bag of pastries. 'I didn't know what you wanted, so got these,' he said, gesturing to the goods with his chin. Luna walked towards her dad and relieved him of his load by taking the cups of tea. Before leaving the shop, she glanced back, looking for the woman, but she had gone.

Luna and Neil both walked home in silence. Her dad lost in his thoughts about Luna's seemingly strange behaviour, fearing that moving had somehow pushed her over the edge, after everything she had been through. Luna, on the other hand, was caught up in the mysteries of Lindull, trying to piece together the information that had come to light in the last twenty-four hours. She had become even more intrigued by the book shop, and who this second woman was; Luna wondered if she was one of those disembodied voices she'd heard coming from the woods the night before. It wasn't just Jack who talked about witches in Lindull woods, there were now others making similar accusations.

As they approached their house, Luna's dad broke the silence. 'I was thinking, as you didn't see nang on your birthday, we could go and visit her after lunch. If you want?'

Luna was still distracted by her thoughts, 'Yeah, okay If you like,' she said sounding disinterested.

'We can stay at home if you would rather. Maybe you could see your friend, Jake was it?'

Luna scowled and corrected him, 'It's Jack. And no, it's okay. Would be nice to see nang.' As Luna uttered her grandmother's name it suddenly occurred to her that nang might be exactly who she *needed* to see. Afterall, she had lived in Lindull her whole life; she was bound to know more about 'Ariella's

Books'. Luna's expression dramatically shifted, and she became animated, beaming with enthusiasm about visiting her elderly relative, 'Yes, actually seeing nang would be awesome. Can we go now?'

Her dad stared at Luna as he unlocked the solid red wooden front door, 'I can't figure you out Luna. You're all over the place. Are you sure you're okay love?' he queried, his brow furrowing with worry.

'Yes, I'm fine. So, can we?' she asked with a sense of urgency.

'Can we what?' Luna's dad was unsure if they were still talking about the same thing, given her unpredictable behaviour over the course of the morning.

Luna was insistent, and impatiently yapped, 'go to nang's of course!'

'Yes, we can. But let's eat first.'

After lunch, Luna and Neil made their way, by foot, to nang's house. Nang lived in a large Edwardian house on Main Road and unlike Luna's house, her grandmother's had a generous front garden, enclosed by a tall black wrought iron fence which ran around the entire property. There was an impressive set of driveway gates which were usually locked shut. The main entry point was a smaller gate further along the front of the property, which hung open. On entering through the gate, a narrow path led to the detached two-story house. At either side of the front door stood stone statues of sphynx-like cats; they looked formidable, quietly observing anyone who entered. Nang's house looked like something out of a gothic horror movie, despite this, Luna found it welcoming and felt at home there. On arrival Luna sprinted towards the front door and opened it - as usual it was unlocked. She trotted down the hallway to the sitting room which was on the right-hand side of the house. 'Nang!' Luna called affectionately, throwing her arms around her grandmother, then squeezing her tightly.

'Put me down,' nang insisted laughing, 'how are you Luna? Did you have a good birthday?' she continued, looking pleased to see her granddaughter. Nang was slender, with white hair cut short, and a gentle face; she often wore quite colourful clothes, which Luna felt reflected her grandmother's liveliness.

'Yes, it was fine.' Luna replied dismissively, trying not to dwell on what had turned out to be a decidedly disappointing thirteenth birthday.

'Oh. Just fine,' nang paused, looking searchingly at Luna, then continued, 'is your dad here too?' nang asked, glancing over Luna's shoulder to see Neil's long tired face appear in the sitting room doorway. Neil had a slim build, with a fair complexion and mousy brown hair. He always looked as though he had something on his mind, and as Luna would eventually learn – he did, carrying his own personal burdens, burdens he did not like to admit to, not even to himself.

'You alright Liz? Thought we'd pop to see you. Did you get that tap sorted? I can look at it while I'm here,' he suggested. Luna's dad was a very practical man, always fixing things that were broken. He was a mechanic by trade, and had his own business back in Leicester, but since moving to Lindull he started working for a local garage. It was still early days, he thought to himself; he had plenty of time to get his business back up and running. In the meantime, he was happy to have a job and tried to keep himself as busy as possible. It was a good way to keep his mind off other things, things he never wanted to think or talk about, because they were too painful.

'Ahh yes Neil, it's still the same. Have a look if you like.' Nang gestured him towards the kitchen from her seat. Neil wandered off to examine the faulty tap, further down the hallway towards the back of the house.

'How has he been?' nang asked Luna looking serious-minded.

'Okay. I guess. He never talks about her. I want to, but he just changes the subject.' Luna looked sad and glanced at her feet as she shuffled them on the spot.

'He deals with things in his own way. As I'm sure you do.' Nang looked at Luna and smiled, knowingly. Her grandmother had an innate wisdom and always seemed to know what to say.

Luna sometimes felt as though her grandmother had some sort of extra sensory perception; when she looked deep into Luna's eyes it was as though her grandmother had climbed inside her mind and knew everything she was thinking. It could be quite disconcerting, yet at the same time, made her feel completely understood.

'Now what brings you here? Really.' Nang probed, looking into Luna's eyes.

'I wanted to ask you about, well....do you know much about 'Ariella's Books'?' Luna seemed hesitant but thought she should get straight to the point. 'The people who work there?' she continued.

Nang momentarily directed her gaze away from Luna and strummed her fingers on the table which was near to her chair; she looked uncomfortable, thinking carefully about how to address her granddaughter's question. As nang lingered in her thoughts, in through the door strutted Mau-Mau, a slender and elegant looking Siamese cat. He circled around Luna's legs, rubbing his head against her and vocalising his delight at seeing her, in that distinctively noisy way Siamese cats communicate. This was a distraction for Luna who quickly scooped him up in her arms. In response Mau-Mau purred loudly and affectionately thrust his head into Luna's chest.

'I love him. He's just the best cat ever. Sometimes I feel like I know exactly what he's thinking.' Luna said serenading Mau-Mau with kisses.

'Maybe you do know what he's thinking. You just need to listen a little more carefully,' nang said, winking.

'I wish I had a cat.' Luna said mournfully.

As Luna put Mau-Mau back on the floor, the cat trilled and skipped off out of the room.

'So...You were about to tell me about 'Ariella's Books'?' Luna reminded her grandmother, who did not seem to want to engage with this question.

'Ahh. Ariella. Why the sudden interest in her book shop?'

'Oh, so she *is* called Ariella then? That must be the owner?'

'Anything else?' nang asked uneasily.

'Well, I just think it's weird how it's rarely open. Although it was today. I've heard, well. Well…' Luna stopped mid-sentence unsure whether to go any further and share the gossip which seemed to be circulating Lindull. She looked at the floor, feeling slightly embarrassed.

'What did you hear?' nang asked her expectantly.

'That she's a…a…oh it doesn't matter.' Luna had a sobering thought, that it was better not to say anymore in case she sounded ridiculous.

'Don't believe idle gossip until you have evidence.' Nang smiled, then got up and headed towards the kitchen to see Neil. Luna could hear them talking in the background as she moved around the sitting room looking at all the different ornaments and trinkets nang had. Boredom was not possible in this house. There were so many rooms, and nooks and crannies to explore, each with their own unique feature. Luna had not spent much time at her grandmother's before moving to Lindull; they rarely visited. Her mum had a strange relationship with nang, it seemed a bit distant at times, which Luna never really understood. As she continued to examine the unusual ornate artifacts on nang's mantel piece, her dad walked in.

'Love, I need to pop out to get a few bits to sort out nang's tap. Did you want to come with me, or did you want to stay here?' he asked, sounding as though he wanted to go alone, which Luna sensed.

'I'll stay here,' she replied with a sigh. Luna felt like her dad was always busy; it was as though he was avoiding something - avoiding her, she often thought.

As Neil left the house, nang returned to the sitting room with a photo album. She sat down on the sofa and signalled to Luna to sit beside her, patting the seat next to her.

'I don't think you have seen these photos. There are some of your mum, when she was about your age. I thought you might like to see her,' nang said smiling, as she opened the album.

Luna glanced over the first page and pointed to a photo of a girl with dark brown curly hair holding a black cat. 'That's mum isn't it?' Luna asked.

'Yes, it is. And that was her cat, Obs,' nang explained.

'Obs? That's a weird name,' Luna said, scrunching her face up.

'Cats are supposed to have odd names,' nang joked and continued to turn the pages of the photo album. Most of the photos were of her mum, nang, and granddad. Luna had never met her granddad; he died when her mum was a teenager. There was always a bit of mystery surrounding him; her mum never really talked about her dad.

As they came to the end of the photo album, Luna noticed that there were several other pictures of her mum with people she did not recognise. She was curious and pointed to a picture taken in nang's sitting room. Her mum was sitting on the sofa, with a woman either side of her. They were all smiling.

'Who are those two ladies next to mum?' Luna asked inquisitively; nang looked more closely at the photo.

'The one on the right is Raven. And the one on the left...*that*, is Ariella,' nang confirmed matter-of-factly, still looking intently at the picture.

Luna looked at her nang, trying to catch her eye, shocked at this revelation.

'Ariella. Ariella? As in...'

"Ariella's Books'? Yes,' nang said quietly, then closed the photo album.

'I didn't realise you knew her. So, you're friends then?' Luna asked, sounding surprised.

'We were, but we don't really speak any more...Poor Ariella,' she said pensively and looked as though she was reminiscing.

'What happened?' Luna was curious but was equally mindful of her nang's sadness as she thought about Ariella.

'Oh, nothing for you to worry about. You don't need to know about all the family dramas today, do you. Maybe another day,' nang said hoping that Luna would stop asking questions.

'Family? Is Ariella family?' Luna asked slowly, not quite

believing what she was hearing.

'Yes. She's your great aunt. She's my baby sister,' nang revealed, sighing. Luna stared at her grandmother, her mouth hung open, trying to take in this news. Luna had so many questions, but didn't know where to start. There was something peculiar about this whole situation, and nang didn't want to discuss it. Luna knew very little about her mum's side of the family; she was unaware of any great aunts, certainly not any who had dark secrets, like being a witch and dancing around trees on a full moon – if that is what witches do of course. Her mum never really talked about her childhood; *why was that? What was she hiding? What didn't she want Luna to know?* Suddenly Luna's mind was racing with hundreds of questions. She wanted to learn more about Ariella and find out the truth about the mysterious goings on in Lindull woods.

CHAPTER 3: A FAMILY OF WITCHES.

It was Monday morning and Luna was on her way to school, not quite awake and wishing she was still curled up under her warm duvet. She had spent most of Sunday pestering her dad about family members who lived in Lindull, but he didn't appear to know very much – or at least that was the impression he gave her. Luna almost got the feeling her dad didn't want to talk about it and she concluded that it was because talking about family in Lindull, would mean he had to think about her mum. Something Neil seemed unable to deal with.

On her walk to school, Luna was still reeling from events of the last couple of days. Wondering if she really did have witches in her family, or if she was letting her imagination runaway with her. As Luna turned onto Primrose Drive, a girl who was walking in the same direction as her and wearing the same school uniform, trotted towards her. She was taller than Luna, had jet black hair tied back and dark skin. Although Luna had no idea who she was, the girl slowed down and started walking next to her, attempting to make conversation.

'You're new here, aren't you? Like, you came here this year? I don't remember you in year seven. We're in the same maths class. I'm Annie,' the girl said anticipating a friendly response. Luna gave a fake but polite smile, then offered a less enthusiastic introduction.

'I'm Luna,' she said blankly.

'How are you finding it here? Teachers are a bit strict aren't they. I hate that we've got to do our top button up. I feel like I'm choking. Mr Porter is cool though, don't you think? Although I can't figure out how his beard is so black. He must dye it...' Annie said giggling to herself. Before Luna had a chance to respond, Annie continued, 'Which form are you in? I'm in Miss Green's. She's alright, but she doesn't stop talking.'

'Really,' Luna said sarcastically, as it had become quite clear that Annie also liked to talk. Luna's sarcasm went completely over Annie's head, and she continued to waffle on.

'I don't usually walk, but my dad couldn't give me a lift today, he's helping nan out at the book shop this morning, not sure why he couldn't drop me off at school, had to walk *all* the way from the book shop, it's quite far really.' Annie barely stopped to take a breath, but it was at that very moment when she mentioned her nan at the book shop that Luna suddenly became interested in Annie and what she had to say.

'Your nan? Is that at 'Ariella's Books'?' Luna asked enthusiastically.

'Yes, my nan. It's her shop,' Annie confirmed, sounding proud of the connection.

'So, you're Ariella's granddaughter?' Luna enquired, feeling excited that this might be an opportunity for her to find out more about the strange goings on in Lindull, but equally flabbergasted that she was suddenly gaining new relatives she never even knew existed.

Before Luna had a chance to go any further with the conversation, they were through the school gates and Annie was speeding off towards her classroom, shouting behind her, 'I might see you later!'

'Yeah! For sure!' Luna called back.

Luna walked briskly to her classroom, feeling confident that she might actually have a reason to enjoy being at school today. Here was an opportunity to learn more about Ariella and her family. Why did there seem to be so many secrets, and how might she solve the mystery surrounding the witches in Lindull – if they were real of course. Her thoughts shifted to her cousin

Annie. Her cousin. Her cousin! She was amazed that she had one, she thought she was the only kid in her family, but suddenly there were more than her. But importantly, she had now learned that there was a cousin who went to the same school as her. Despite Luna's dislike of maths, today she longed for that final class of the day, knowing that Annie would be there too. She wondered if she would be able to sit next to her, so she could learn more about her mysterious family.

The day at school seemed to drag. Luna had hoped to see Annie during lunch break, but she barely had time to eat, let alone socialise. There had been some sort of drama in the school canteen at the start of lunch, as a small fight had broken out between two year nine boys. This resulted in significant disruptions in the canteen, with everyone having to wait much longer than usual to be served food. Luna sat in her English class, watching the clock on the wall, willing the minute hand to move more quickly, so she could go to her final class of the day. She counted the last remaining minutes until the bell sounded for the next period. Luna raced out of her English class in hope of getting to maths before Annie. She pushed her way through the busy corridor and up the stairs, then sprinted to her maths classroom; she was the first one there. Luna was out of breath and rested her back against the wall peering down the corridor to see if Annie was on her way. Mr Porter opened the door and beckoned Luna in, 'You're keen this afternoon. Come in,' he said encouragingly. Luna hesitated, preferring to wait for Annie, but felt compelled to accept his invitation. Luna sat in her usual place; her body strained around so she could see the classroom door. Mr Porter noticed and said, 'Are you waiting for someone?'

'Just looking for my friend Sir. Annie.'

'And here she is,' Mr Porter replied as he watched Annie saunter into the classroom.

She spotted Luna immediately and walked toward her asking, 'Sir, can I sit next to Luna?' Mr Porter nodded in agreement and started writing something on the whiteboard.

'I tried looking for you at lunch, but that fight meant I didn't get to eat for ages,' Luna said sounding irritated.

'Oh yeah, that fight. Idiots them two.'

'Do you know them? They're in year nine, aren't they?'

'Yeah. I do. Oscar and Arthur. Arthur is my brother believe it or not,' Annie said quietly, sounding embarrassed.

Luna could not believe it. Another cousin. How many people was she related to in the school.

'There was something I wanted to tell you this morning but didn't get a chance.' Luna paused, wondering how to phrase it without sounding like she was making it up, and equally concerned about what Ariella, and her family, thought about nang. She decided to be direct. 'Ariella is related to my nang, I mean nan. She's her sister. Her name is Liz. Liz Le Fai.' Luna said with some trepidation but also felt excited at sharing this news.

Annie's expression changed, and she beamed at Luna.

'Oh my…I can't believe we're related. What does that make us?' Annie squealed excitedly, but tried to hush her voice in case Mr Porter asked her to move.

'Cousins. Well second cousins, but, same thing really,' Luna said enthusiastically, joining in with Annie's excitement.

'Why haven't I met you before? I didn't even know great aunt Liz had any other relatives. So, who is Liz's…'

Luna cut her off. 'My mum. My mum was her daughter, Aggie.' Luna hesitated, then continued, 'But she died last year.' Luna's tone became sombre, and she stared out of the window. Annie wasn't sure what to say and hesitated, trying to find the right words.

'I'm sorry. I had no idea. Can't be easy,' she said compassionately but felt awkward in case she said the wrong thing.

Annie tried to shift the sudden low mood, and changed the subject, 'Do you have any brothers or sisters? I've just got Arthur, unfortunately.'

'It's just me and my dad. We only moved here about a month ago. I thought it was boring here, but I think I might have been wrong.' Luna suddenly forgot who she was talking to and was about to share her thoughts about Ariella.

'I don't know. I think it's pretty dull. Why do you think it's called Lin – dull,' Annie said mockingly, and her and Luna started laughing.

Luna paused and thoughtfully twisted one of her long curls around her finger, 'Do you think there are witches here?'

'Witches. What makes you ask that?' Annie sounded interested, but guarded, then gave Luna a probing look.

'Oh nothing. Just heard stuff about witches in the woods at the full moon,' Luna said cautiously, being very careful not to say too much to implicate Ariella. Annie went quiet, as though she was thinking carefully about what Luna had just said.

'Where did you hear that?' Annie said, her tone sounded slightly defensive, which made Luna panic she had said too much.

'Oh, I just overheard something in the shop. Probably just gossip,' Luna said quickly, hoping that would be enough to move on to something else.

'There are a lot of narrowminded people in Lindull who have nothing better to do than spread vicious rumours about people they've no understanding of! Who they don't even really know!' Annie spat with scorn as her body became rigid in her seat, seething over the rumours.

Luna looked sheepish, 'Yes, sorry. I didn't think,' she said guiltily, aware that this had somehow touched a nerve.

Annie closed her eyes and took a deep breath and said 'No. I'm sorry. It's not your fault. There are just, well, some really horrible people that have said some nasty things about my family over the years.' Annie looked sad and gazed at her desk. Luna felt awful, realising Annie must have figured out who she was talking about - she decided it was time for a reality check. How could she have been so stupid and thoughtless. Believing unfounded gossip and jumping to conclusions about an old woman who she didn't even know, who wasn't just any elderly person, but her family. Suddenly Luna had other relatives in her life, aside from her dad and nang. She had a cousin, who seemed really nice, and there were more people in her family she was still to meet. Perhaps Lindull wasn't that bad after all.

At the end of class, when Annie and Luna got up to leave, Mr Porter stopped Luna and asked her to stay behind. Annie widened her eyes, shrugged and whispered in Luna's ear, 'Wonder what you have done? See you tomorrow.'

As Annie and the remaining students left the classroom, Mr Porter walked over and closed the door behind them, then went to his desk and sat down, beckoning Luna over. He stroked his thick black beard as she approached the table. Luna felt anxious, wondering if she had done something wrong, which prompted Mr Porter to reassure her 'Why do you look so worried? You're not in trouble. I just wondered how you were getting on here. I know you haven't been in Lindull very long, and well, Mr Jackson told me about your mum.' Mr Porter looked at her, his eyes appeared soft and his expression gentle; he seemed genuine and trustworthy.

'Yeah, I'm fine. I didn't like being here at first, but actually, it's all good now.' Luna sounded quite upbeat and continued. 'I've made some friends, so yeah, I'm okay,' she reassured him.

'I noticed you're friendly with Annie?' Mr Porter said, with curiosity in his voice.

'Yeah. I really like her,' Luna confirmed, sounding even more enthusiastic.

'Good. Good. Glad everything is going well.' Mr Porter looked at her earnestly, his head tilted to one side. Luna thought how lucky she was to have such a caring teacher, one who seemed genuinely concerned about her. She thought about how everything suddenly felt so much better, so much brighter, and that maybe moving here was the best thing that had happened in a long time.

As Luna walked home from school, thinking about the last few days, she started to chuckle to herself: what on earth had she been thinking. She decided it was time for a new start, time to turn over a new leaf and forget all the silly thoughts she's had about Ariella. Luna swore to herself that she would spend time getting to know her family in Lindull and daydreamed about meeting other unknown relatives. Her train of thought was interrupted. 'Luna! Over here!' called a voice from across the road. It was Jack.

Luna was pleased to see Jack and dashed across the road to join him. She desperately wanted to tell him about what had happened since their last conversation. Luna still couldn't figure out why she felt so comfortable with Jack, and why he seemed so familiar.

'Jack you're not going to believe it. You know Ariella? Well, turns out she's related to me! Like, she's my great aunt, and my cousin, her granddaughter, goes to my school!' Luna enthused.

'No way. So does that make you a witch too,' he teased jabbing her in the ribs.

'That hurt! And no, it doesn't.' Luna sounded irritated and jabbed him back.

'So does that mean you're a Le Fai?' Jack asked sounding curious.

'No, I'm a 'Woods', but my nan's last name is Le Fai.' Luna confirmed. She wondered if her family had some kind of local celebrity status for Jack to know the Le Fais.

'So, you know my family then?' she asked.

'Yeah, well sort of, I used to be friends with some of them, but, well, not seen them for a while.'

'Oh, why? How come?'

'Dunno.' Jack paused, furrowed his brow as though he was thinking about something, and continued, 'anyway, if you're one of them...'

Luna cut Jack off and scornfully asked, 'What do you mean by one of 'them'?'

'A Le Fai. You should know about all that stuff they get up to,' he said leaning into Luna and arching his eyebrows.

Luna was caught between intrigue and irritation, then snapped, 'They're *not* witches, if that's what you mean! That's just nasty gossip from narrowminded idiots.'

'So, I'm a narrowminded idiot?! A narrowminded idiot who has seen the Le Fai witches in action!' Jack barked back.

'What do you mean? In action? Flying on their broom sticks,' Luna said sardonically, throwing her arms in the air dramatically, signalling her agitation.

'You really think I'm lying, don't you? Maybe you should come with me and see,' Jack urged.

Whilst Luna did her best to remove herself from the rumours about the Le Fais, part of her remained curious and felt an inclination to go with Jack. 'Well, I can't now. I need to go home. But, see what anyway?' Luna didn't know what to think. He sounded so sure, and sincere. Maybe there was a tiny possibility he was telling the truth.

'Okay, as long as it's not going to take too long?' Luna said resignedly.

Jack tugged her arm and headed in the direction of Ariella's book shop, but this time they went down a little cut which led to some garages at the back of the shops. Luna wondered where they were going but continued to follow Jack as he tiptoed up a flight of metal steps. At the top there was a fire door which looked like it was broken and unable to close properly. Jack slowly opened the door and guided Luna in. He put his mouth to her ear and whispered, 'Don't make a sound.'

'What the hell are we doing?' Luna said anxiously, trying to keep her voice as quiet as possible.

'Shhh.' Jack pulled her into a small walk-in cupboard, and closed the door, but left a small gap for them to see out of.

'Just listen and wait. You'll see,' Jack whispered his instructions.

Luna's heart was beating hard in her chest, her palms were clammy, and she felt on the brink of tears. Wondering what she had got herself into, her stomach sank as she thought about how perfect everything seemed an hour ago.

'Listen,' Jack quietly directed, putting his index finger against his lips to encourage her silence.

Luna could hear voices, which became more audible as they

both waited and listened. Out of the gap in the door, Luna spied Ariella, followed by a younger woman with long blonde hair, and a man with a bald head, walk into a room opposite the walk-in cupboard. They did not fully close the door behind them and continued with their conversation.

'He has been putting pressure on me again. I have told him I don't know where the amulet is!' an older voice exclaimed, sounding exasperated – Luna assumed this must be Ariella.

'Mum, what can he do? We've enough protection around us all; any hexes would bounce back on to him. He can't do anything,' the man said reassuringly.

'It'll be okay Ariella. You must stop worrying. We can't do anything but keep ourselves protected. We just have to ride it out, I guess. He'll give up when he realises, we don't have it,' the younger woman said softly.

'If he got that amulet, I really don't know what he would do. He isn't rational! The way he is, we could all be in trouble! The power he would have! Sometimes I wish it had never been brought into our family. I feel awful,' Ariella lamented, with an edge of frantic urgency in her voice.

'Have you spoken to auntie Liz?' the woman asked tentatively.

'No. You know things are difficult between us. She still blames me for...Oh it's such a mess...I'm not sure if I can forgive myself,' the old woman started to weep. Luna wondered what nang blamed Ariella for. What was it that Ariella couldn't forgive herself for. Luna's head was spinning – there was too much to take in and make sense of. It wasn't ordinary, everyday stuff thirteen year olds have to deal with – it was inexplicable and fantastical. Luna was starting to feel as though she had been propelled into a parallel universe, thrust into an alien world where nothing made any sense. Luna couldn't help but fret about everything she had heard. But there was one detail, in particular, which kept running around her head - witches, her family were witches. So, what did that make her?

CHAPTER 4: THE AMULET

Luna and Jack remained in the cupboard listening to the three voices conversing in the room opposite. Ariella was still crying, and the other two were continuing to reassure and comfort her.

'Why don't I talk to auntie Liz? This can't go on. We need to stand strong together,' the woman declared, sounding exasperated.

'It's no good. She has made up her mind,' Ariella lamented, continuing to weep.

'Mum, I'm sorry, I really have to go. Annie and Arthur are waiting for me to take them home. I'll call later. It'll be okay. I promise.'

Soon after, the man quickly exited the room. As he swiftly walked past the walk-in cupboard, he stopped dead in his tracks, as though he sensed something, then turned his head and glanced at Luna's and Jack's hiding place. For a split second the man looked as though he was going to walk back and open the cupboard, however, he was interrupted by a girl calling up, 'Dad. Come on! What are you doing up there?!' It sounded like Annie. Luna's stomach plummeted. She felt terrible, now filled with regret about betraying her new friend by spying on her grandmother, Ariella. Suddenly the voices in the room started up again.

'It has always been hard for us. People not understanding our ways. I sometimes feel persecuted!' Ariella sounded desperate, and Luna felt overwhelmed by her feelings of guilt.

'It *is* hard. But we *must* carry on. I know you don't want me to, but I'm going to talk to Liz. She needs to know how bad things are getting,' the woman asserted, but maintained her gentle tone.

'The amulet. She's the only one who knows where the amulet is now,' Ariella confirmed.

'I need to talk to her. It's for the best,' the woman sounded determined.

'Yes, yes, Suzie. You're right,' Ariella agreed resignedly, taking a loud audible sigh.

After a few minutes of silence, the two women left the room and headed down the stairs, their voices disappearing into the distance. Luna and Jack waited until they could no longer hear them talking, and crept out of the cupboard, through the fire door, and down the metal steps. As they got to the bottom of the stairs, Jack directed Luna to another cut through, which led onto a housing estate. Jack stopped and looked at Luna, silently, not knowing what to say at first.

'Are you okay?' he asked after a few moments, looking at Luna's bewildered face.

'Not really. How am I supposed to feel about it. It's not normal is it...It's like my life has been a lie,' Luna said sounding somewhat dazed.

'Maybe they just didn't want to put you in danger,' Jack said thoughtfully.

'I would rather know what's going on. Looks like my nang must be a witch. What about my mum? Was she a witch? Am I? I don't even know how it works. Are people born witches or do they choose to become them?' Luna's head started to hurt. It was all too much to take in. She felt exhausted at the weight of it all.

'I don't know. Maybe you need to ask your nang,' Jack suggested sensitively, shrugging his scrawny shoulders. But Luna stood there gazing into space. Looking despondent and lost.

'Maybe I should walk you back home?' Jack said softly.

After a few moments of standing together in silence, they

sauntered to Luna's house.

As they approached her front door, Jack held back and said, 'I'll maybe see you tomorrow, Luna. Try not to worry. Things are never as bad as they seem,' he smiled, then turned and ran back towards the end of the cul-de-sac. Luna lifted her arm to bid him goodbye, but he was already out of view. She then walked into her house and traipsed upstairs to her bedroom. Luna sat on her bed motionless and started to weep.

There was a gentle knock on the door, and a soft voice asked, 'Can I come in love?' It was her dad. He came in and quietly sat down next to her on the bed. He didn't say anything, he just put his arms around her and continued to hold her as she cried.

'I wish things were like they used to be. I wish we hadn't come here,' Luna blubbed, tears flooding her face.

'Has something happened Luna?' her dad sounded concerned.

'I...I...don't know. It's just all so confusing,' she said between sobs, sounding frustrated, but not making much sense.

'What's confusing love?' he asked softly.

'Oh, just everything.' Luna gave a vague answer, not wanting to say too much; determined not to implicate anyone. She pulled away from her dad, got off the bed and walked over to her bedroom window. Luna stared into the woods, thinking. She wondered if she should confront nang about the amulet and the family secrets. Luna wiped her eyes and took a deep breath.

'Sorry dad. I'm just feeling a bit fed up. It's nothing to worry about,' she said trying to shake off her distress and formulate a plan that would help her get some answers.

Her dad stood up and walked over to her at the window and put his arm around her. 'You're allowed to feel upset love. It's been tough for both of us. I know I'll never be like your mum, but I'm here for you,' he said kissing her on the head.

'I know. I'm okay. I'm okay now,' she replied still looking into the woods.

'Okay love,' he said lovingly. They both continued to look out of the window, staring out in silence for some time, when Neil broke the stillness, 'I really should get a fence up at the bottom

of the garden. God knows who goes through those woods.'
He tutted, rubbed Luna's back affectionately, then turned and
walked to the bedroom door. Luna thought about his words,
'God knows who goes through those woods' and decided that she
would need to explore Lindull woods if she wanted to find out
exactly who was going there, and what was really going on in the
woodland. But first she needed to confront nang.

'Dad. Wait. Is it okay if I go to see nang after tea?'

'Yes, of course. Just remember you have school tomorrow, so
don't be there too late.'

After Luna had eaten, she walked over to nang's house, ready
to ask her more questions about Ariella and the rest of the
family. As she walked through the gate, and down the path to the
front door of her grandmother's house, she heard talking inside.
Luna slowly opened the door and walked in. Standing in the
hallway she was faced with the woman she had seen earlier at
Ariella's book shop, the same person who had been with Ariella
and Annie's dad in the room upstairs.

'And here she is,' nang said smiling. The woman turned to
look at Luna; she was tall, slim with long blonde hair. She flashed
Luna a broad smile, her teeth were intensely white, emphasised
by her bright red lipstick.

'Hello,' the woman said sounding friendly.

'Hi,' Luna responded, nervously, not knowing what to do with
herself, standing awkwardly in nang's hallway.

'Your nan has just been talking about you. She was telling me
you're settling in well.' The woman elegantly tossed back her
long golden locks; Luna thought she looked quite glamorous,
like she could be in a movie.

'This is my niece, Suzie,' nang explained. Luna gave a weak
smile, and walked further along the hallway towards the
kitchen, not knowing what to say. Suzie and nang continued to
talk.

'Please think about what I've said. It's important,' Suzie said
earnestly to Luna's grandmother, before giving her aunt an

affectionate squeeze.

'I will. Now take care,' nang replied, as the two women moved towards the front door. Luna was still standing further down the hallway, and could hear them talking in hushed tones, as Suzie gave a final goodbye. Once Suzie had left, nang walked over to Luna and gave her a searching look.

'This is late for you. Is everything okay?' nang asked seriously.

'Yes. Well. No. Not really. Can we go and sit down?' Luna said uneasily, which deepened nang's concern.

'Yes, let's go into the kitchen. Would you like a drink?' nang asked gently, but her tone was laced with worry.

'Yes, okay. I don't mind,' Luna agreed quietly.

Luna and nang walked into the kitchen, saying very little to each other. The atmosphere was tense. Luna sat down at the kitchen table while nang put the kettle on.

'Would you like a hot chocolate? I've got those ones in that you like,' nang said affectionately. Her grandmother was feeling apprehensive about the nature of Luna's visit.

'Thanks. That would be nice,' Luna said politely. Both remained silent whilst nang made the drinks and brought them over to the table, sitting down opposite her granddaughter. Luna looked down into her cup, mustering the courage to speak up.

'Is everything okay Luna? You seem, upset?' nang asked, her face now showing her worry more prominently.

'I know about the family secret,' Luna replied quietly, still staring into her mug.

'What family secret dear?' nang said, her tone suddenly flat.

Luna lifted her head up to look at the elderly woman and said, coldly, 'That you, and the rest of them are witches.' Nang's expression was neutral, and her eyes locked with Luna's, both refused to look away. They were silent for some time, until Luna diverted her eyes back onto her drink.

'Your mum didn't tell you?' nang was buying time, thinking about how to deal with this. She was fully aware that her daughter had not shared this information with Luna.

'No. She didn't. But I now get why she kept away,' Luna said caustically. Nang sighed, thinking about what to say, then spoke.

'She was also a witch Luna. In the end she chose to live a very different life from the rest of us. That was her choice, and I respected it.' Nang sounded very matter-of-fact. Luna's heart started racing; she couldn't believe her mum had kept such a big secret from her. 'She never told you because she didn't want this life for you. In her own way she tried to protect you,' nang explained, sounding softer.

'Protect me from what? Well, she didn't do a very good job, did she?' Luna spat, refusing to look at her grandmother. She felt that the nang she once knew and loved was not the person sitting in front of her. Luna felt betrayed, by her grandmother and her mum.

'Witches are not all bad Luna. Like everybody else, there's good, bad, and somewhere in-between,' nang said trying to catch Luna's eye.

'Well, I don't want to be a witch. I'm *not* a witch. And I never will be.' Luna asserted, glaring down at the kitchen table.

'The truth of the matter is, whether you like it or not, you *are*. You were born that way,' nang said bluntly, refusing to accept Luna's conclusion.

Luna felt the anger twist up inside her; she looked at nang, her face contorted with contempt. 'I'm not. I will *never ever* be one,' she said angrily and glared up at her grandmother.

'You *are*, but you don't need to lead the life of a witch, if that's what you decide. You can take the path your mother wanted for you. But I do have to warn you. As much as you try to push it away, it will always come looking for you. You will always be called back to it,' nang said emphatically, staring intently into her granddaughter's eyes.

Luna felt enraged at her grandmother's bluntness and shot up out of the chair, spilling her drink all over the table. Nang remained seated and seemed unphased by her granddaughter's outburst. She looked at Luna and calmly said, 'I think we had better clean that up.'

Luna stomped over to the sink to fetch a dishcloth, her

anger polluting the air. Despite this, her grandmother remained calm and unaffected. Luna aggressively mopped up the hot chocolatey liquid from the table and then threw herself back in her seat. Folded her arms, crossed her legs, and swung her foot signalling her agitation.

'I understand how you feel. It must be confusing for you. But you have always felt you were somehow different. That you saw things differently from others, as though you had some sort of unexplainable superpower. That's your witch blood Luna,' nang paused for a moment, then continued, 'I would have rather told you myself, but it seems you learned about it from people outside of the family,' nang concluded, still looking at Luna intently – she was searching for a clue to learn how her granddaughter had discovered the truth. Luna remained silent, trying to brush away the angry and intrusive thoughts which were cascading through her mind.

'It's okay to feel angry, but it won't change anything.' Nang took a long sip from her cup of tea and continued. 'You must have lots of questions?' she posited, inviting Luna to speak. Luna stared at the table and vigorously swung her leg back and forth as she considered what to say next.

'People will hate me if they find out. I won't have any friends,' Luna said woefully.

'Maybe some people will, but they're not the sort of people you need as friends. The right people will accept you as you are. Whoever we are in life, we will always come across those who don't like us. Do you like everyone?' nang sounded softer, and her wisdom jolted Luna out of her self-pity.

'I guess…I guess you're right,' Luna said sounding less petulant.

'Now. What would you like to know?' nang again invited her granddaughter to ask questions. Luna felt calmer, and more rational. She sat silently thinking about where to start.

'Do you do magic?' Luna sounded less agitated and more curious.

'Sometimes, but only when necessary,' nang confirmed.

'What sort of magic?' she asked her grandmother, apprehensive that the answer might not be what she wanted to hear. She knew nang was a good person, but she still couldn't help thinking that being a witch involved something sinister and dangerous.

'All sorts of magic. The last spell I performed was a protection enchantment. Nothing bad about that,' her nang said reassuringly and then paused to consider what to say next. However, she was interrupted by Luna.

'Are there any bad witches in our family. Ones who do....dark magic?' Luna asked nervously.

Nang took a sharp breath in through her nostrils.

'Yes. In the past. But not for a long time.' She could see Luna's eyes widen with fear. Nang quickly jumped in to reassure her granddaughter.

'There's nothing dark about the Le Fais. Certainly not now. You really need not worry about that.'

'I can't help but worry,' Luna looked thoughtful, paused to consider, and then continued, changing the subject, 'do you think Annie knows she's, a, you know?'

'A witch?' nang said anticipating Luna's question.

'Yes, a, witch.' Luna's voice was uneasy. She looked uncomfortable and once again lowered her gaze towards the tabletop.

'I think that's a conversation for you to have with her,' nang suggested wisely.

'Nang, what can you tell me about the amulet? Is it magic?' Luna lifted her head to make eye contact, but then had a sudden fear her grandmother might wonder *how* she knew about it. However, nang's response came as a surprise.

'The amulet. Yes, it is magical.' Nang paused and looked at Luna ponderingly, 'I'm surprised you never asked me before now.'

Luna looked confused.

'Why?' Luna said uneasily, crumpling her brow.

'Because *you* have the amulet,' nang said emphatically.

'I. I, have it? I don't understand?' Luna was bemused at nang's claim.

'Yes. It was your mum's, and I believe it now belongs to you.'

Luna still looked baffled, but then, without understanding why, something deep inside of her nudged her thoughts to the crystal pendant.

'Oh. You mean, in the 'goth' box. You mean the crystal pendant?' Luna widened her eyes, showing her surprise.

'Yes. That's the amulet,' nang confirmed, smiling.

Luna stared at her grandmother, thinking about how to react, wondering how this magical object had been sitting in a little wooden box under her bed this whole time. She could not work out why or how the amulet had been in her mum's possession for all those years, and yet no one else, apart from her grandmother, knew where it was. Luna had a sudden urge to run home and examine the amulet. She felt privileged to have it amongst her belongings, and special, knowing that she was inadvertently part of a big secret. However, along with a burst of excitement, came a rush of fear - unsure of what this would mean for her given that there were people, probably other witches, desperate to obtain it.

CHAPTER 5: UNEXPECTED ENCOUNTERS

When Luna got home, she went straight to her bedroom and retrieved the 'goth' box from underneath her bed. She took the padlock key from the top drawer of her bedside table and carefully opened the container and slowly pulled out the amulet. Luna scrupulously examined every part of it, feeling a strong sense of awe and wonder about what magical properties it had. The main part of the amulet was a crystal which appeared to be about the size of a small conker. The crystal was embedded in a silver casing, which resembled half a walnut shell, and hung from a silver chain. The stone had a rough, uneven surface, and was purple and translucent. Whilst Luna liked the colour, its appearance was not particularly alluring, and Luna wondered how something so ordinary looking, could be so special, and hold such power. She held it in her hands, as she often did, and closed her eyes, wondering if now that she knew its qualities, it would somehow allow her to connect to its magic. Despite Luna's vocal rejection of the Le Fai witches and their ways, part of her was enchanted by the idea of living a magical life. Luna squeezed her eyes shut, but did not feel any different. She opened them, feeling disappointed, and placed the amulet back in the box, throwing herself down on her bed. She laid there staring at the ceiling for some time, thinking what to do next. Luna closed her eyes once more and said to herself 'Maybe this is all rubbish.

Maybe they're all mad,' she sighed, then took the amulet from the box, put it around her neck and laid back down on the bed. Luna had never worn the pendant before now, but without understanding why, she felt a sudden urge to put it on. Within a couple of minutes Luna's body felt unusually heavy, it was as though she was being pulled; her head began to whoosh, and she sat up in a panic. Luna yanked the amulet off from around her neck and threw it in the box, she was shaking and wondering what had just happened. She took a few deep breaths, then slowly took the amulet back from the box and again placed it around her neck. Almost immediately Luna felt a heavy pull on her body, the intensity of this increased, her head started to spin again. Luna held her nerve, slowly breathing to control her anxiety. She closed her eyes, willing the strange sensations to stop, then unexpectedly her body seemed to adjust, and the sensations came to a halt. Luna felt a strange jolt in her body. There was a sudden, and inexplicable feeling of connection to the Le Fais. It was as though there were invisible cords connecting her to generations of witches in her family. She felt somehow changed, like she was a different person being born into a new life. Luna's senses felt sharper, as though she had sight of everything. This amulet was hers; it was as though it told her so, communicating with her in a unique and unexpected way that is not humanly possible, and which she could not explain. Luna felt absorbed by this new supernatural insight. As she marvelled in the power she felt from the amulet, she suddenly heard a voice. This was not a voice she recognised; it sounded like multiple voices speaking at the same time in perfect synchronicity. It said, 'You are the keeper'. This was unsettling and driven by a sense of horror she ripped the amulet from around her neck, forcing it back in the box. This time she snapped the container shut; her hands were shaking so much she struggled to close the padlock. Luna grabbed the box and pushed it back under her bed as far as it would go. She then sat on the edge the bed and tried to steady her breath, and calm her mind, as surging thoughts were causing the panic to bubble up in her stomach.

'It's all in my head. It's all in my head. This isn't real. It's all in my head,' Luna thought to herself, frantically battling with her anxiety about this experience. Hearing voices was not something she wanted to entertain; it offered a glimpse of a new world, one which although enticing, was in many ways overwhelming, and potentially terrifying. It made everything feel much more real.

Luna heard a knock on the door. It was her dad. 'Are you okay? Thought you were asleep,' he asked through the wooden door, sounding tired and concerned.

'I'm fine. Just about to go to sleep,' she lied, trying her best to sound calm. This seemed to work as Neil said goodnight and went off.

Luna sat for some time on the edge of her bed, trying to quieten her mind. She remembered how her mum had always told her to be brave and embrace the unexpected. This was good advice, especially now, as she had been unexpectedly immersed in an unfathomable world. Luna was exhausted, physically and mentally, with everything that had happened over the last couple of days. She yawned and got ready to go to sleep. She then tucked herself into bed, throwing the duvet over her head in a further attempt to block out all the chatter which was now racing through her mind. She needed to get some sleep. Luna focused on her plans for the next day. First, she would see Annie at school and try to gauge what her cousin knew about the Le Fai witches, and then, she would take the amulet to nang. Luna didn't really want it near her. It frightened her; she was worried about what it would do to her. She had so many more questions, but now she needed to get some sleep. As Luna drifted off, those haunting words *'You are the keeper'* played out in her head.

The next morning Luna left for school earlier than usual; she was hoping to bump into Annie before registration. Luna lingered outside the school grounds and paced up and down near the school gates. Her behaviour must have looked unusual as it provoked a few odd looks from other pupils walking into school. Luna continued to survey the road, looking for Annie, but became mindful that it was almost time to go into school. Just as she was about to head through the school gates, Annie appeared, enthusiastically waving as she approached her. 'Luna! Luna! Wait!' Annie called, racing up to her as quickly as she could. Annie pushed whisps of her hair off her face and continued, 'I was hoping I would see you. I told my parents all about you. They said you should come over sometime, maybe one day after school? Maybe you could come for tea?' Annie sounded excited, her smile widening as she spoke.

'Oooh. Yes, that would be great,' Luna said eagerly.

'Yay! Do you want to meet me at break? We could meet near the science block. Don't get as many annoying people there,' Annie suggested. Luna laughed and nodded in agreement, understanding exactly what her cousin meant by 'annoying people'.

'Too many 'normals' everywhere.' Luna said dryly, then giggled.

'Hah! Yes, exactly! 'Normals' Ha! I like that,' Annie said giving a satisfied smile.

Annie and Luna walked into school together, and parted ways as they headed to their classrooms.

At break time Luna made her way to the science block and waited for Annie. There seemed to be a few other people there, milling around in small groups, mostly chatting; some looked awkward and not fitting with the other kids at her school. She thought they were probably a lot like her, and Annie for that matter.

'Luna, sorry, just had to run across from the art block,' Annie said puffing, sounding out of breath.

'It's okay, I was just people watching,' Luna said, spotting Annie's brother across the way, talking to two other boys she did not recognise. She was surprised he was still at school after the commotion in the canteen the previous day. In her last school that would have definitely led to a suspension, if not an exclusion. 'Annie, that's Arthur, isn't it? I wanted to ask yesterday, but, well…what was that fight about?' Luna asked gesturing towards Annie's brother.

'Oh, dunno. Probably someone they've both got a crush on,' Annie said, then pretended to stick her fingers down her throat, emphasising how this situation felt pretty disgusting to her - this made Luna chortle to herself.

'He doesn't get on with Oscar. My parents know his dad. They don't like him, either. Not sure what it's all about, but, well, the Blackthorns and the Le Fais don't get on,' Annie said shrugging, genuinely unaware of what was underlying the conflict.

Luna couldn't help but wonder if it was something to do with the Le Fais being witches. Perhaps Oscar's dad was one of those 'narrowminded people' Annie had scolded her about the day before.

'I like Oscar. He has always been nice to me,' Annie confessed.

'Did he used to be friends with your brother?'

'Not really, but they've never had a fight before,' Annie said starting to sound bored at the direction of the conversation. Luna could see Annie was losing interest so tentatively changed the subject onto the other matters she was intent on asking her about.

'Annie. We're cousins, right?' Luna said slowly, sounding uneasy.

'I believe so,' she replied smiling, pulling out a packet of crisps from her bag.

'So. I'm, er, guessing you know about the er, you know?' Luna widened her eyes and looked directly at Annie searchingly.

'Errr, know what?' Annie looked confused, then opened her packet of crisps and offered Luna one.

'No thanks,' Luna shook her head, and continued answering Annie's query, 'You know? About the Le Fais?' Luna felt she might be treading on thin ice, and could easily say the wrong thing, putting her new friendship in serious jeopardy. She really liked Annie, and didn't want to ruin anything.

'You have lost me,' Annie admitted, looking blankly at Luna.

'I know my nan's a witch, and that's fine. I'm not saying it in a horrible way, she tells me I'm a witch, not sure how I feel about that, but yeah, anyway, that's what I meant.' Luna spoke at such a fast pace, even Annie took a few moments to process it.

'Oohhh.' Annie paused, stopped eating her crisps and shifted her eyes around thinking what to say next.

'Well, yesterday I thought you were being stuffy about it, but then realised no one must have told you. Well, no one in the family. I guessed you'd just heard it from others. I did mention it to dad, and he thought you maybe didn't know. I found it a bit weird cos would have thought your mum would have told you. Sorry to bring her up, but...'

'No, she never told me anything. Nang thinks she was trying to protect me. Said she didn't want to be a witch or something,' Luna said pensively, trying to make sense of it herself.

'Really. Didn't want to be a witch? God, can't imagine that. I wish I was.' Annie said sorrowfully.

'But you are, aren't you? Your dad is a Le Fai? You're a Le Fai?' Luna asked sounding puzzled.

'Well, not exactly. Not like you,' Annie hung her head down and looked sad. Luna didn't know what to say at first and felt as though she had perhaps started a conversation that she might regret.

'Annie. What do you mean?' Luna said gently.

'Well...I'm adopted. I'm a Le Fai, but not biologically,' Annie explained lifting her head to meet Luna's eyes. Luna felt guilty, worried she had upset Annie.

'Sorry. I had no idea. But you were brought up as a witch, so that really makes you more of a witch than me,' Luna said trying to reassure Annie and lift her mood.

'Apparently it doesn't work like that. But I love my family, and I'm proud to be a Le Fai,' Annie suddenly sounded more positive and cheerier. In that moment, Luna felt like her and Annie would be good friends, great friends in fact. She thought about how much she hated leaving Leicester and especially Alex, but that all seemed like a hundred years ago. Things were really starting to feel different; she had found a friend who truly understood her.

'I'm so glad we're cousins. I couldn't ask for a better one,' Luna said beaming and hugged Annie, who blushed, but seemed happy with Luna's friendly declaration.

'Me too. Can't believe we've never met before now. Well, it doesn't matter, we know each other now,' Annie said, sounding delighted.

After school had finished, Luna waited for Annie near the main entrance; they had arranged to meet each other there earlier that day. As Luna waited, she saw Mr Porter, her math's teacher, talking to Oscar Blackthorn, the year nine boy who had been fighting with Arthur the previous day. Although Luna could not hear what the conversation was about, from observing their body language she could tell that they were having some sort of minor disagreement. Mr Porter turned and made eye contact with Luna. As their eyes met Luna looked away feeling embarrassed about being caught watching the interaction between him and Oscar. When Luna turned back, they had both disappeared. She wondered what it was about. It seemed Oscar was on everybody's radar for one reason or another.

'Luna. You okay?' Annie noticed she seemed distracted.

'Yeah, I just saw Oscar and Mr Porter. It looked like they were arguing,' Luna said looking thoughtful.

'Oh, really. Probably been causing trouble again,' Annie suggested, shaking her head patronisingly, sounding like a disappointed teacher or parent.

'Maybe. It was weird, seemed sort of private,' Luna said suspiciously. Annie suddenly looked past Luna. She could see her brother, Arthur, approaching. He was tall, slim, with very short black hair and dark skin.

'Why not ask Arthur. He might know,' Annie said looking directly at her brother as he continued to walk towards her.

'Ask me what?' he said bluntly. Luna spun around to see Arthur looking her up and down as though he was trying to figure out if she was trustworthy.

'About your best mate Oscar,' Annie said sarcastically, 'Luna said he was arguing with Mr Porter.' Arthur just looked blankly at Annie and Luna and seemed irritated at being asked.

'How would I know? But, just keep away from Oscar. He's not the sort of person either of you should be around. He's trouble.' Arthur sounded serious, and flashed Luna and Annie a stern look.

'Trouble. Says you! *You*, who had a fight with him,' Annie said haughtily, glaring at Arthur.

'I'm serious Annie. He's, well, dangerous.' Arthur's voice dropped off at the end of the sentence as though he regretted using the word 'dangerous'. Annie couldn't help herself and started laughing at her brother's description of Oscar. Arthur stared at his sister until she stopped mocking him. As the three of them stood by the school gates, a black Land Rover, with blacked out back windows, and a number plate which read: TODD13, pulled up near to them. As they watched the driver lower his window, Oscar pushed passed them and jumped into the passenger's side. Luna couldn't help stare at the driver; he was dressed in a black pullover, had short dark brown hair and was clean shaven. There was a visible tattoo of a large spider on his neck, which to some, might look intimidating, however, Luna found it curious, and familiar. It reminded her of her mum, who had a similar tattoo on her leg, she thought this was a strange coincidence. For a moment, she pondered on this, but suddenly the driver turned his head to look out of the window. He caught Luna staring at him and glared back, but rather than turn away Luna felt herself being pulled into his eyes, which were like dark and sinister enigmatic pools. As she continued to stare, she felt the same overwhelming sensations which ran through her body the first time she tried on the amulet. This time, it felt like it would not be a passing thing, and as though something was suffocating her. The longer she locked eyes with him the worse those feelings got, her head started to spin, and she began seeing black spots in front of her eyes.

'Luna? Luna? What's wrong?!' Annie shrieked as Luna started to collapse, her eyes rolling in her head. As her falling body made contact with Annie's, Luna started to come around and steadied her fall by anchoring herself onto her cousin's arm.

'What happened?' Luna sounded dazed and confused.

'One minute you were looking over at the car,' Annie said frantically gesturing to the Land Rover, 'and the next you were falling on me. I think you passed out. You, okay? Should I get my dad to come from the shop to take you home?' Annie genuinely sounded concerned about her cousin. As Annie tended to Luna, the Land Rover sped off.

'I told you he was trouble. Him and his family. Keep away from the Blackthorns,' Arthur instructed sternly, then swaggered off, leaving Luna and Annie trying to make sense of it all. Luna could not understand why she had collapsed. She wondered if it was an after effect from the amulet. Luna thought it might be time to see her grandmother again and get some answers about everything that had been happening to her.

CHAPTER 6: LUNA AND THE FLYING GIRL

It had been a couple of weeks and Luna had not yet visited nang, despite her plans to return the amulet and quiz her grandmother. The magical object was still tucked away underneath her bed, locked in the 'goth' box. Luna decided it would be better to wait before doing anything. The truth was, Luna was still in a state of denial about the strange experiences she had with the amulet, and her mysterious encounter with the driver of the Land Rover outside Willow Way High. Luna believed the driver to be Oscar's dad – there was a striking resemblance between them. Everything had made her feel uneasy and understandably confused. Luna had gone from being a regular girl, to a witch – an identity she was still uncertain about.

Today Luna had arranged to go to Annie's after school. It was the first time she would be meeting Annie's family. Her family in fact – Luna still couldn't get her head around this. The new and unexpected relationships in her life were both a comfort and a distraction for her, taking her away from the other dramatic events which had unravelled in the last few weeks. Luna had managed to temporarily bury it, blocking it out as much as possible. She was trying her best to get on with her life like any other thirteen year old should. Annie and Luna had become inseparable at school, spending their breaks together outside the science block, feeling like a powerful duo who stood out from the rest, calling themselves the 'anti-normals'. In this time Luna had forgotten all the upheaval of leaving her old life behind in Leicester. Her dad, Neil, had noticed how much more positive and happier Luna was, which made him feel at ease about his decision to move to Lindull. In some ways things were starting to feel perfect again, and Luna was grateful.

Luna walked down Hubble Road on her way to school and smiled to herself, thinking about her plans with Annie that afternoon. As she continued to ponder her newfound friendship, Luna suddenly thought about Jack, realising she hadn't seen him for a while. Luna wondered if he was okay, and when she would next see him. As those thoughts lingered in her head, she became aware of a presence behind her, and without really understanding why, she knew exactly who it was.

'Jack?' Luna said slowly, second-guessing her intuition.

'Luna. You okay?' Jack said putting his hand on her shoulder. Luna turned to see him smiling.

'You not at school again?' Luna asked, noticing that he didn't have a school uniform on.

He simply shrugged and said, 'Not today.' Luna screwed up her face and shook her head, puzzled, but did not dwell on it. Jack continued to walk next to her down Hubble Road.

'I'm going to my friend's, Annie's, today.' Luna beamed, pleased to be sharing news with Jack.

'I see. That's good then.' Jack paused and continued, 'I wondered if you were okay, after, you know, what we heard at the book shop. Hope you aren't too upset by it all,' Jack said softly. Luna lifted her head and sniffed haughtily.

'I'm fine. I'm trying not to think about it right now. Just getting on with my life,' Luna said sounding irritated at being reminded.

'Fair enough. But, well, it doesn't matter to me if you *are* a witch,' Jack said earnestly. Despite the sincerity in his voice, it seemed to intensify Luna's irritation.

'Stop it Jack. Let's talk about something else,' Luna said firmly, bringing their conversation to a halt.

'Enjoy school! I'm off. See you later Luna.' And with that, Jack sped off and disappeared into the distance.

Luna could not figure him out. She wondered why he was always rushing about. *'Where is he going? Not school? Home maybe?'* Luna quickly dismissed her speculation and continued to walk towards Willow Way High, thinking again about her plans with Annie.

At lunch time Luna and Annie met outside the school canteen and went in together. As they queued up in line for their food, and chatted about their day so far, a blonde girl pushed her way in front of them. Luna found this rude and challenged the girl.

'Excuse me!' Luna snapped. The girl turned around and flashed a smug smile at Luna and Annie, before turning away again.

'How rude,' Luna said firmly, unable to stop her retort. The girl turned back around, and this time she didn't look smug, she looked angry.

'Who do you think you are? Little girl!' the irritated pupil said disdainfully, looking Luna up and down. This infuriated Luna, who felt a sudden burst of rage, which continued to bubble up inside her.

'Little girl!? Don't call me a little girl!' Luna blasted, and then without thinking she went to push the girl, while Annie watched on, transfixed, and taken aback by the speed of the altercation. As Luna made contact, the girl quickly retaliated and gave Luna a hard shove, causing her to stumble into Annie, who lost her footing and fell over. Luna felt another surge of anger, her heart was beating out of her chest, but this time, everything around her appeared to change pace and play out in slow motion. As Luna watched on, and without even touching her, the girl appeared to lift into the air, fly across the canteen, then descend and crash into a table on the other side of the food hall. As the girl landed on the floor, time seemed to speed up and revert to a normal pace. Luna stood there shaking unable to comprehend what she had just witnessed. Annie was still on the ground but now sitting up staring on. Everyone in the canteen was quiet, unable to comprehend what had just happened. Luna muttered, 'I didn't even touch her. I didn't even touch her.'

Mrs Clarke, one of the teachers on lunch duty, ran over to see if the girl, who was now sitting up on the floor looking dazed, was okay – apart from being in shock, she was surprisingly uninjured. Luna stood there staring at the chaos in front of her, frozen and muted, trying to make sense of it all, when she heard Mr Porter's voice, he sounded calm, but assertive, 'Come with me Luna.' Luna exited the canteen with her maths teacher, who led her away. Mr Porter was head of sixth form and had the luxury of his own office. He was almost always on lunch duty, and Luna had seen him take other students in that direction when they had caused some sort of disruption. She never thought that this would be her one day. On entering his office, Mr Porter quietly walked over to his black leather chair and sat down, then silently pointed to the seat on the opposite side of his desk, signalling Luna to take a seat. He never uttered a word. He simply sat there and looked at Luna, his face expressionless. He didn't look angry. He didn't look upset, or disappointed. He just looked blank.

'Would you like to tell me what happened in there Luna?' Mr Porter asked maintaining his composed demeanour.

'I don't know, Sir…One minute she pushed me, and the next…I don't know…she just…I don't know.' Luna was so confused by what had just happened she was unable to offer any explanation to her teacher.

Mr Porter took a sharp breath in through his nostrils and stroked his beard thoughtfully. He leaned back, still looking at Luna, gently swivelling in his chair. This silent treatment made her feel uneasy. She didn't know where this was going.

'I believe you Luna,' Mr Porter said gently and sincerely. His expression changed, and he titled his head to the side, looking at her with soft eyes, appearing empathetic. Luna looked at him, relieved, but unsure why he was being so understanding after what had happened.

'I want you to promise me to keep that temper of yours under wraps,' he paused for a moment and continued to look at her in a way that made her feel safe and understood. 'Now, move along. I'll see you in maths this afternoon.' Mr Porter said dismissively, gesturing her towards the door. Luna reluctantly stood up and stared at him furrowing her brow. 'You look confused Luna. You can go. I'll see you this afternoon.'

Luna quickly walked toward the exit, fearful that he might change his mind. She momentarily paused at the door, wondering why Mr Porter had been so incredibly lenient. She turned and looked searchingly at his face for clues, but once again he was expressionless. Luna then opened the door and exited, shutting it as quietly as possible so as not to draw attention to herself. As Luna walked away, she looked down at the floor avoiding eye contact with any passing students and headed out of the building toward her next class.

During the next hour Luna sat quietly in her class, making every effort not to arouse any attention. She could feel eyes fixed on her from around the room and was aware of audible whispers which uttered her name. The incident at lunch was not any ordinary fall out between two students, it was unfathomable. Luna replayed events repeatedly in her mind, dissecting every moment to try to find a rational explanation. Not only was she filled with regret but was completely flummoxed by how the incident had unravelled. Luna considered all the possibilities of how her perception of time had momentarily changed, enabling her to see everything in slow motion. She could not find any logical explanation. Then she thought about how the girl appeared to fly across the entire stretch of the canteen, without Luna making physical contact. After running this over in her mind several times, she reasoned that she must have blocked out pushing her, she must be mistaken. But even if Luna had pushed her, how did she muster enough strength to force the girl's body to shift across such a distance. Again, Luna didn't have a rational explanation. She then thought about how Mr Porter dealt with her in his office. There was no punishment, no retribution, just:

'I believe you.' Surely, there had been a mistake. Maybe the head teacher would walk in the room at any moment and remove her from the class and send her home. None of it seemed possible. None of it could be rationalised.

At the end of her English lesson, Luna waited for the rest of the students to leave before she skulked out of the classroom, her head down, once again avoiding any kind of eye contact. She made her way over to the science block, where her maths lesson took place. As Luna walked over, she wondered what Annie would think of her. Her heart sank, fearing that her behaviour would cause her cousin to think she was a horrible person, a person she no longer wanted to associate with. Luna walked into the classroom and quickly jumped into her usual seat, and fixed her eyes on the desk, continuing to look away from everyone. As she sat there, staring at her exercise book, she heard a warm and familiar voice talking in hushed tones.

'What happened? Are you okay? I saw you disappear with Mr Porter. I didn't expect to see you here,' Annie said, making every effort to keep her voice low so no one else could hear her apart from Luna.

'Luna? Are you okay?' Annie asked her again, sounding concerned about her cousin. It was clear that there was not any animosity or disappointment in Annie's voice.

'I'm okay. I...I'm sorry for what happened. I...I don't know how it all happened,' Luna said sounding a little dazed and upset.

'I can tell you what happened. You were awesome! Emily is horrible! She's in year ten and goes round like she owns the place. Loads of people are scared of her. Not anymore. Think you might be the Willow Way High hero,' Annie said, still speaking in hushed tones, but sounding increasingly animated.

'I don't think I am. It wasn't the right thing to do. I should've... I should've walked away,' Luna said sorrowfully, indicating her regret.

'None of us know how you did it. She literally went flying. It was awesome!' the volume of Annie's voice increased, which caught the attention of Mr Porter. He made a 'Uhhum', signal for her to quieten down.

'No. It wasn't awesome at all. I don't even know how it happened. One minute she was there and the next, she was…on the floor,' Luna lamented, her voice trailed off. Annie started to recognise how upset Luna was and decided to stop revelling in the incident.

'What happened with Mr Porter?' Annie asked, trying her best to steady the excitement in her voice, and sound a little more understanding.

'Nothing,' Luna said flatly.

'Nothing? Like no detention or anything.' Annie sounded surprised.

'Nothing. Nothing at all. He said I could go. It was…weird. I can't get my head round it.' Both girls looked at Mr Porter in puzzlement as he got ready to talk to the class.

'We can talk later. But, honestly, I know you don't see it this way, but no one holds it against you. We're all just, well, amazed,' Annie said reassuringly, looking at Luna directly in the eye emphasising her sincerity.

It was the end of class, and Luna and Annie got up to leave. Luna started to feel more positive but still felt guilty about what had happened to Emily. She wondered if she should check to see if she was alright, and apologise, but when she suggested this to Annie she was cut off with a firm 'No way!'

As Luna went to exit the classroom, Mr Porter gently tapped her arm to get her attention and asked her to stay behind. She thought, *'This is it. I knew I wouldn't get off lightly. Probably going to give me detention or tell me to see the head.'* He looked at Luna and Annie and said, 'It won't take long.' Annie nodded and waited outside, a little further down the corridor. Mr Porter waited for the last couple of students to leave the room and lightly closed the classroom door. He remained standing near to the exit, opposite Luna.

'I wanted to talk to you about what happened at lunch time. I realise this must all be very confusing for you. It's important not to overthink it. Put it out of your head. When you come back on Monday, no one will be interested in what happened in the canteen. Every day is a new start, Luna.' He looked her directly in the eyes, which reminded her of the way her grandmother looked at her – it was as though he was searching inside her mind. Luna did not know how she felt about this and broke his gaze.

'Thanks Sir. And, I'm sorry,' Luna said regretfully, looking down at the floor.

'I think your friend is waiting for you' Mr Porter said, lightening the mood, and opened the classroom door indicating it was time to go. Luna walked out feeling some relief but still shaken by what had taken place at lunchtime. She was also unsure why Mr Porter had not punished her, and why he seemed so relaxed, given she sent a girl flying across the canteen. Something about this made her feel uneasy. Luna then thought about the fight between Oscar and Arthur; they too did not appear to receive any punishments. Mr Porter was also on duty that day. Was there something connecting the incidents? Then she had a sudden idea – witches, perhaps this is the connection. Luna wondered if Mr Porter knew that her and the other Le Fais were witches, and that this scared him, resulting in their exemption from any sort of punishment. However, on further reflection, she realised that Mr Porter didn't seem remotely fearful, he was relaxed – almost too relaxed. Luna wondered why everything was so opaque, so out of the ordinary. As much as she had tried to push events which had taken place over the last few weeks, to the back of her mind, and with some success, it was as though it wasn't possible to block everything out completely. Something always seemed to jolt her back to her new reality. The reality of being a Le Fai witch.

CHAPTER 7: DINNER WITH THE LE FAIS

'What was all that about?' Annie asked as Luna walked over to her in the corridor.

'I don't really understand it. He didn't tell me off, he just tried to reassure me. Telling me to put it out of my head. Reckons no one will be bothered next week.' Luna shrugged, feeling bemused.

'Weird,' Annie said, sounding perplexed.

'Do you think he treats us differently?' Luna wondered, hoping Annie had an answer.

'What do you mean, us?

'Le Fais. Cos we're witches.'

'Dunno. Maybe. I suppose, thinking about it, my brother didn't get into trouble the other day after that fight. Which is odd.'

'That's what I was thinking. None of it makes sense.'

They both exited the school grounds and waited further along Primrose Drive for Annie's dad to pick them up. Luna felt quite nervous about meeting other family members, she had not only never met, but didn't even know existed until very recently. She wondered what they would think of her. Luna still felt guilty for her initial thoughts about Ariella, wishing she had not followed Jack into the back of the book shop that day, spying on the Le Fais.

Annie's dad pulled up next to the curb in a silver Honda. The girls both got into the back of the car and put their seat belts on. Annie's dad turned his head to look at Annie and Luna, his face warm and friendly. The Le Fai family resemblance was clear to Luna, he had the same eyes as her and her mum, and the same heart-shaped face. This familiarity made Luna feel comfortable and she had a sudden sense of familial belonging. Annie's dad smiled at Luna and said, 'We finally meet. Annie hasn't stopped talking about you. Good to meet you. I'm Nick.'

Luna gave a nervous smile and said, 'Hi.' She suddenly noticed that there was another man sitting in the passenger seat next to Nick.

He turned his head to speak to Luna, smiled genially and said, 'Hi Luna, I'm Daniel.'

Luna looked at Annie, raising her eyebrows in a way that denoted her curiosity about who Daniel was.

'Oh, he's also my dad. I've two.' Annie confirmed grinning proudly. It was clear that Annie loved her dads very much; there was a strong sense of family unity and love, which was almost palpable. Daniel was black, with very short dark hair and almond shaped eyes which were filled with an abundance of kindness. Even though she had only just met Nick and Daniel, Luna felt an instant connection, the same connection she felt with Annie.

They drove for some time, until they reached their destination which was a small village called Thornberry, on the outskirts of Lindull. As the car pulled up onto a long-cobbled driveway, next to a detached farmhouse, Luna and Annie unplugged their seat belts and hopped out of the car. Luna looked around at the view and noticed that Annie's house was surrounded by an expanse of green landscape, comprising of farmland and woodland. At the back of Annie's house there was a brook, which weaved through the village before joining the river in the nearby market town, Ruxluth. It was so quiet, that Luna could hear the brook rushing between rocks, it almost sounded like it was whispering to her. Annie and Luna followed Nick, and then Daniel, to the front door. On opening the door, they were greeted by a playful brindle-coloured boxer dog who bounded straight up to Luna, almost knocking her down in its attempt to smother her with kisses. Luna loved dogs, so enjoyed this attention, and encouraged the pooch to give her more affection.

'I'm really sorry Luna,' stressed Nick as he pulled the dog away from her.

'No, its fine. I love dogs, and cats, well, all animals.' Luna said grinning, getting down to the dog's level and giving him a fuss.

'It's a good job then,' Daniel said sounding relieved.

'He's called Dex. He's their baby, now that I'm getting older,' Annie said trying to sound mature.

'You'll always be our baby,' Daniel said kissing his daughter on the top of her head. Annie quickly blushed, then rolled her eyes and put her fingers down her throat, pretending to be sick.

'Are you both okay with a stir-fry? Or did you want something else?' Nick asked attentively, as he hung his coat up and headed to the kitchen.

'Stir-fry is fine by me, thank you,' Luna replied politely, and Annie put her thumbs up to show her agreement.

'Okay. I'll call you when its ready.' Nick said.

Annie went upstairs, with Luna following behind, heading in the direction of Annie's bedroom. On entering, Luna immediately noticed that her cousin had several framed pictures of fairies on her walls – some were hand painted, and others were charcoal sketches. Luna wondered why at almost thirteen years old, Annie had pictures of fairies around her room, finding it somewhat childish. Part of her believed that liking fairies at their age was definitely *not* okay by most people's standards. However, Luna thought better than to cast too much judgement on her cousin and kept her initial thoughts to herself. But then without thinking Luna suddenly blurted, 'I didn't know you liked fairies.'

'Well, yes, of course! I'm a Le Fai,' Annie said sounding surprised at Luna's question, as though she expected her to understand. But Luna did not.

'I don't know what that means,' Luna said uneasily; she couldn't help but feel excluded from the Le Fai family culture and traditions. It was almost as if her mum had never been a Le Fai.

'The name Le Fai. We actually got it from the faye. The fairies. Slightly different spelling, but anyway that bit isn't important,' Annie said waving her hands about, then continued, 'some of our ancestors, many, many years back were fairies,' Annie sounded very matter-of-fact, which threw Luna. Witches were one thing, but fairies - surely this was some childish fantasy.

'Fairies.' Luna said in disbelief, clearly unconvinced by Annie's claim.

'Yes. Fairies. Le Fai literally means 'the fairy',' Annie said, looking at Luna as though she was stupid.

'Oh. Weird. So, fairies are real then?' Luna looked puzzled by Annie's conviction, not quite sure why she was even asking, as it seemed so far-fetched.

'Yes, of course they're real! Not that I've met one, but not everyone can see them. Some of our family can, well, have seen them. Suzie's mum, Raven, could. Raven was my nan's twin.'

'Your nan's twin. Really. I saw a picture of her next to my mum. Nang showed me. There's so much I don't know or understand...But, I'm sorry, I find it hard to believe fairies are real.'

'They are,' Annie said firmly.

Luna walked around the bedroom and looked at the pictures more closely. Some of them appeared to be quite old. One of the pictures Luna examined was hand painted – she found this one particularly captivating. The fairy looked authoritative, was dressed in a floaty emerald-green dress and had long dark brown flowing hair. Inscribed below, it read, *Aurora - Queen of the Elm*, and in the corner of the picture was a small artist signature, which read, *Raven Le Fai*. Next to the picture of Aurora was a hand sketch of a little girl, sitting next to another fairy. The little girl looked familiar. Inscribed below it read, *Little Aggie with Trixella*. Luna widened her eyes and said out loud, 'Aggie! As in

Agatha?! My mum!' This caught Annie's attention who scooted over and looked closely at the picture.

'Your mum? Oh yes, Aggie, of course!' Annie said sounding astonished.

'There's so much I don't know.' Luna sighed regretfully.

'Yes. I guess there is. Sorry. I was waffling on and should've been more thoughtful.'

'It's okay. Do you think that picture is real? I mean of my mum and a...a fairy?' Luna could not believe she was starting to entertain the idea of *fairies*.

'Well, yes. I told you fairies are real Luna,' Annie said sounding sincere, with a note of impatience in her voice.

As the friends continued to look at the pictures, Daniel called up to Annie and Luna to come down to eat. They made their way downstairs and into the dining room then sat at the long oak table with Nick and Daniel.

'I hope this is okay for you Luna?' Daniel asked as he served her a plate of food. She nodded and thanked him.

'Dad, you knew Luna's mum, Aggie, didn't you?' Annie said tentatively looking at Nick.

'Yes, of course. She was my cousin. We used to play together when we were kids,' Nick said, trying not to sound uncomfortable, but there was a trace of unease about embarking on this conversation.

'What powers did she have?' Annie asked bluntly, which caused Daniel to almost choke on his noodles.

'Annie!' Daniel scolded her for being so direct.

'It's okay. I want to know,' Luna said quietly, looking at Nick and Daniel hoping they would answer Annie's question.

Nick took a deep breath and smiled at her, uncertainly.

'Annie said you didn't know anything about the family. So, I suppose it's your right to know. Your mum, well, she was very magical. Had a bit of a temper though, so it was a bit out of control at times, until she learned to harness her powers. But wow she could do things.' Nick said reminiscing, as though he had been taken back in time.

'Like what?' Annie butted in looking intrigued. Daniel looked at her reproachfully.

'She could see and hear things that few of us could. She could transport into different dimensions without much effort. I think she spent a great deal of her childhood with different elementals and faye folk.' Nick looked at Luna's face and could see her briefly frown, indicating a sense of disbelief.

'I know this must all sound strange and unbelievable to you, but…. It's real,' Nick contended, with Daniel nodding in agreement. Luna couldn't help but feel they were being genuine, despite her own reservations.

'Do you think that's why Emily went flying across the room Luna. Maybe it was your powers,' Annie said suddenly interrupting again, forgetting herself, temporarily oblivious to her parents sitting with them at the table.

'What girl? What are you talking about Annie?' Daniel asked, looking slightly confused.

Luna and Annie looked at each other, then down at their food continuing to eat, trying to avoid the question.

'Has something happened?' Daniel said, sounding serious, but still maintaining that kind undertone, which reflected a deeply embedded geniality in his character.

'I got into an argument with a girl at lunch. I didn't mean to but…' Luna said quietly, drifting off at the end of her sentence.

'Luna didn't even touch her, but Emily just went flying across the canteen! It was pretty awesome to be honest,' Annie trilled, once again forgetting herself, and revelling in the moment.

'Annie. That's enough,' Daniel said firmly but kept his voice low.

'I feel horrible about it. When it happened, I honestly didn't do anything to make it happen. I went to, but, but…everything just slowed down, and I could see her moving across the canteen in slow motion…and then…well, she stopped mid-air and then dropped to the floor. Everything seemed to speed up again, and, and…I just, just…I've no idea how it happened,' Luna said regretfully, as though she was reliving it again, consumed with guilt, and looked on the brink of tears. Nick stood up, walked over to her and gently rubbed the top of her shoulders to offer her some reassurance and comfort.

'It's okay Luna. It's okay. You weren't to know,' Nick said soothingly.

'I knew it was you Luna! Amazing!' Annie sounded even more excited, which prompted a warning look from Daniel.

'Your mum was the same. We ended up getting into lots of trouble when we were kids.' Nick paused for a moment, then continued. 'You'll need to get that under control quite quickly. Has this ever happened before?' Nick asked her, then went back to his seat, maintaining eye contact with Luna, keeping her engaged in the conversation.

'No. First time…but I guess when I think back. I always felt I knew things, like I could see things coming, or if I wished hard enough for something, it sorta felt like I could make it happen… I don't know. Maybe, I'm imagining it differently now.' Luna said sounding baffled, then paused as her thoughts jumped to the amulet, and how it had made her feel when she wore it. Part of her wondered if it was something to do with that, perhaps it had somehow increased her powers, but decided it was better not to mention it.

'You should talk to your nan Luna. She'll be able to help you. She's an incredible witch,' Nick said admiringly.

'And teacher,' Daniel added, sounding equally enthusiastic about Liz Le Fai.

'You need to be careful who you talk to about being a witch. You can't trust everyone.'

'Like who dad?'

'Keep away from Oscar and his family. They're *not* good people,' Nick stated firmly.

'What do you mean? Is that why Arthur told us to keep away from them? Is that why he had a fight with Oscar?' Annie caught her dads' expressions; they glared at her clearly unaware of the altercation between Arthur and Oscar.

'What fight?' Daniel snapped, trying to hold eye contact with his daughter. However, Annie did everything to evade his stare, looking down at her plate of food.

'Err…they maybe had a little bit of an argument. That's all,' Annie lied. She did not sound very convincing.

'Annieee,' Nick said, directing her to tell them exactly what she meant.

'It wasn't that bad. Just, well, Arthur and Oscar, sort of, well, had a fight in the canteen. No one was hurt. It was just a little bit of a fight.' Annie looked sheepish and glanced at Luna.

'Did you know about this too Luna?' Daniel said appealing to her for more information.

'Errr, well yeah,' Luna reluctantly answered.

'What happened then?' Daniel looked at Luna, the worry in his face, and the warmth in his eyes made her want to tell him everything she knew, but she suddenly looked down at the table not sure what to say.

'They did have a fight during lunch time, and no one seemed to get hurt, but I think it was, well…' Luna felt like she was in a difficult position, not wanting to lie to Annie's dads, but equally she didn't want to get Arthur into unnecessary trouble. Daniel recognised the dilemma that Luna was faced with and stopped pressing her.

'It's okay. We'll talk to Arthur later. Please girls, though. It's important to stay away from the Blackthorns. This must sound dramatic, but we have our reasons,' Daniel warned, turning to Nick and flashing him a knowing look. Whilst Luna was paying attention to Daniel's advice, Annie appeared to be lost in her thoughts; her brow crumpled as though she was trying to calculate something. Suddenly her eyes widened.

'Luna! Maybe that's why you nearly passed out. You know, that day when Oscar's dad pulled up in his car? You were looking at him, remember?'

'What are you talking about Annie?' Nick asked sounding concerned, shifting his eyes from his daughter then quickly to Luna.

'I was just looking at Oscar's dad. I don't know why, but I

couldn't help it. He was looking back. Staring at me, and then I started feeling weird, and, and…well I sort of blacked out,' Luna recalled.

'She means she collapsed on me!' Annie corrected Luna, sounding melodramatic.

Nick and Daniel looked at each other serious faced. This piece of information prompted Nick to go into more detail about Oscar's family.

'I wasn't going to tell you this, but well, I think you need to understand why it's in your best interests to keep away from them. Oscar Blackthorn and his family are also witches. But they're not the sort of witches you want to be involved with. They're…dark witches.' Nick paused, and could see that this had caught Luna's attention, so he continued. 'You were lucky Luna. That incident could've been much worse. We'll need to talk to the others about increasing the Le Fai protection; this must now extend to you. You see…oh I can't believe I'm telling you this… Oscar's dad, Todd, has been after something that has been in our family for years. It's a long story, and not one for today, but, it's something that he *mustn't* have. Fortunately, only one person in the family knows where this thing is. It's easier this way.'

Luna knew what Nick was talking about. She knew exactly what it was that Todd Blackthorn wanted. He wanted the amulet. Luna concluded that it must have been Oscar's dad who had been pressurising Ariella for the magical family object. It suddenly dawned on Luna that she was now involved in something far more complicated, and potentially dangerous, than she first thought. She didn't realise how powerful witches could be and never truly believed, until now, that some might use dark magic to harm *her*. Luna had a sudden thought - she needed to get rid of that amulet, quickly. She needed to get it out of her bedroom and to someone who she could trust – it was time to see nang.

CHAPTER 8: TO BE A WITCH

Luna had spent most of Saturday at home, helping her dad clear the bottom of the garden, so he could put a fence up to create a secure boundary around their home. There was initially some resistance from Luna, not just because she would rather do other things - more interesting things - but because she was worried the fence would restrict her access to Lindull woods. However, on reflection, she concluded that as she may be at threat, with the amulet still in her possession, having that additional barrier between her and the woods was a good idea.

It was now Sunday morning. Luna was sitting with her dad in the kitchen for breakfast. However, she was too distracted by her thoughts to eat and instead used her spoon to push the pieces of cereal around her bowl, like they were tiny ships in a milky ocean. Luna was thinking about the amulet, wondering when the right moment would be to return it to nang.

'Are you going to eat that?' Neil asked, frowning, wondering what was on her mind, given she looked so distant. Luna looked up blankly, not registering his words, and continued to play with her breakfast cereal. Her dad shook his head, paused, then changed the subject in an attempt to engage her in conversation. 'You will have to ask Annie if she wants to come round next week. Would be nice to meet her,' her dad stopped to consider how to word the next part, mindful of how sensitive Luna had been since moving to Lindull. 'You know, I'm sort of relieved you have made some friends. You have seemed much happier this last week or so. I have to say I was getting worried about you,' Neil tentatively confessed, taking a light sip from his cup of coffee.

'I just wish mum had told me more about her family. I can't believe you didn't know either. It's just so weird.' Luna looked at her dad for some kind of recognition of how odd the whole situation was. However, he just sheepishly glanced back, gave a vague smile and continued to sip his coffee. Luna observed his reaction, and it made her sense something wasn't right. He wasn't telling her something.

'I'm assuming she didn't tell you? That you didn't know she had a family, other than nang,' Luna said, sounding slightly put out, suspicious that the deceit had gone even further than she first thought.

'Well, I didn't meet them, but I did know about them,' Neil said awkwardly, looking down at his cup as he set it down on the table.

'You knew, and you didn't tell me! Well, that's great. Thought you didn't know?! Can't even trust you now,' Luna said indignantly, then forcefully pushed her breakfast away, turned her legs from her dad and folded her arms. She looked quite petulant, but Neil felt she was justified. He regretted not telling her about the existence of her relatives in Lindull.

'I know I should've, but your mum didn't like talking about her life here. So, we never spoke about it, really, and then, well, I just never thought to say anything to you, even after...' Neil cut himself off, then took a moment to think before continuing, 'I wasn't really sure where they all were, really. It's as much of a surprise to me as it is to you that they're living here...But I'm sorry...I should've thought,' Neil said appealing to Luna for her understanding, however, her face did not show any glimmer of forgiveness. She looked at him with hostility.

'Should've but didn't! Story of my life!' Luna spat bitterly, then abruptly stood up and left the kitchen to go to her bedroom. Neil did not stop her. He was sympathetic and felt responsible for her feelings of distrust and frustration. In retrospect, he would have done things differently; but hindsight always presents us with different and more favourable paths, which, perhaps, we were never really meant to take.

Luna stomped to her bedroom, went in and slammed the door behind her, forcefully throwing herself onto the bed. She laid on her back and stared at the ceiling, thinking about her mum and all the secrets she had harboured. Her mum was not who Luna thought. As she pondered on this, her mind drifted to the amulet. It was still under her bed in the 'goth' box. She had been too scared to touch it, too scared to transport it to nang's – but, driven by anger, Luna thought that now was the time to be brave. To get the amulet, and everything associated with it, out of her life. Luna jumped up and got off the bed, then reached underneath to retrieve the 'goth' box. She took the key from the top drawer of her bedside table and stuffed it in her pocket. Luna stood there looking at the little wooden container, wondering what to put it in, then grabbed an old drawstring bag, which was hanging on the handle of her wardrobe. She carefully put the 'goth' box in the bag, and left her room, walked downstairs, and headed back to the kitchen.

'Sorry dad. I didn't mean to get cross. It's not your fault,' Luna said apologetically, leaning into the doorframe of the kitchen, her body language indicating her regret for snapping at her dad shortly before. Luna was very good at apologising, even when she didn't really mean it. Even when she still felt angry inside; this had proven to be an effective strategy in the past.

'It's okay. I understand.' Her dad gave a weak smile and carried on washing the pots.

'Err...am I okay to pop to nang's for a bit?' Luna asked cautiously, trying not to raise any suspicion about why she was visiting her grandmother, and in the hope, he wouldn't ask to come along.

'Yes love. Might do you some good,' her dad said, again vaguely smiling, still feeling a sense of guilt following their earlier conversation.

Luna left the house and walked down Hubble Road, en route to nang's. She had not got far when she saw Jack; he always seemed to suddenly appear out of nowhere. Luna found this intriguing but accepted their spontaneous meetings as normal.

'Luna! You off somewhere?' Jack said briskly, eyeing the bag on her back.

'Yeah. Just nang's. You should come sometime. You'd like her,' Luna said affectionately. Jack was now more interested in what his friend was transporting in her bag.

'What you got in there?' he asked, giving the bag a nudge, causing it to shift uncomfortably across Luna's back.

'Stop that. None of your business' Luna barked, pulling the bag away from him.

'Jeez. Only asked,' Jack scoffed, stepping back.

'If you must know, and I don't know why I'm telling you this. But…I've got the amulet,' Luna confessed, wondering, in the back of her mind, why on earth she had just shared such an important secret with him.

'Amulet?' Jack looked at her blankly.

'Duh. *The* amulet. You know, the one Ariella was talking about, when we were, you know…' Luna didn't like acknowledging that they had spied on her elderly great aunt. She still felt regretful about how she had behaved and couldn't help thinking she had somehow betrayed Annie.

'How have you got that? Did you find it somewhere?' Jack suddenly sounded interested, which made Luna feel important for having such a magical object in her possession.

'You mustn't tell anyone Jack. You better swear.' Luna looked at Jack intently, then continued to share her plan with him. 'No one knows apart from nang, and well, you, now. I'm going to take the amulet to her. I think it's better off there with her. She'll know what to do.'

'My lips are sealed.' Jack actioned zipping his lips closed. 'I can't believe you've got it. Can I see it?' Jack asked, hoping to get a glimpse of the treasured pendant.

'Definitely not! It's staying in my bag 'til I get to nang's,' Luna asserted, clasping the strings of the bag, making sure it was still secure on her back.

'Maybe I'll walk with you, just to make sure you're okay. Never know who might be around, eh?' Jack suggested nervously, suddenly looking as if he was on high alert, his eyes darting around the street.

'Make sure I'm okay? I'm sure I can look after myself.' Luna scoffed snootily, feeling offended that Jack thought she was too vulnerable to be trusted to safely transport the amulet to her grandmother's house, 'But, I suppose the company would be nice,' Luna said, sounding slightly aloof.

They continued walking together to Luna's grandmother's, with Jack remaining vigilant for potential threats, with any noise causing him to flinch and spin in that direction. Luna found this somewhat irritating, but equally endearing. He was being very considerate and protective, like a big brother. Jack and Luna soon approached Main Road into town, where nang's house was situated. They walked down the road chatting, with Jack continuing to monitor the street, when they got closer to nang's house.

'Nang only lives a few doors down, sure I'll be okay now. You look so, well, so anxious,' Luna said trying to stop herself from sniggering at Jack's behaviour.

'I'm fine. Just being look out,' Jack said nervously, twitching his head, keeping a close eye on his peripheral vision.

'Jack. I'll be okay now. Maybe I'll see you around later?' Luna indicated, trying to gently encourage him to stop being her chaperone.

'Okay. Maybe I'll just stay here and watch you walk off a bit further up the road. Just in case I need to, you know, do some kung fu moves,' Jack said, mimicking a few swift whip punches, which made Luna shake her head and sigh.

'Whatever. See you later Jack.'

Luna turned away from Jack and walked up the road towards her grandmother's house. On arrival, she turned back and could still see Jack standing there, vaguely waving at her. Luna gave a quick lift of her arm to indicate she had arrived at her grandmother's, then headed to the front door of the old Edwardian house. As she put her hand on the door handle, it suddenly opened, and nang was standing there smiling.

'I thought you would be coming today,' nang said, looking at Luna in that piercing way which made her feel keeping secrets from her grandmother was difficult.

'I've brought something for you,' Luna said, walking in the house, and then on towards the sitting room. She removed the bag from her back and sat down on the sofa, waiting expectantly for nang to sit with her. Luna clutched the bag looking uneasy. Her nang sat down slowly on the sofa next to Luna leaving a space between them, then turned her body towards her granddaughter and rested her hands in her lap.

'What do we have here?' nang asked gesturing to the bag Luna was still clutching.

'The 'goth' box. I've brought the amulet,' Luna said emphatically, widening her eyes, expecting an urgent response.

'Oh, I see. And why have your brought it to me?' nang asked casually, looking relaxed.

'Because I don't want it. It's. It's. Dangerous,' Luna said, quickly pushing the bag towards her grandmother.

'It belongs to *you* now. So, *you* should keep it,' nang asserted, slowly pushing the bag back towards Luna.

'I don't want it,' Luna stressed, pushing it back at nang and turning her legs away from her grandmother.

'Luna. It was bestowed to *you*. It's meant to be with *you*,' Nang said slowly, trying to emphasise the importance of keeping the amulet with her granddaughter.

'I don't understand what that means. I don't understand anything! I barely know who I am anymore!' Luna blasted.

'The amulet was given to my mother by her mother, then to me, then to *your* mum, and now to *you*. We did not choose who it went to. The amulet chose us, and now it has chosen *you*,' nang said calmly and slowly, maintaining eye contact with Luna as she spoke.

'How can it choose someone? That doesn't even make any sense.' Luna said scathingly, looking at her grandmother in disbelief.

'As you have already said. Nothing really does make any sense, so it shouldn't come as any surprise, should it?' nang contended with a hint of sarcasm in her voice. She then opened the bag and took out the box, setting it on her lap.

'Do you have the key Luna?' nang asked. Luna reached into her pocket and warily passed her the key.

'I don't think you should do that,' Luna warned. Her nang momentarily stopped what she was doing to look at Luna but then continued to unlock the 'goth' box. Her grandmother opened the little treasure chest and carefully pulled out the amulet, examining it, smiling to herself. Luna shuffled towards the opposite end of the sofa, as far away from nang as she could go without having to get up.

'You're not going to put it on, are you?' Luna asked her grandmother, sounding worried. Her eyes tightly shut, and her face scrunched up, anticipating that something awful was about to happen.

'No, my dear. You're going to wear it,' nang said moving towards her granddaughter with the amulet in hand.

'Me? No, I can't. Last time I did that, I started hearing voices, and my head started feeling weird!' Luna recalled sounding agitated.

'That's all very normal. The first time can always be quite unpleasant. It can take a bit of getting used to. I would never make you wear it if I thought it would hurt you,' nang said coolly, first smiling at Luna and then glancing admiringly back at the amulet.

'What do you mean? Why did I hear a voice?' Luna asked, now sounding more interested than anxious.

'That voice you heard was the amulet talking to you. The crystal part of it, is an amethyst. A useful tool for many witches – it's said to be the most powerful and spiritual stone there is. But this is no ordinary amethyst. It's not from our world you see, it came from another realm. It's a stone of the faye. This was given to our Le Fai mothers, generations ago. It came from the fairies of the elm. It only goes to those it has chosen as its keeper. As you will learn, it should *only* be worn by who it chooses. This is important.'

'What happens if someone else wears it? What would happen if I gave it to someone else to wear?' Luna asked, apprehensive about nang's answer, thinking about how Oscar's dad longed for it.

'It would certainly break the promise made by our ancestors, damaging generations of trust our family have built with the faye.'

'What would happen if the wrong person got it?'

'You mean the Blackthorn family, I'm assuming? Well, that could cause problems. You see the amulet can open endless possibilities. But should be used with caution, and only for good. The amulet is attractive to those who want more power, who want to take control of everything and anything they can. Do you understand?'

'So, they want it to do bad? To...to increase their power?' Luna said slowly, part of her still in disbelief about what her grandmother was telling her.

'Something like that. Todd Blackthorn is quite a powerful witch already, but he wants to be even more powerful,' nang paused, as though she was momentarily taken back in time, reflecting on the past, then continued, 'he's always been quite arrogant. I've known him for a *very* long time.' nang said taking a slow deep breath before pursing her lips together.

'He's a witch? I thought women were witches and men were wizards?'

'Nooo. That's just in stories. We're all witches, although some might prefer to call themselves sorcerers or magicians. Todd Blackthorn prefers sorcerer. So, I would rather call him a witch,' nang said with a wry smile.

'Nang, do all witches have powers?'

'Yes, of some sort. Some are gifted at healing others, some at spells, some at communicating with spirits, some at divination, and some of us can do all of that, and much, much, more,' nang said with a wink.

'What do you mean? You can do all that, and, and, even more?' Luna said sounding curious and amazed at what she was hearing.

'Yes, and so could your mother. And so can you. You just need to pay more attention and follow your instincts a little more. You need to work this out for yourself. You will start to understand what your abilities are over time,' nang explained, looking deeper into Luna's eyes. As she did this, Luna felt a strange rush of cold air around her, which made her shudder.

'I...I don't know. I can't imagine I can do what you can,' Luna said, unconvinced she could be that powerful. She paused for thought, then continued, 'What other things can you do?' Luna was becoming increasingly absorbed in her grandmother's narrative, which was reflected in her body language as she leaned in towards nang anticipating her answer.

'My sister Raven, your mum, and me, and others, generations before us, could communicate with the faye folk. We were lucky enough to be able to physically cross over the boundary into their world. Not all witches can do that. They may be able to feel their presence, and even visit their world in spirit, but not in their physical state. In time, I suspect you can also do this. There are several portals in Lindull woods that our family have used for generations, to cross over into the fairy realm, but also into other worlds.'

'Oh, is that why Ariella goes to the woods during a full moon? For the portals?'

'Ariella? No, no, I doubt it. My sister is a gifted diviner and visionary, which is the main part of her practice, but I doubt she has any interest in traipsing round Lindull woods. She wouldn't waste her time. What made you think that?'

'Oh, just something I heard. Well, saw, actually. A few weeks back or so, during the full moon, there were people with torches at the back of my garden going through the woods. I just assumed...'

'Assumed that it was Ariella? What did I tell you about believing idle gossip? Those people you saw may very well be a coven of local witches, but maybe not. Those woods attract lots of different people, for lots of different reasons. It doesn't mean they're all witches. It doesn't mean they're doing anything they shouldn't either. Be careful not to jump to conclusions and be careful who you believe. There're lots of people in this world who spread misinformation. Misinformation which could be damaging,' nang said gently, but firmly.

'Sorry. You're right. I should've thought,' Luna paused, to think for a moment about her grandmother's wise words, then continued, 'so, what does it actually mean...being a witch. Why am I a witch, but Annie isn't? How does it work?' Luna asked, wanting to learn more about her identity.

'To be a witch, brings with it an understanding and wisdom which allows you to see the world in a different way from everyone else. But, we also have what some people might call supernatural abilities, which are usually passed down in families. However, we're still people. In the past our abilities got us into lots of trouble, and in some places, sadly, they still do. Today most people don't believe witches have any powers. They think it's all make believe. And we prefer it that way. It means we're left alone. It's wise not to share your abilities with everyone. Be selective with who you tell. And take care not to let it go to your head and *never* think of yourself as better than people who aren't magical. We're all equal, whatever our talents.' Nang's astuteness mesmerised Luna.

'Nang, if I wear the amulet, can I take it off again, or is that it? What will happen to me?' Luna asked, sounding a little uneasy.

'Why not try it on and see?' nang suggested, passing her the amulet to try on. Luna cautiously took the crystal pendant from her grandmother and, closing her eyes, slowly fastened it around her neck. Instantly, she felt a rush of energy fill her body - although it was less intense this time - and ended as quickly as it started.

Luna opened her eyes and looked around the room, spotting her favourite cat, Mau-Mau, skipping through the sitting room doorway. He trotted up to her legs, coiling himself around them. Then immediately gazed up at Luna, 'Good afternoon. I am pleased to see you have finally decided to stop being silly and wear the amulet'. Luna shot up out of her seat and stood back away from the cat, who looked on unimpressed by her dramatic reaction. 'Do sit back down and then I can hop on your knee. You know I love a bit of affection,' her feline friend purred, his words drawn out in a slow and steady pace.

'I'm hearing voices again! I don't like this!' Luna went to remove the amulet from around her neck but was stopped by her grandmother who quickly stood up and gently stroked Luna's arm to reassure her.

'Well, I can hear Mau-Mau perfectly well,' nang said smiling.

'It's this amulet! It makes weird things happen,' Luna said sounding jittery, her body quivering slightly.

'It's not the amulet. It's *you* Luna. *You* have always been able to do this. You just weren't listening properly. The amulet might have helped you along a bit, but if you take it off you will still hear Mau-Mau,' after a short pause, nang continued, 'you see, although the amulet has chosen you, you never did need it to increase your powers.' Nang looked directly into Luna's eyes and clasped the tops of her arms firmly, looking at her intently, as though she wanted to make sure her granddaughter took in every word she was about to say, 'Luna, you're already very powerful. Wear the amulet and it'll help you control those powers. But the amulet is for *you*, and *you* alone.' She let go of Luna's arms, and relaxed her expression, 'It's strange how the amulet works. It gives the person who wears it what they need, if used properly, but, it can also be used to grant our wishes, our deepest desires. It's this which makes it so attractive to witches like Todd Blackthorn. He desires great power. But do not fear him too much. The amulet will protect you while you wear it, and by wearing it, you will also protect the amulet from people like him.

You see, no one can take the amulet from you. They can only take it if *you* give it to them. You have to surrender it. I realise this is a lot to take in, and it probably doesn't make much sense, but things will start to become clearer. Luna, you have been given a lot of responsibility as the keeper of the amulet, but it's just the way it is.'

'I'll do my best,' Luna looked down at the amulet, then reached out to hug her grandmother.

'Oh, do stop that. When are you going to sit down so I can hop on your knee,' Mau-Mau purred impatiently at Luna. Nang and Luna looked back at the cat, and both started laughing at the indignation of their feline friend.

Luna spent the remainder of the morning with nang, quizzing her about the amulet, and trying to learn more about Todd Blackthorn's attempts to retrieve it. However, her grandmother did not give much detail, and left Luna wondering why she was holding back information.

As lunch-time approached Luna's stomach was groaning at her, which made her realise that in her haste to visit nang she had not finished her breakfast, so decided to stay longer than planned to get something to eat, keeping her hunger at bay.

'Thanks, nang, for everything. But I had better go back,' Luna said getting up to leave, but as she did her grandmother suddenly stopped her.

'Just a minute. There's something I think you might find useful.' Nang gave a mysterious smile, then walked over to an old oak bureau and opened the top drawer. She reached in and pulled out a rolled-up piece of old looking parchment and handed it to Luna.

'What is it?' Luna asked curiously, examining it.

'Now be careful who sees this. It was given to me by my mother. It's a map. A Le Fai map of Lindull woods.'

'A map?'

This sparked Luna's interest, and her eyes lit up.

'Yes, it marks out most of the portals in the woods. It's important that this does *not* get into the wrong hands,' nang said, giving Luna a warning look.

'Thanks! I'll look after it. Promise,' Luna vowed, packing it into her bag.

CHAPTER 9:
LINDULL WOODS

Luna left nang's house feeling brighter and more confident about who she was and what she could do. Everything was starting to make sense and fall into place – for now anyway. Luna had experienced a whirlwind of emotions, overwhelmed and confused, at times, by contradictory and erratic thoughts about living in Lindull and being a witch. Luna couldn't wait to see Annie at school and share everything with her. But then, she suddenly thought about her cousin. She thought about how Annie had been a Le Fai all her life yet wasn't a witch. Annie, who would love nothing more than to be magical, and share her family's talents. Luna felt guilty. Perhaps going into detail about being a witch was not the right thing to do. It would be cruel. It would make Annie think about everything she wasn't, but so desperately wanted to be. As Luna pondered on this, she heard a whisper in her ear, which seemed to get louder as she walked. It was a familiar voice. It was of course Jack, but he was nowhere to be seen.

'Jack? Is that you?' Luna asked, looking around to see where his whispers were coming from.

'Psst. Psst, over here,' replied a quiet voice, which seemed to be coming from one of the bushes near the edge of the path. Luna walked towards the talking greenery and peered her head into the shrub border to see a pair of blue eyes staring back at her.

'What on earth are you doing in there?' Luna asked astonished to see Jack hiding out in the undergrowth.

'Just keeping lookout. Thought it was better to keep out of sight,' he said climbing from the shrubbery.

'You're so strange Jack,' Luna declared, smirking.

'If you say so. Anyway, what did nang say? Did she take the amulet back?' Jack asked urgently, desperate to learn what had happened.

'Errr, well, no. She didn't,' Luna said evasively and then carried on walking in the direction of home.

'Well...are you going to tell me?' Jack probed, trotting along next to her. Luna continued to look straight ahead but occasionally peered at Jack out of the corner of her eye. The truth was, Luna was bursting to tell someone.

'What are you doing now? If you come to my house, I can tell you more. Probably best not tell you here,' Luna said mysteriously, quickening her pace, rushing to get home so she could reveal all.

'Okay. Why not. Got nothing better to do.' Jack agreed, now marching next to Luna to keep up with her speed-walking.

It wasn't long before they arrived outside Luna's house. Her dad was outside working on his car, which was up on jacks, with Neil busily buried underneath, his legs only visible. Luna stood next to the car, with Jack beside her looking awkward.

'Dad, I've got Jack here,' Luna said, in a half-hearted attempt at an introduction.

Neil did not come out from under the car but called out, 'Nice to meet you Jack', as he continued to work out of sight. Jack didn't say anything, he just looked at Luna waiting for her to tell him what to do next.

'Come on Jack,' Luna instructed as she led him into the house and up the stairs to her bedroom. She sat on the floor and motioned him over to sit with her.

'I've got lots to tell you,' Luna said, removing the bag from her back, opening it, taking out the 'goth' box, pushing it back under her bed, and then pulling out the map given to her by her grandmother. Jack's eyes were fixed on the rolled-up parchment; he looked intrigued. 'I also still have this,' Luna said happily, pulling up the amulet from underneath her top to show Jack. The silver of the magical pendant glistened as it reflected the autumn sun light, which burst through Luna's bedroom window. Luna gazed admiringly at the amulet, suddenly finding it less ordinary looking, recognising its magnificence.

'Nang said it was bestowed to me, or something like that. Think that was the word she used, said it has been in the family for years, and now because it has chosen me, I have to wear it. Cos, they made a promise to the fairies, you see. Oh, and turns out I'm quite a powerful witch who can talk to cats and make people fly across the room. Hard to believe I know. But yeah. So, lots has happened.' Luna said all of this at lightning speed, unable to stop the flow of words as they seemed to spontaneously fire from her mouth. She wasn't sure why she had given so much detail in such a quick-paced way. On reflection, this all sounded extremely farfetched, and quite unbelievable. Jack looked on, considering how to react. It wasn't the sort of news he was expecting, and Luna sensed he wasn't convinced.

'Well, are you going to say something Jack?' Luna urged him to answer; she was feeling anxious and impatient for his response.

'What do I say to that. Wow. Just wow...I always knew there was something weird about you, but, well...' Jack joked, causing Luna to roll her eyes.

'This is a map of Lindull woods,' Luna said, carefully untying it and slowly unrolling the parchment. They both fixed their eyes on the hand drawn detail, which showed various routes leading to different areas of the woodland. Each path had been given a name, some of which appeared to be related to corresponding trees, plants, and animals associated with the track. Luna read some of these out loud.

'Look at this. *Great Oak Way, Rowan Walk, Nettle Rash Lane* - I don't like the sound of that one. And what's this, *Path to the Fairy Elm*.' Luna paused, then had a sudden thought, 'Jack, this must be the track to the fairy elm tree in the picture I saw at Annie's!' Luna said excitedly, forgetting Jack had no idea what she was talking about.

'Eh?' Jack looked on bemused at this new insight.

'Oh. Oh. Of course. I forgot to tell you that bit. Basically, my mum, nang and great aunt Raven used to hang out with fairies. Amazing, eh? Annie has pictures in her room that Raven drew of her and my mum with the fairies,' Luna enthused, but Jack just looked on at her and raised an eyebrow, marking his disbelief.

'Sounds like *you* are away with the fairies,' Jack scoffed quietly.

'What's that supposed to mean!?' Luna was irritated by Jack's sarcastic remark.

'I think you really are weird.'

'That's really horrible Jack! It's not nice! Fairies are real,' Luna said haughtily and continued to quietly look at the map, doing her best to ignore him.

'Sorry. It's just hard to believe...fairies. I mean witches are one thing, but fairies,' Jack said defending his views, but quickly recognised that he had upset her, 'sorry...I suppose anything is possible...' Jack sighed resignedly, then shrugged his shoulders.

'What's that?' Jack asked pointing to one of the circles drawn on the map. Luna leaned in closely to read it.

'Portal to the Undines of Trelorth?' Luna read, uncertainly.

'What are undines?' Jack sounded equally mystified, Luna shrugged and continued to read the map.

'Look here, there are more portals. *Portal to Scorpius' Cave, Portal to Cauldron of Fire*...look, look *Portal to the fairies of the elm*!' Luna beamed at Jack, who was unsure what to think.

'We should go Jack! Let's go and explore the woods!' Luna looked eagerly at her friend, willing him to agree.

'I suppose we could, but...' Jack sounded hesitant.

'But what? Come on. Are you a scaredy-cat?' Luna teased.

'I mean...well it might not be safe,' Jack said slowly, sounding uneasy about it.

'I can't believe you're being so scared! Well, I'll go myself then!'

'You can't do that! Okay, I'll go with you, but when?'

Luna sat there silently thinking, putting together a plan of action in her head. She had to be practical. Luna looked at her watch. It was already two o'clock.

'Maybe we should go now?' Luna suggested.

'Won't there be people walking round there now?' Jack said, trying to delay the adventure because he was secretly a bit nervous about what they might find.

'Yeah. Maybe...but we can at least track out where the different paths and portals are? We can always go back when its dark...though it's school tomorrow, so probably not the best idea,' Luna said, stopping to think about how to proceed.

'Let's just go now,' Luna decided, standing up, rolling up the map, and putting it back in the drawstring bag. She put the bag on her back and pulled on Jack's arm to go. He loyally followed her, although there was a definite reluctance about his pace as they left the bedroom and went down the stairs towards the front door. On exiting Luna could see her dad's legs still visible from underneath the car. She stopped to talk to him.

'Dad we're going for a walk. I'll be back for tea,' Luna said quickly, hoping that he wouldn't ask too many questions. Luckily her dad was too engrossed in what he was doing to really pay attention to the detail and gave a distracted response.

'Yeah, okay, love. Just finishing this off.'

Following Neil's brief acknowledgment, Luna and Jack walked to a cut through near Luna's house which led them directly to one of the main entrances into Lindull woods. On entering the wooded area, there was a visible natural pathway, marked by trodden-down earth which weaved around the trees and undergrowth. Luna and Jack looked ahead, unsure of which direction they should walk in, as the path split off in several directions. As they walked a little further into the wooded opening, Jack suddenly jumped back.

'What's wrong?' Luna asked, quickly turning to her friend. He pointed down to the floor of the woodland.

'That!' Jack shuddered. Luna's eyes followed Jack's gaze down to see a snake slithering around the area directly next to her feet, its oscillating forked tongue tasting the air as they looked on.

'Careful Luna, don't move suddenly. It might bite you,' Jack warned keeping his voice low, squeezing his eyes shut. Luna briefly frowned back at him, then crouched down to examine the snake more closely.

'It's an adder…they usually go into hibernation round now,' Luna said thoughtfully as the snake weaved in and out of the undergrowth, staying close to her feet.

'An adder! They bite Luna!' Jack panicked, taking a step back.

'No, I think he's okay,' Luna said calmly. When she looked at the adder, she felt an unexpected familial connection, as though they were old friends, reunited. Luna didn't understand this sense and brushed it off.

'It's a male adder. You can tell by the black and white markings. I had a thing about adders when I was little…first time I've seen one properly, close up. He's beautiful.'

'You just get weirder.' Jack winced, still keeping his distance. Luna leaned in even closer to the snake and heard a whisper from the reptile.

'Be careful…sssss…these woods have hidden dangers….sssss….take care…we will meet again…sssss.' Luna's eyes widened, she quickly stood up and the snake slithered away. Luna's ability to communicate with creatures, other than humans, was something she would have to get used to.

'Has it gone?' Jack asked, darting his eyes around the floor of the woodland to see where it had gone.

'Yes, he's gone. Come on Jack.'

Luna took out the rolled-up parchment from her bag, opened it, and examined the detail closely, trying to make sense of how it mapped against the area they were standing in.

'I can't make anything out,' Luna said sounding frustrated and spinning the map around attempting to identify any clues to indicate where they were. Jack scanned the map and pointed to an entrance.

'Look. That entrance there, must be where we are now. If you see behind us,' Jack turned around and pointed at two giant oak trees which looked like impressive wooden pillars framing the entrance to the woods.

'If you see on the map, there are two big oak trees there,' Jack pointed at the position on the map, which clearly highlighted two grand oaks at the entrance.

'But how do we know. There are oak trees everywhere,' Luna said sounding slightly flummoxed.

'Well, let's take a chance and see if I'm right. I bet you I am.' Jack held out his hand for Luna to shake, to agree to the gamble.

'Okay. Let's go this way and keep straight. But I'm not betting with you,' Luna said haughtily, pushing his hand away. They both walked further forward keeping on the path directly in front, becoming more enclosed by the trees, still looking at the map and ensuring they were walking on a recorded route, until they reached a fork in the track. Luna looked more closely at the map.

'Ah ha. If we keep going ahead that should take us to *nettle rash lane*, and if we go to the left, that should take us to that portal there,' Luna said pointing at a cluster of trees on the map, with an unnamed portal. It simply had an 'X' written next to it. 'Why doesn't that have a name?' Luna asked, sounding cautiously interested in what might be there.

'It has an 'X' next to it though, so maybe we should head there. You know like 'X' marks the spot,' Jack suggested, keen to go in that direction, as though he was going to unveil some hidden treasure.

'That 'X' could mean anything. Might not be a good thing. Problem is, I don't know,' Luna said sensibly, wondering if this whole adventure might turn out to be a bad idea.

'I vote we head for the treasure!' Jack said starting to sound like he wasn't taking this very seriously at all, which seemed to irritate Luna.

'Stop being silly. We don't even know what's there…but, actually, we could go and look. I have protection.' Luna said clasping her amulet.

Luna and Jack stayed on the path, as marked on the map in search of portal 'X', occasionally stopping to check that they were walking in the right direction. They continued walking for some time, when Luna realised, she hadn't been consulting the map. She quickly unwound the parchment to ensure they hadn't wondered off the recorded pathway.

'Let me see,' Luna said carefully examining the map, tracing her finger along the marked-out track, then looking ahead of her to check her bearings.

'Oh. Oh no. I think we might be going in completely the wrong direction,' Luna said sounding flustered, frantically re-checking the map. She looked around expecting to see Jack, but noticed he was no longer with her. Panic set in as she could not see him anywhere, and she realised she had no idea where she was. One minute she was walking with Jack, following the well-trodden trail, and the next she was off the beaten track, lost on her own in woodland she had no knowledge of. Luna could not understand where Jack had got to. She called out to him. 'Jack! Jack, where are you? This isn't funny.' Luna was hoping he would suddenly jump out at her, but there was no answer and no sign of him. She kept shouting his name, but nothing. *'People don't just vanish like that,'* she thought to herself. The panic escalated and Luna's heart was thumping uncomfortably in her chest; she felt suffocated as though the woods were somehow closing in on her. Scared and without any sense of where she was, Luna sat on the ground, curled herself up into a tight ball and started to cry. This dramatic display seemed to silence the woodland, which had been filled with the sound of birds chirping and the wind moving through the trees. It was as if Lindull woods had stopped to listen to her weep. Luna continued to sob, unable to move, when something hard hit her directly on the top of her head. It startled her; she looked up at the tall oak tree towering over her. Luna wondered if it was one of the acorns, dropped by a squirrel, or perhaps the crow which was perched above looking down at her. The black feathered creature appeared to be watching her, tilting its head from side to side, as though it was deciphering her cries. It unexpectedly swooped down, as though it was taking a closer look, and then flew off into the woods. Luna buried her head into her knees once more and began to cry again. Then, she felt another sharp knock on her head. Luna stopped crying and looked up at the oak tree towering over her. As she continued to gaze up at the tree, she heard a deep voice, which seemed to echo around the woods.

'You have stopped crying. Good.' Luna looked closely at the branches wondering where the voice had come from, when it started up again.

'You can hear me little one?' the voice said sounding surprised, but maintained its low and deep tone, which was strangely soothing.

'She can hear us.' Luna heard another voice emerging from the trees, this was followed by a wave of whispering, which moved through the woodland.

'How can she hear us?' posed another, more distinctive voice.

'Quieten down. You will frighten the poor child,' commanded the original low deep voice. Luna looked around, unable to comprehend what she was hearing and where it was coming from.

'We mean no harm little one. We don't often come across humans who can hear us. I could feel your sadness and thought the acorn would get your attention and distract you from your sorrow. I did not expect to be heard,' the voice continued.

Luna reluctantly stood up and bravely spoke out.

'Are you a squirrel? Or a bird? I can hear animals.' She sounded uneasy, not understanding exactly what was happening, but she had experienced so many unusual and unexpected things recently, Luna was starting to feel prepared for the fantastical.

'A squirrel? A bird? No, no, no little one. I am the tall handsome one who stands before you,' the voice said laughing, maintaining a friendliness. Luna followed the tall thick trunk of the oak tree up to its splendid network of branches in absolute wonder.

'The oak? You're a tree. I can hear the trees?' Luna said slowly and quietly, in disbelief.

'Yes, little one,' the great oak confirmed. Luna wanted to pinch herself.

'I'm talking to a tree?' Luna said uncertainly, still trying to come to terms with this new ability.

'Yes. And not any tree. The finest oak in the entire woodland,' the voice said jovially, which prompted other trees to quietly mutter and laugh.

'Can you help me find my friend Jack. He was with me, but, but...he's gone. I'm worried something has happened to him,' Luna said, sounding tearful once more.

'Now try not to get upset little one...I did not see anyone with you, but perhaps I can call upon the others to ask,' the great oak said reassuringly, then called to the other trees, 'can we help this little one find her friend. Spread the word.' As the oak uttered these words, Luna could hear whispers move through the trees like a gentle breeze, away from where she was, and then back again.

'It seems your friend did not get too far. Something stopped him from moving forward. I'm afraid that's all I know. I suspect he left the woods soon after,' the great oak confirmed, as the information was fed to him by the other trees.

Luna sighed with a strong sense of relief; she was no longer worried about Jack, but now realised she needed to return home. Going on into the woods, alone, would not be a good idea, she decided.

'Can you help me get back home?' Luna asked tentatively, hoping that she would not be stranded in the wood for the rest of the day.

'We can do that for you little one. Listen to the trees and they will lead you out from where you came. Do come back to visit. It is always nice to make new friends,' the oak tree said fondly.

'Thank you, and yes, I will. Thank you so much.' Luna gently stroked the bark of the great oak, said goodbye and was then guided out of Lindull woods, following in the direction of the trees' voices.

On exiting the woods, Luna thought about Jack, wondering why he had turned back. She found it strange, given he didn't let her know he was leaving the woods, and had seemed keen to join her in search of the portals. Luna looked back at the woods, confident that next time she would not let anything stop her, determined to learn more about a place which seemed to hold important family memories and secrets.

CHAPTER 10:
FRIEND OR FOE?

It had been almost two weeks since Luna and Jack had set out to explore Lindull woods. Luna had seen Jack a few days after being separated in the woods, however, she was unable to get a clear answer from him about what happened during their trek. His version of events did not mirror Luna's. From Jack's perspective, it was *Luna* who vanished, unexpectedly, shortly after they set off in pursuit of the portal marked 'X'. He was then compelled to turn back, leaving the woodland. Luna could not decide if Jack was telling the truth. Part of her wondered if it was her who had somehow been propelled forward into the woodland, leaving Jack alone. But maybe Jack simply got scared and headed back – not wanting to admit this in fear of looking cowedly. Luna remembered that the trees said something had stopped Jack in his tracks, preventing him from moving ahead; but this just added to her confusion. Like so many things in Luna's life right now, there did not appear to be a logical explanation.

Luna had still not confided in Annie about anything that had happened in the woods, or about the amulet; she hadn't told her that she could talk to animals, or trees. Luna was worried about hurting her cousin. Worried it would make Annie feel excluded. Luna didn't want to sound as though she was bragging about being a witch, so decided silence was the best course of action. However, this was not working out how Luna intended and subsequently caused her to be distant and increasingly grumpy as time went on. Annie wondered if Luna had tired of their friendship and no longer wanted to hang around with her. They spent most of the last week or so just engaging in small talk, with Luna barely making conversation; this eventually provoked Annie to react.

Luna and Annie were on their lunch break at school, hanging around their usual spot outside the science block. It was a dreary day; the sky was grey, and it was wet outside from the heavy rain which had fallen during the morning. Luna had got caught in it walking to school and her clothing still felt damp, making her uncomfortable, adding to her grumpiness. Both girls stood in silence. Luna was leaning with her back against the science block wall, as Annie looked on at her friend munching on an apple.

'Do you have to chew so loudly.' Luna tutted, indicating her crabbiness. Annie stopped and stared at Luna, not sure if to chastise her for her irritability or to ignore it. She decided to ignore it and move on. Luna just stared ahead, looking into the distance.

'Not looking forward to English this afternoon. I didn't get my homework done. I know I'm going to get in trouble...how was art this morning?' Annie said trying to break the tension. Luna didn't appear to hear Annie, or perhaps she chose to ignore her. She just carried on gazing ahead.

'Thank God its half term next week. Need a break from this hell hole...' Annie suddenly stopped talking, aware that Luna was still not listening to her.

'Luna. Luna, are you even listening to me?...You have been really off with me.' Annie sounded frustrated, unable to keep a lid on her irritation.

'No, I haven't. I'm...I'm just tired,' Luna snapped back.

'I don't believe you. Have I done something wrong? Tell me if I have. I hate this silent treatment,' Annie complained, sounding hurt.

'What makes you think that? I told you I'm just tired.' Luna said petulantly, looking ill tempered.

'Well, if you're not going to be honest with me, we may as well not bother being friends!' Annie blasted storming off across the school grounds.

Luna looked on at her cousin, wishing Annie had not stomped off, but felt too proud and sulky to follow her. Luna was feeling sorry for herself, despite it being self-inflicted, and remained propped up against the wall, scowling as she looked forward. It was not long before Luna's self-indulgence was interrupted, as a boy approached her. He was tall, lanky, with a pale complexion, dark, almost black-looking eyes, and dark brown hair – which was short at the back and sides, but long on top, with a fringe which he frequently flicked away from his eyes. Luna didn't turn to look but could see him walking closer in her peripheral vision - it was Oscar Blackthorn.

'You're Luna aren't you. Hang around with that Le Fai, don't you?' Oscar stated sounding superior and aloof, looking at her intently. Luna remembered what Annie's dad and nang had said to her about the Blackthorns, which instantly made her clam up. She kept staring ahead not answering him at first, but she could feel his dark eyes bore into her as he waited for a response.

'Yes, why do you ask?' Luna said flatly, feeling pressure to say something – she tried not to sound worried, even though she was uneasy about the conversation.

'You're one of them.' He paused to think, 'But you're different.' Oscar gave her a perceptive look, which seemed to rattle Luna, and she glared at him, attempting to stare him out.

'Depends. Depends, what you mean by different,' Luna said coldly, still maintaining her stare.

'You look like a Le Fai...I don't have an issue with *you*, it's only that idiot Arthur I can't stand,' Oscar admitted, sounding bitter as he uttered Annie's brother's name.

'What's wrong with Arthur? He seems perfectly fine to me.'

'If you say so, but you know what happened in the canteen, don't you? That wasn't my doing, that was all his. He hates my family.' Oscar sighed, then paused momentarily looking away,

'His dad hates my dad. I just get caught in the middle of it all,' his tone now less self-important, sounding unsettled and regretful. This caught Luna's attention and made her relax slightly, recognising a glimmer of softness in him.

'I didn't think of it like that. Your family are like, the Le Fais aren't they, witches?' Luna asked, her voice trailing off. She was still looking at Oscar, but she had softened her gaze.

'Yeah, we are. I am too, obvs,' Oscar gave a coy smile, briefly glanced at Luna, and then down at his feet.

'What can you do?' Luna was curious, reluctantly drawn in by his sudden openness. Oscar started to seem quite different from how she imagined. He seemed friendly, and there was a gentleness about him she didn't expect.

'Different things, but well…I can talk to creatures. I can hear animals speak like we are…weird, huh?' he said still looking down at his feet.

'No, no not at all…I can too.' Luna lowered her voice, secretly thrilled that there was someone else just like her. Someone around the same age, who might understand her, and she could even talk to about stuff. Oscar looked up at Luna.

'Can you? My dad's not impressed. Thinks it's a waste of time. It's not what Blackthorns do. But, well, it suits me. Prefer talking to animals than people sometimes.' Oscar smiled to himself, then looked into Luna's eyes, 'Can't believe… you're like me,' Oscar said slowly, then gave a broad grin.

'Listen I've got to get off, the bell's about to ring anyway. Maybe see you around sometime, Luna?' Oscar suggested, sounding sincere.

'Yeah. Sure,' Luna replied, quietly. Oscar walked away, looked back at her smiling, then slowly lifted his arm to gesture goodbye. Luna blushed and smiled to herself, feeling an odd connection with him she didn't quite understand.

After English, Luna made her way to her maths lesson, which she wasn't looking forward to, knowing she would have to face Annie after their disagreement. Luna walked into the classroom,

Mr Porter made eye contact with her and gave a slight nod of his head as a subtle greeting. In response she flashed a half smile and scuttled to her seat, then pulled the maths workbook out of her bag. Luna flicked through the book, wondering if she should avoid talking to Annie or try to make small talk in hope that their fall out could be forgotten. Annie approached the desk sighing loudly as she sat next to Luna.

'I'm sorry. I shouldn't have gone off like that,' Annie said, avoiding eye contact with Luna in case her apology was not welcomed.

'No, I'm sorry. I've been really horrible...you're right, I was being unreasonable. I...I really wanted to tell you some stuff that had happened the other week after I was at your house, but... well. I just couldn't. I didn't want to upset you. Oh, I feel so guilty,' Luna confessed uneasily, still looking at her workbook. Annie turned to face her and placed her hand gently on Luna's shoulder, showing affection for her cousin.

'It can't be that bad. What's there to feel guilty about?' Annie asked, smiling nervously, unsure whether she really wanted to hear her friend's response. Luna slowly turned her head and looked at Annie, then smiled and crumpled her brow apprehensively.

'You're my best friend. I know we haven't known each other long, but, well, we just clicked, didn't we? I feel so lucky to have you as a friend, and it's a bonus we're family, so, I don't want to ruin that...I don't want to ever make you feel pushed out. You have been a Le Fai all of your life, right, so I feel like I'm this imposter who came along, and can, well do all this stuff. All this stuff you can't. I'm sorry I didn't mean that to sound big headed. It's not coming out right.' Luna lowered her voice and looked down at the desk, avoiding eye contact with Annie, but continued to speak, 'I don't want you to feel bad that I can do stuff, if you can't. It's not fair, is it? I feel so bad about it.' Luna admitted to Annie.

'Luna it's okay. I'm used to it. Sure, I would love to be like the rest of the Le Fais, and sometimes it upsets me, but I would never hold it against you or not want you to have your powers... it makes me feel special to be part of it all. If you know what I mean,' Annie said earnestly, trying to make eye contact with Luna who was gazing down at her workbook.

'Only if, you're sure. If I ever make you feel rubbish about it, then tell me to shut up. I wish I had talked to you about this earlier. Wasted the two weeks worrying about it.' Luna sounded relieved but equally annoyed with herself for not being open with Annie in the first place.

'Let's not fight again. I'm dying to hear what has been happening,' Annie said positively, squeezing Luna's arm excitedly. Luna grinned back at Annie, 'We can catch up later. Why not come to mine at the weekend?' Luna suggested, but suddenly spotted Mr Porter watching her and Annie, so she decided it might be better to stop talking and retreat into her workbook.

'Talk later. Mr Porter has given me the look,' Luna whispered, glancing back at her teacher out of the corner of her eye.

'Oh, remind me to tell you the latest with Mr Porter and Oscar,' Annie said quietly opening her workbook. The mention of Oscar's name spiked Luna's interest.

'Really? What do you mean?' Luna asked casually, trying not to sound as interested as she felt.

'Later. Mr Porter is coming over.' Annie quickly pretended she was engrossed in her work as her teacher approached the desk.

'Luna, can I see you after class please? Nothing to worry about,' Mr Porter asked in his usual friendly manner, smiling at her.

'Yes, sir,' Luna said hesitantly. As Mr Porter walked away, seeing to another student, Luna turned to Annie, widening her eyes and raising her eyebrows, displaying her uncertainty about why he might want to talk to her after class. Annie looked equally baffled and shrugged, then returned to her work.

At the end of the lesson, all the students left the classroom in a hurry, excited about it being the end of the school week, and the start of half term. Annie remained with Luna, and hovered near the door, which prompted Mr Porter.

'Annie, she won't be long. I would appreciate it if you could wait outside. Thank you,' Mr Porter said instructing her to leave the classroom. Annie exited the room and closed the door behind her, remaining nearby in the corridor. Mr Porter looked at Luna and smiled reassuringly.

'I suppose you're wondering what I wanted to see you about?' Mr Porter said stroking his thick black beard.

'Er, yes sir,' Luna replied politely but felt apprehensive about what he was going to say next.

'I wanted to talk about the incident with Emily...from the other week.' Mr Porter paused, and smiled gently, his eyes soft. As he did this, Luna wondered why he was suddenly bringing it up again – part of her panicked about his intention. He looked at her perceptively, as though he knew this was bothering her, and quickly tried to alleviate her concerns.

'You're not in trouble Luna. I just wanted to explain, well, why I was so lenient.' Mr Porter stopped briefly, smiled again, then continued, 'I wanted to stop any speculation. You see, I understand what it's like to be, a, well, an outsider. I understand what it's like to be in your position Luna. How hard things are for you, and well, I want you to know I'm here for you. I don't want you to feel like you're alone. You see, I really do understand what you're going through. I'm here if you need someone to talk to,' he said genuinely, looking Luna in the eyes, emphasising his sincerity.

'Thanks Sir, that, er, means a lot.' Luna looked down at the floor, feeling slightly awkward.

'Now, I believe Annie is waiting for you.' He peered out of the glass in the classroom door at Luna's cousin, who was now standing directly outside. Luna smiled at Mr Porter as she left and was quickly greeted by Annie who was eager to find out what their teacher wanted. Luna and Annie walked together down the corridor in silence, waiting until they got outside the building before talking. Once they exited, Annie bombarded

Luna with questions.

'What was that all about? Are you in trouble?'

'No. He just wanted to let me know he understands how I feel and, well, that he's there for me. Said he didn't want to be hard on me when that stuff happened with Emily, cos of what I've been through, or something like that,' Luna said shrugging her shoulders, suggesting her puzzlement, but sounding relieved she wasn't in trouble. Annie went quiet as though she was thinking, formulating her own interpretation.

'Hmmm. Weird isn't it. He seems to be different with you and Oscar. He says he 'understands you',' Annie said cryptically, still grappling with her thoughts about Mr Porter.

'What d'you mean?' Luna asked, not clear about Annie's reasoning.

'Well, the other day, must have been Wednesday, that thing I wanted to tell you about happened. You know about Mr Porter and Oscar? Well, I didn't tell you, cos you know, you were a bit weird with me...But anyway, Charlotte in History told me that Oscar and Mr Porter were in his office for ages that lunch-time, like the whole time. No one knows why. Seems to be a bit of a mystery about it. Charlotte reckons he was getting told off, cos there was apparently a lot of tension between them when Oscar came out. Well, that's what she reckoned...So weird.' Annie, paused for thought, then carried on, 'Mr Porter seems to be on his case...and now he's showing interest in you...makes you wonder, doesn't it?' Annie said elusively, but hoping Luna would work out what she was implying.

'Makes you wonder what? Spit it out Annie,' Luna said impatiently.

'Well, you and Oscar are both witches, aren't you? So *maybe* it's something to do with that? *Maybe*, that's what connects you all. All three of you,' Annie said staring hard at her cousin, wondering how long it would take for the penny to drop.

'I don't get you,' Luna said sounding confused.

'Duh. Mr Porter is probably a witch *too*!' Annie contended, tapping her forehead with the palm of her hand and rolling her eyes, indicating her frustration at how slow Luna was being to grasp her theory.

'A witch? Mr Porter?' Luna said in disbelief, pulling a face.

'Yes. A witch. Would explain why he's paid so much attention to you and Oscar, and why he 'understands you',' Annie explained, using her fingers to give air quotation marks, to emphasise her point, 'bet he knows Oscar is up to no good and wants to deal with it in his own way. Explains why my brother didn't get a detention for the fight, as well, doesn't it? There can't be any other explanation,' Annie determined, confident that she had solved the mystery.

As Luna and Annie left the school grounds, Luna mused over the possibility of Mr Porter being just like her: a witch. She thought about how wonderful it would be to have a teacher she could trust and talk to about it. Luna wondered if this would make things easier for her at school. Mr Porter might even be able to help her learn to control her powers. Perhaps he was helping Oscar too, taking him under his wing, teaching him how to be a good witch. Luna then thought about her conversation with Oscar at lunch-time, and about how nice he seemed; he was not what she expected. It made her think about all the judgements she had made over the last month or so, jumping to conclusions about members of her own family, getting things so wrong. Maybe Oscar deserved a chance, a chance to be understood, and not tainted by the reputation of the Blackthorn family.

CHAPTER 11: A WEEKEND OF SURPRISES

Luna and Annie left the school grounds, heading in the same direction. Annie was to meet her dad, Nick, at Ariella's book shop for a lift home. Luna continued to walk with Annie until they were at the crossroads which split off towards the town centre in one direction and Hubble Road in the other; it was here that the friends would go their separate ways.

'Why don't you come with me to my nan's shop? You can meet her then. You will love her,' Annie enthused, smiling proudly - once more Luna was reminded of the deep affection Annie held for her family. 'I've told her all about you. She would love to meet you.'

Whilst Luna was eager to connect with the rest of the Le Fai family, she could not get over her deception, when only weeks earlier, her and Jack hid in the cupboard listening to Ariella's conversation with Nick and Suzie. Luna didn't want to disappoint Annie, so gave a weak smile and reluctantly agreed. As they made their way to the book shop, they discussed their plans for half term, with Annie suggesting they spend a good deal of it together. Luna started to feel butterflies in her stomach as they approached the four shops on Main Road, and she held back.

'You okay? You look worried?' Annie said sounding slightly concerned, tilting her head and looking at Luna, her brow furrowing.

'Yeah, just thinking about everything that has happened over the last few weeks. It's all been a bit, well, overwhelming,' Luna lied, trying to make excuses for her hesitance.

'Yes, it has been wild, hasn't it,' Annie said forgetting herself, smiling at Luna, then led the way into the book shop. Luna was instantly hit by that smell of books and incense, which reminded her of the first time she visited. She remembered browsing through the books and being spoken to by a mysterious elderly woman. Until that moment, Luna had not really thought about her. She wondered if the woman was another Le Fai, thinking how much she looked like her grandmother, and Ariella for that matter. It suddenly clicked – the shadowy lady in the book shop must be Raven, Ariella's twin sister. These thoughts temporarily distracted Luna from her reluctance about meeting Ariella.

'Nan? Nan? Are you through the back?' Annie called as they made their way further into the shop.

'Yes sweetheart, I'll be with you in a minute,' Ariella called back, her voice sounding very much like Luna's grandmother's as she listened closely. It wasn't long before Ariella joined them in the front of the shop. She walked towards Annie, gave her a gentle hug and then turned to Luna.

'My goodness, there's no mistaking who your mother is. You look just like Aggie. You must be Luna? Annie doesn't stop talking about you,' Ariella said giving Luna a warm and welcoming smile.

'Hello.' Luna smiled faintly, awkwardly swivelling her feet on the spot.

'Nan, is dad through there?' Annie asked making her way into the back of the shop, with Luna trailing behind her.

Nick was sitting at a small desk, checking through some paperwork. Luna could not help noticing that there was a smaller table tucked away in the far corner of the room with a purple silky cloth pulled over it, and a chair on either side. In the middle of the table was a thick white candle, which was embedded with several burned down incense sticks. On one side of the table there was a small purple and black crocheted draw string bag, containing what looked like a thick deck of cards. Next to that, was another small black cotton drawstring bag, about the same size, but the shape reminded Luna of a bag of marbles. Annie noticed Luna examining the table and its contents.

'That's where nan does her readings,' Annie whispered, leaning into Luna.

'Oh. Like a fortune teller?' Luna suggested, sounding fascinated.

'Hmm I wouldn't call it that. She's a psychic, but people don't call themselves psychics to the 'normals',' Annie said winking at Luna. The term 'normals' had become something of a private joke between the cousins – describing people who were conformist and often didn't like Luna or Annie.

'What do psychics call themselves then?' Luna was even more curious.

'Intuitives. Same thing as psychic, really. Nan said it's just more acceptable,' Annie explained, her voice now more audible, which caught the attention of Nick.

'Hello girls. I'm just finishing this off for mum,' he said flicking through the papers in front of him.

'Why not take Luna upstairs?' Nick suggested, sounding distracted by the task in front of him.

'She can't stay that long. Just popped in to meet nan. Also, I wanted to ask if I could go to Luna's this weekend?'

I don't see why not...If it's okay with Luna's dad,' Nick said still engrossed in the paperwork.

Annie turned to Luna and gave her a broad grin, which was reciprocated. Ariella returned to the back room carrying a small pile of books and put them down on the desk where Nick was sitting. She then turned to talk to Luna.

'How is your grandmother?' Ariella asked cautiously, avoiding making eye contact with Luna, and focusing on her cardigan as she buttoned it up.

'Errr, yeah, she's okay.' Luna answered uneasily knowing that nang and Ariella were not on speaking terms. Nick overhead the brief conversation and interjected.

'I keep telling them both that it's about time they caught up with each other. It has been a while,' Nick said looking disapprovingly at his mother. Luna understood the context of his words and felt the tension which was almost palpable.

'Oh, dad. Maybe Luna and her nan could come over around Halloween?' Annie innocently suggested, unaware of the conflict between Ariella and Luna's grandmother.

'That might not be a bad idea,' Nick agreed sarcastically, flashing his mother a warning look. Ariella subtly rolled her eyes, but did not comment.

'You're more than welcome Luna. You would get to meet the others. Ask your dad if it's okay,' Nick suggested.

'Yeah, okay. I'll ask him.'

'What are the plans for tomorrow then? Shall I come to yours in the morning? Dad is probably back at the shop, so you could meet me here? I don't know where your house is, so...' Annie asked.

'Yeah sure, what time?' Luna agreed, feeling upbeat about the prospect of spending time with her.

'Dad what time are we coming here tomorrow?'

'Probably about ten. But I can drop you off at Luna's.'

'Bonus. What's your address?' Annie asked sounding pleased, her eyes twinkling.

'We're on Hubble Road, number seventy-seven.' Luna glanced at her watch, 'I had better go.'

Luna said goodbye to Ariella and Nick, then walked to the book shop door with Annie. As she passed the rows of books, her mind returned to the elderly woman she had previously seen there, wondering if it was Raven.

'Oh, I meant to ask. I saw another lady in here who looked just like your nan. Thought it might be Raven?'

'When?' Annie asked sounding slightly curious, furrowing her brow.

'Errr?' Luna said uncomfortably, hoping this wouldn't spiral into an awkward conversation about why she had visited the shop in the first place.

'When was it you saw her?' Annie interjected quickly, thinking Luna was being slow.

'Oh. The other week,' Luna said, being careful to remain vague in her answer in case it led to further questions.

'It couldn't have been Raven then. She died a couple of years ago. Must have been someone else.' Annie shrugged, seemingly disinterested in exploring Luna's query any further, which came as a relief.

'Oh. Okay. Must have been someone else then…Anyway, see you tomorrow,' Luna said giving Annie a quick hug and leaving the shop.

The next morning, Luna was up early, excited about spending the day with Annie. As Luna got dressed and made her bed, she planned their day ahead, thinking that perhaps they could venture into the town centre together. Making plans with Annie in this way made her think of her friend Alex who was back in Leicester. Luna had not heard from Alex since moving – which still occasionally played on her mind. Whilst this was upsetting, getting to know Annie had been a good distraction for Luna, until now. Today was the first time in a while that Luna felt a surge of sadness rise inside her when she thought about Alex. Luna considered whether she should try to call her old friend, wishing she had her own mobile phone, and thinking how much easier it would make things. So many people her age had them; she found it unfair that she was not allowed, although Annie didn't have one either. As Luna began to ponder on the injustice of not having her own phone, it distracted her from her sadness about Alex. Then her dad called up, 'Luna, I think Annie is here. Are you coming down?'

Luna swiftly exited her bedroom and bounded down the stairs to the front door, then pulled it open to find Annie and her dad, Nick, standing there.

'Hi! Come in.' she beckoned Annie in enthusiastically. Neil was standing behind Luna, then approached the door towards Nick, side stepping the two friends who looked on as their dad's interacted.

'Hi, I'm Neil,' Luna's dad said holding out his hand for Nick to shake.

'Hello, I'm Nick. Those two are inseparable,' Nick said to Neil smiling as he shook his hand. Luna and Annie ran up the stairs towards Luna's bedroom, but they stopped on the landing, hidden out of view, listening to their dads, wondering what they were going to talk about.

'Come in,' Neil offered, gesturing Nick in, getting the impression he was waiting for an invitation to enter the house.

'Thanks, I won't stay long. I've got to help my mother at the shop.' Nick came in and stood in the hallway looking around at the pictures on the wall, spotting one of Aggie.

'Luna looks so much like her...I'm sorry. Things can't be easy on your own,' Nick said gently.

'It has been difficult, but Luna keeps me going,' Neil said uncomfortably, gazing at the photo of Aggie, his eyes softening with sadness.

'I know we haven't had anything to do with each other, but as far as we're all concerned you're as much family as Aggie was. If you need anything, just let me know,' Nick said earnestly, looking intently at Neil, his eyes filled with kindness.

'Thanks. That's good of you. I'm sorry we haven't met until now. But well, lots happened, and well, maybe you know the rest...the decision that was made. She didn't want her to know.' Neil said lowering his voice and checking behind him ensuring that Luna and Annie were not in hearing distance.

'I'm not sure that's an issue anymore...you see, she knows.' Nick said soberingly.

'She knows. Christ. How? Was it Liz?' Neil looked alarmed and rubbed his forehead with the palm of his hand anxiously, worried about what might follow.

'I think Luna worked some of it out for herself, but Liz filled in the gaps I suspect. I was amazed Aggie never told her…I don't know what happened to make it such a dark secret for her, and you?' Nick locked eyes with Neil, his stare was unwavering as he searched him to find out more.

'It's complicated, I'll er, well, tell you another time.' Neil was becoming aware of movement on the landing and gave Nick a look to silence the discussion.

'Listen, I need to get off. You and Luna should come down to the house this week. There's a family get together at Halloween. You should come along,' Nick suggested as he walked back towards the door.

As Neil followed him and watched him leave, Luna stood on the landing with Annie, silently staring at the wall, her face filled with disbelief and betrayal. She gulped and turned to Annie, 'Come on, let's go out,' Luna said, clutching the amulet through her jumper. Annie silently nodded in agreement and followed her down the stairs. That initial feeling of excitement on Annie's arrival to the house, had been replaced with tension and frustration, which hung in the air like an unpleasant smell. Neil passed Luna and Annie at the bottom of the stairs. Luna glared directly at her dad, and said coldly, 'We're going to walk into town. Be back later.' She then pulled on her shoes and coat, and stomped out of the house, Annie traipsing behind her.

Annie and Luna walked in silence down Hubble Road, en route to Main Road into the town centre. Luna was too angry to make conversation. For once, Annie was unsure how to ease the tension and remained muted until Luna broke the silence.

'I hate him, and I hate my mum. They both lied to me. My dad knew she was a witch. He knew about everything. Everything! He never told me anything!' Luna scorned, her pace increasing as the anger boiled inside her.

'I'm really sorry Luna. I don't know what to say,' Annie said uneasily, trying to catch up with Luna's fast pace.

'What can you say. My dad isn't who I thought he was. I really didn't think he knew. This is all so confusing.'

'I…I don't think they meant to hurt you. I'm, I'm sure they had their reasons,' Annie said bravely, which caused Luna to shoot her a reproachful look.

'How can even I trust him now. After everything.' Luna complained, her agitation reflected in her pace as she marched on.

'Luna, wait up, slow down!' Annie asserted, pulling on Luna's arm to stop her. Luna reluctantly came to a halt and stared at Annie, her face twisted by her intense feelings of anger and disappointment.

'Sorry, but you know now. And well, maybe none of this was meant to come out before. Maybe things have happened the way they were supposed to. My nan always says things happen as the Universe intended, and we should accept our fate, the good and the bad. I'm not sure what that really means, but, well I *think* it means it doesn't really matter. At least now it's all out in the open. It means you can talk to your dad about it?'

In the short space of time that Luna and Annie had known each other, their friendship had become very close. Annie was able to reason with Luna in a way no one else, apart from her grandmother, could.

'Spose. But…I just feel like they've let me down. I don't understand why dad didn't say anything,' Luna said, her face starting to soften.

'I get why you feel like that, but maybe it wasn't the right time…it'll be okay. You've got me. You're like the sister I never had,' Annie said throwing her arms around her cousin, trying to cheer her up.

'Sorry Annie. I didn't mean to get so cross. I'm such a hot head.'

'Yes, yes you are!' Annie and Luna both started chuckling and continued walking on Main Road into the town centre.

As they reached Lindull High Street, Luna and Annie headed in the direction of the local shopping mall, where some of their school peers often hung out on the weekends. Annie thought it would be a good opportunity to pick out the annoying 'normals' from school and construct their own amusing narratives about each one they could identify - as though they were a different species. As they walked into the shopping mall, Luna glanced into the phone shop next to the main entrance and spotted Oscar Blackthorn and his dad browsing the mobile phones. She nudged Annie, urging her to look.

'D'you see who it is? Let's hang around here a bit,' Luna suggested, lowering her voice and trying to position herself out of the Blackthorns' view.

'What *are* you doing? Why don't we just go upstairs. You know what my dad said?'

'Yeah, I know, but I'm just curious. Don't see how they can hurt us. I have this, see,' Luna said pulling out the amulet to show Annie. Since wearing the magical object, Luna had taken care to conceal it, wearing it underneath her clothing.

'What's that?' Annie said sounding intrigued, eyeing the amulet closely.

'It's an amulet from the faye. It was my mum's, and nang's before that, and her mum's before that, and so on. Apparently, it has to go to the person it chooses. And, well, nang said it has chosen me, so I have to wear it,' Luna whispered, her face animated as she explained its history to Annie who seemed transfixed by the magical pendant, which now hung on the outside of Luna's jumper. Luna looked back at the shop, and watched Oscar leave, with his dad still inside talking to one of the shop assistants. Oscar spotted Luna and waved, smiling cooly, then flicked his heavy fridge out of his eyes. Annie watched the interaction as Luna blushed, waved, then started twisting her hair around her fingers.

'OMG Luna, you fancy Oscar Blackthorn! What the...' Annie declared sounding shocked.

'Shut up! No, I don't...OMG he's coming over. Be quiet.' Luna fretted uncomfortably, trying her best to look less embarrassed than she actually felt.

'Hi. What you up to?' Oscar said smoothly to Luna, then

acknowledged Annie with a nod of his head.

'Er, not a lot, just hanging out. Saw you in the phone shop with your dad,' Luna said feeling increasingly uncomfortable, aware that Annie was watching her closely. Luna caught Oscar eyeing the amulet, which was still hanging on top of her jumper, visible from the gap in her unzipped jacket. She pulled her coat together, pretending to shiver, giving her an excuse to zip up her coat.

'You okay? It's not that cold in here,' Oscar said smirking.

'Yeah, I'm fine. So, do you come here often?' as Luna spoke, she cringed at her question, which was compounded by Annie who turned her head away clearly embarrassed by her friend's words. Oscar didn't seem to notice, and as he continued to talk to Luna, his dad walked over. Todd Blackthorn was dressed in black - Luna wondered if all the Blackthorns dressed the same, only ever wearing dark colours. It was starting to seem that way. He looked around the same age as Luna's mum and dad, was tall, thick-set, with bitterness visibly etched on his face - Luna wondered if this was permanent, or brought on by seeing his son talk to members of the Le Fai family. As Oscar's dad got closer, Luna noticed he had several tattoos on his hands, some of symbols on his fingers she did not recognise.

'What do we have here Oscar. Making friends with the Le Fais now,' his dad sneered, looking the cousins up and down contemptuously, then fixed his stare on Luna. Luna instantly felt her temper rise, her face reflecting her irritation, as she glared back at Todd Blackthorn. 'Luna, isn't it? Aggie's daughter.' Todd sounded cold. He paused as though he was thinking, still looking at Luna, 'Just like your mum,' a frown appeared on his face, and he narrowed his eyes.

Annie observed her cousin's fists tightening as the rage started to swell inside Luna; she squeezed Luna's arm and whispered, 'Just ignore him. He's trying to get you worked up. Keep it under control. Remember what my dad said.' Luna stopped herself and took a deep breath, then unclenched her fists.

'Think we'd better go Oscar. Say goodbye to your friends,' Todd said dismissively, walking away expecting his son to obediently follow. Oscar reluctantly walked after his dad, momentarily turning to Annie and Luna giving them a weak smile and miming 'bye'.

As the Blackthorns disappeared, Annie turned to Luna.

'What da hell was all that about?' Annie posed, sounding relieved that Oscar and his dad had gone.

'I dunno. But...I could feel something build inside me,' Luna said thoughtfully.

'Yeah, you really are a hot head. I thought you were gonna punch him.'

'No, not that. Something else. Like...I don't know. Like something was gonna happen. Like when that thing happened to Emily in the canteen at school.'

'Maybe it was just the anger?'

'No, well, maybe, but it's like when I focus hard on something or someone, I feel it. Think it has always been there, but I can feel it more now.'

'Maybe you need to get your nan to help you use it. Like my dad said. She could teach you.'

As they continued to talk, Annie and Luna walked towards the escalators and headed up to the next floor of the shopping mall. As they stepped off the escalator, Annie spotted Suzie in one of the card shops, so went in that direction with Luna tagging along.

'Suze, just saw you and thought I'd say hello. This is Luna,' Annie said amiably indicating towards Luna with her hand.

'Yes, we've met before, haven't we?' Suzie replied smiling, looking at Luna, who reciprocated the friendly gesture.

'What you up to?' Annie asked noticing that Suzie was looking at wedding cards.

'Oh, going to a wedding soon, just looking for a card.' As she spoke Mr Porter appeared from the aisle next to where they were all standing and put his hand on the small of Suzie's back. This came as a surprise to Annie and Luna, who briefly glanced at each other, their eyes reflecting their astonishment.

'Hello Luna, Annie. How are you both doing?' Mr Porter asked, sounding as friendly as ever.

'They're both in one of my maths classes, Suze,' Mr Porter confirmed as Suzie looked at him, wondering how he knew Luna and Annie.

'Oh, yes of course, I keep forgetting you teach at Annie's school,' Suzie remembered, then looked back at Annie and Luna.

'We've been dating for a while now. Frank will be meeting the others at the Halloween get together. I'm bringing him along,' Suzie swooned, turning back to Mr Porter, her expression bursting with affection for him.

'Oh, okay. Well, we'll see you there then, Sir. I mean Mr Porter. Actually, what should we call you?' Annie asked clumsily. Mr Porter and Suzie grinned at each other.

'Frank is fine, but Mr Porter at school,' Frank said with a wink, looking back at Annie.

Luna thought how perfect this was turning out to be. Her favourite teacher dating one of her relatives. This also confirmed everything she thought about him - he genuinely was a good person. Annie also thought that this was unequivocal evidence that Mr Porter was, indeed, a witch.

'Have things been okay Luna?' Mr Porter asked gently, looking deep into her eyes, reflecting the same sincerity he did each time he spoke to her.

'Yeah, really good actually. Thanks.' Luna beamed, now starting to feel happy again about the direction her life seemed to be moving in, despite all the secrecy and trouble with Todd Blackthorn.

'I'm pleased. Now look after yourself and enjoy the rest of your holiday.' Mr Porter flashed both Luna and Annie a broad smile, then put his arm around Suzie as they both headed in the direction of the tills.

Luna and Annie said goodbye and left the shop.

'Well today has been full of surprises hasn't it,' Annie said marvelling at all the new information which had come to light.

'Yeah. And, well, there's more. More that I need to share with you Annie...some of the other stuff I wanted to tell you, that, well I never got to...'

As Luna and Annie headed to get a milk shake from one of the eateries on the top floor of the shopping mall, they talked about what had happened to Luna in the weeks leading up to now. Luna explained how she discovered she had the ability to communicate with animals and trees – at the same time still trying to get her own head around it. She also explained about the map given to her by nang and her adventure with Jack in Lindull woods. Finally, Luna told Annie how Todd Blackthorn wanted the amulet.

'I can't believe all of this. Wish you had told me earlier. Can't believe about Oscar's dad. Luna, you need to be careful,' Annie said seriously. Luna looked sheepish and vaguely nodded in agreement.

'Maybe we could go to see nang on the way back from town,' Luna said looking at her watch, noticing it was already lunchtime, 'Are you hungry? Could grab something to eat and head back?' Luna suggested, with Annie nodding eagerly in agreement.

As they queued to order their food, Luna felt a tap on the shoulder - it was Oscar.

'Sorry about dad. He can be a bit of a...' Oscar said guiltily.

'It's okay. Don't worry about it,' Luna said still looking ahead, wondering whether it was a bad idea to carry on the conversation.

'Listen, a few of us are going to the woods on Halloween for my birthday. We'll be doing some, well, you know...magic.' Oscar leaned further in whispering his plan to Luna and Annie.

'It's your birthday on Halloween...cool,' Annie said, thinking aloud.

'Why not join us. And don't worry, my dad won't be there. Just a couple of my mates. They're like us. You should both come along. We're meeting at the entrance to Lindull woods on Cashmere Road at 8pm,' Oscar confirmed quietly.

As they looked around, Oscar was walking off, briefly turning to wave, looking directly at Luna. She felt that it was her, in particular, who Oscar was interested in, and whilst Luna secretly liked this special attention, a voice in the back of her mind was urging caution.

'Sounds awesome…But do you think we can trust him?' Annie said, sounding unsure, deep in her mind she was conscious of her dad's and brother's warning about the Blackthorns, as well as the new knowledge that Todd Blackburn was after Luna's amulet.

'I mean, well, what if Oscar gets your amulet and gives it to his dad. That would be serious, wouldn't it?' Annie worried, anxiously nibbling at the skin inside her mouth.

'It'll be fine. He can't take it from me. It doesn't work like that. I think I have to give it to him. And I'm not going to do that,' Luna explained, then paused for a moment, considering if she was being naive about it, but decided to trust this judgement, 'I think he's okay. I just think he's caught in the middle of everything. Like, just because his dad is horrible doesn't mean *he* is,' Luna said thoughtfully, remembering her conversation with Oscar at school. She looked at Annie hoping for her approval.

'I guess, and to be honest I always liked Oscar.' Annie took a moment to think, then agreed, 'Okay. Let's go. But we'd best not tell *anyone.* We'd get into trouble. Make sure you don't let it slip to Arthur. You know what he would say.' Annie gave an exasperated sigh, starting to begrudge the hostility between her brother and Oscar.

'Er, well. I think *you* are the one who lets things slip.' Luna teased Annie, chortling to herself, then giving her a gentle and friendly push causing Annie to stagger.

'Ha…yeah, I know. I'll *try* to keep quiet…This is going to be so cool,' Annie said grabbing Luna's hand in excitement and squeezing it.

Annie and Luna made their way out of the shopping mall, and

headed home, intending to visit Luna's grandmother on the way back. However, they were not prepared for what was about to happen; things were about to head in an unexpected direction.

CHAPTER 12: THE COMA CURSE

Luna and Annie made their way to nang's house, which was situated on Main Road almost halfway between town and Luna's home. Annie had never been to Liz Le Fai's house until now, although she had previously met her. However, Ariella's fragile relationship with her sister had caused a rift which meant that the two were rarely seen together, excluding Luna's grandmother from many of the family celebrations. As the girls walked towards the front door, Annie looked up at the big Edwardian house in admiration, thinking how much it resembled something from a spooky tv show – this appealed to Annie, who loved anything creepy – or so she told herself. Luna tried the handle of the door expecting it to open, however, for once, it was locked.

'That's odd.' Luna frowned, trying the door again.

'Weird. It's usually unlocked.' Luna sounded slightly worried, pulling at the handle.

'Maybe she's out?' Annie said, offering a practical suggestion.

'No, I don't think so.' Luna was sounding more concerned and used the big knocker to bang on the heavy black oak door. After a few moments, they heard the front door being unbolted and unlocked; it opened to reveal a serious and pale-faced nang, who ushered them in.

'Come in girls. Quickly.' As soon as Annie and Luna stepped into the house nang locked and bolted the door behind them.

'Annie, your dad has been looking for you. I'll give him a

call to let him know you're here. Luna, you stay here with me.' Luna and Annie wondered what could have possibly happened to cause nang to issue these instructions, and sound so serious in doing so.

'Has something happened nang?' Luna enquired anxiously, which showed in her face.

'I will be back in a minute. I'm just going to call your dad Annie. He'll explain when he picks you up. Luna, I'll talk to you once Annie has been collected,' nang said mysteriously, maintaining her serious tone. Luna and Annie walked on to the sitting room while nang called Nick. They sat on the sofa waiting in silence, continuing to ponder over what could have happened to cause such tension and urgent behaviour from Luna's grandmother. Luna started to panic that her family had somehow found out about her and Annie's encounter with the Blackthorns in the shopping mall. She panicked that they had been tipped off about their plans to meet Oscar in the woods at Halloween. Luna's thoughts continued to spiral; she began to fret about the impact her interactions, earlier that day, might have on the feud between the Blackthorns and the Le Fais. She worried her and Annie would be held to account for any repercussions and might even be forbidden from seeing one another.

As Luna continued to agonise over her racing thoughts, nang walked into the sitting room, took a deep breath to compose herself, and then plastered on a braver face.

'Your dad is on his way Annie. Now, what have you girls been up to?' nang's tone was suddenly different, less severe and more welcoming. Annie and Luna gave each other a puzzled look.

'I don't understand what has happened? Can you just tell us?' Luna pleaded, desperate for some clarity to help alleviate the suspense, in the hope it would bring a halt to her over thinking as it was causing her stomach to tie up in knots.

'I'll talk to you soon. Annie's dad won't be long Luna.'

Luna puffed and threw herself into the back of the sofa, then sunk down, slouching, and tapped her foot impatiently on the floor. Annie remained perched on the edge of the sofa looking uneasy. All three were silent, which heightened the edgy atmosphere. This was soon interrupted by three sharp knocks on the front door, which prompted Luna's grandmother to march back to the door and open it. It was Nick. Nang walked him to the sitting room, chatting in whispers as they approached.

'Annie, sorry to end your day with Luna, but we need to get home. You can see each other in the week,' Nick said calmly, standing in the doorway of the sitting room.

'Do I have to go now? We only just got here dad,' Annie moaned, frowning at him.

'Annie, I'm sorry, but yes, we need to go. You can call Luna later.' Nick paused then looked directly at Luna, 'Sorry Luna. I know you were both looking forward to spending the whole day together. Your dad is going to bring you over to ours on Halloween. We had a chat earlier. Anyway, Annie, we'd better go.' Nick then turned to Luna's grandmother, 'Thank you Liz. For everything. We'll talk later.' He leaned into hug her, then gestured to Annie to get up and leave with him. His daughter reluctantly followed, giving Luna a quick goodbye hug.

After Annie and Nick left the house, Luna and nang sat in the sitting room silently for a few moments, when the quietness was broken by Mau-Mau, who entered the room and hopped onto Luna's knee. He looked up at her adoringly and purred, 'I've missed your attention. I just love the way you scratch behind my ear.' This softened Luna, distracting her from the anxious thoughts which had dominated her mind since she had arrived at her grandmother's house. Luna looked fondly at Mau-Mau and stroked him, giving him a little kiss on his head.

'Luna, I need you to come with me. There's something you need to see,' nang said standing up, her solemn tone returning. Luna glanced up at her grandmother's face; her expression gave Luna the impression she had better comply with nang's request. Luna lifted Mau-Mau from her knee and gently placed him on the seat next to her, then stood up to follow her grandmother, who promptly exited the sitting room and headed towards the stairs. As they walked up the staircase, nang began to speak again, issuing new instructions.

'Luna, now I don't want you to be frightened by what I'm going to show you. There's nothing to worry about. All is in hand, but you need to know what our family is up against. As the keeper of the amulet, it's your right to know.'

As they reached the top of the stairs, nang led Luna to a locked room at the end of the landing. The elderly woman pulled a key from her pocket and proceeded to unlock the door; she held it open for Luna and then quickly locked it behind them. Luna looked around the double sized bedroom. There was a mahogany wooden dressing table by the window, and two matching antique wardrobes situated either side of an open fireplace. Opposite the dressing table on the other side of the room pushed against the wall, was a king-sized bed. As Luna glanced at the bed, she noticed that underneath the covers was an ashen faced elderly woman. The covers were pulled up to the woman's chest, with the top of her purple cardigan on display. Luna crept over to the bed and cautiously peered at the woman's face, taking a closer look. It took her a moment to realise who it was.

'It's Ariella!' Luna gasped, stepping back in shock.

'Yes, Luna. It's my baby sister, Ariella.' Nang sounded calm, but her voice was laced with sadness. She walked over to the bed where her sister lay, bent down and gently kissed Ariella on her forehead.

'What has happened? Is she, is she, alive?' Luna's voice was quivering, worried about her nang's answer.

'Yes, she is. But she's in a very, very, deep sleep, brought on by a powerful curse – the coma curse. Nick found her like this at the book shop, after he dropped Annie off at yours this morning.'

'Is she going to be, okay? Will she wake up?' Luna said uneasily, looking on at Ariella, trying to understand how this happened.

'She'll be okay, eventually, but it'll take some time to bring her back. It's not like a normal state of sleep. She has been put into a deep trance and is trapped in another dimension. We're not sure where she is yet. Nick believes Todd Blackthorn is responsible for this, but we can't be sure,' nang hesitated, before continuing, 'we thought our protection was enough, but somehow our defences have been broken. Nick thinks we underestimated his powers.'

'Todd Blackthorn did this? Is there anything I can do?'

'No, no, this is for the rest of us to figure out. You will have enough to think about. She'll be safe here with me…I wanted to show you what has happened to Ariella so you could understand the seriousness of what you're now involved with, as keeper of the amulet. Todd Blackthorn wants the amulet, but there are others too, no doubt, who find it as attractive as he does…' nang broke off for a moment, as though she was holding something back, then continued, 'as you can see, people won't stop at anything to get it…As the keeper of the amulet it's important that you continue to wear it and do *not* give it to anyone, not even Annie. No one. Remember, giving it to someone like Todd Blackthorn would be *very* serious. The consequences would be, well, unthinkable,' nang warned, turning again to look at her sister, who looked pale, but strangely peaceful.

'Would it not be better to return the amulet? Back to the faye? It seems to have caused nothing but trouble.'

'I wish it were that simple. You see, it would be disrespectful to return their gift. That might cause other problems,' nang sighed, 'although our family have maintained a good relationship with the faye, it's better to not provoke them. They can be, well, not as sweet and cute as the tooth fairy. The faye are powerful and can be dangerous, if you offend them or they take a dislike to you.' This surprised Luna who had a very different image of the faye in her mind from the one her grandmother conveyed.

'You must be brave and be strong. You must keep that amulet, until it chooses someone else. So, for now, I'm afraid that the amulet is here to stay. I'm sorry that you have the responsibility of looking after it. I must emphasise that as its keeper, by keeping it with you, you also protect the rest of us.' Nang suddenly hung her head down, looking regretful. In that moment, Luna couldn't decide if her remorse was because of Ariella, or because of the responsibility imposed on her as the amulet's keeper. Wanting to ease her grandmother's predicament, Luna reached out and gently rubbed nang's arm.

'It's okay. Like you said, Ariella will get better. And, well, as for the amulet. It isn't anyone's fault…I sorta feel like it's an honour I was chosen. Sure, I'm a bit scared about it, but, really, it's, quite exciting. I'm up for it. I'll do everything I can to protect it…and if it means it keeps us all safe, well, I have to. No, I *want* to,' Luna said maturely, trying to reassure her grandmother.

'I'm confident you will do that just fine darling.' Nang hugged Luna and stroked her hair as she pulled her granddaughter into her arms for an embrace.

'Nang, I need you to teach me. Teach me how to use my powers…I know I can do stuff, I, I just don't know where to start.'

'Well, perhaps it's about time you learned what it *really* means to be a witch.'

Luna and her grandmother left the bedroom, locking it behind them. Nang walked Luna to another room on the landing and pulled out a different key from her pocket, unlocked the door, directed Luna in, and switched on the light. This room was different from the one Ariella was in, which had looked like an ordinary bedroom; in this room the curtains were drawn and there wasn't a bed, just a table with various objects on it. Next to the table was a tall narrow cupboard. Luna walked over to the table and picked up a Victorian vanity hand mirror and gazed into it, but instead of seeing her own reflection, she observed the face of an older woman who was smiling back at her. Startled by this, Luna dropped the mirror on the floor.

'Did she frighten you? You probably weren't expecting to see the reflection of your great grandmother looking back at you. Take another look,' nang said, gently instructing her granddaughter to return to the mirror. Luna slowly crouched down to retrieve it, then reluctantly looked back at the reflection, seeing the same face as before.

'This is my great grandmother? Your mother?' Luna asked sounding amazed.

'Yes, I'm Seraphina, your great grandmother,' the reflection replied.

'Why is she in the mirror? Is she trapped?' Luna asked, turning away from the reflection to face nang.

'She isn't trapped. She can leave whenever she wants to. She asked to be drawn into the mirror. It isn't all of her, only a small fraction of her spirit.' Luna looked puzzled at this and returned to look at her great grandmother's reflection.

'It seems strange meeting you this way,' Luna said to Seraphina.

'Life is full of oddities, even I haven't yet figured it all out.' Seraphina replied philosophically. Luna put the mirror back down on the table and picked up an old looking pocket watch.

'What does this do?' Luna asked her grandmother inquisitively.

'What do you think it does Luna?'

'Let's you travel through time?'

'No Luna. It's a watch. We use it to tell the time,' nang teased dryly. Luna smiled to herself and then placed the pocket watch back on the table and opened a small wooden box, which contained several different crystals. As Luna carefully examined the contents, nang began to speak.

'We use crystals from time to time in magic, and for various other things. But I want you to pick up that mirror again.'

Luna closed the box and returned to the hand mirror. She picked it up and looked at the reflection of her great grandmother, who had a more serious expression this time.

'Luna, I want you to draw her out of that mirror and into this room,' nang instructed.

'What? I can't do that.'

'Yes, you can. You just need to focus your mind and use your will.'

'My will? How do I do that?'

'Use your will. Want it. Ask for it. Demand it.'

'I don't understand.'

'Your will is where your power is, Luna.'

'I really don't think…'

'Just do it,' nang said bluntly, interrupting her granddaughter. Luna sighed, then closed her eyes, trying to focus on the reflection of her great grandmother; but it was no good, she kept losing the image in her mind.

'I can't do it.' Luna moaned sounding defeated.

'You haven't even tried Luna. I know you can do it. Now you don't need to close your eyes. Look deep into the mirror and imagine you're pulling her out with your eyes. Focus your mind on what you want to happen, and it *will* happen,' nang directed assertively.

Luna took a deep breath, then stared hard at the reflection of her great grandmother. As Luna stared and concentrated, something felt different inside her; it was the same feeling she had earlier that day when Todd Blackthorn had confronted her, and when Emily flew across the canteen at school. Luna focused her thoughts, shutting everything else out of her mind apart from her intention to pull Seraphina from the mirror. As she did this, those inexplicable feelings continued to grow and consume her, reaching a climatic point at which her great grandmother's spirit was pulled from the mirror and into the room. Luna did not notice immediately, but felt a coldness wrap around her body, and sensed something next to her - a presence. Luna looked closely at the mirror and noticed that Seraphina was no longer staring back at her. Luna slowly turned towards the presence to see her great grandmother standing next to her in the room.

'Well done! I knew you could do it. You were quicker than I thought you'd be,' nang trilled proudly, giving Luna a broad smile.

'I did it. I did it,' Luna said slowly, trying to grasp what she had just achieved.

'Not bad. Not bad at all. Now you need to put me back into the mirror,' her great grandmother said encouragingly.

'Do what you did before Luna, but this time, imagine drawing my mother back into the mirror. You must *will* her reflection to stare back at you.' nang instructed, her eyes twinkling.

'Okay. I'll give it a go.' Luna sounded determined, took a deep breath and stared at the mirror, visualising her great grandmother's reflection gazing back at her, willing the mirror to suck Seraphina back in. Once again, the same powerful feeling began to build inside Luna, until it consumed her. In a blink of an eye her great grandmother was back in the mirror. Luna beamed at her relative's reflection and then turned to nang.

'I just can't believe it! It was easier that time,' Luna boasted, her face glowing.

'You're doing *very* well. But don't get ahead of yourself. You'll need to practice,' nang advised but couldn't hide her own delight at Luna's quickness to learn.

'Can I do *anything* at will?'

'Well, you can, but that doesn't mean you *should*. You should only use your powers when absolutely necessary, and only for good, Luna.' Nang gave her a warning look, then peered into her granddaughter's eyes, 'It's important you don't use your powers to hurt others, however angry they make you. Lots of witches get caught out that way and it has backfired. Unfortunately, I know a few of those...' nang said sighing regretfully.

'Backfired? How? Who?' Luna asked quickly, but nang just stared back at her and pursed her lips together; she was not going to satisfy Luna's curiosity.

'I won't do anything stupid nang.'

'I hope not Luna.'

'But what am I capable of doing?' Luna asked eagerly.

'Whatever your will desires. But, practice with caution and do *not* show off to others. And, be careful around other witches. They do *not* like show-offs. They might find ways to hurt you if they think you're too powerful. Psychic attacks are an unfortunate reality for us. The amulet will protect you, but it won't make you invincible. Don't forget that.'

'I won't. Promise.'

'Now pass me that old pocket watch,' nang asked, smiling at Luna. Her granddaughter reached across the table to pick up the watch, when nang stopped her.

'Tut, tut. No, don't pick it up. Think.' Luna quickly realised what her grandmother was asking of her. Luna stared at the pocket watch, concentrating and focusing her mind, willing it to travel towards nang. This time it all seemed to happen much more fluidly and quickly. As those familiar feelings began to rise inside of Luna, the pocket watch leapt off the table and flew swiftly across the room into her grandmother's hand.

'I did it!' Luna marvelled at her abilities and skipped over to nang throwing her arms around her.

'Thank you. Thank you so much,' Luna squealed, beaming at her grandmother.

'It wasn't me, Luna. It was all you darling.'

That afternoon Luna practised moving and retrieving objects, willing them to fly in different directions, and testing herself to see if she could beat the original speed at which she transported things. She was able to learn things very quickly, and in a short space of time it started to feel so normal and natural to her, as though she had always been able to work magic. Luna felt complete, as though she finally understood who she truly was; she felt like the person she was always meant to be - a witch. A Le Fai witch.

CHAPTER 13: A POWERLESS WITCH MAY AS WELL BE A DEAD WITCH

That evening Luna spoke to Annie on the phone about events over the last twenty-four hours. However, it soon became clear that Annie did not know about everything that had happened. Her dad hadn't revealed that Todd Blackthorn put a curse on Ariella and that as a result she was now in a deep trance - victim of the coma curse. Nick had told Annie that there had been more threats from the Blackthorn family, but that Ariella had gone away to stay with friends for her own protection. Luna felt it better not to unveil the truth to Annie - even though she didn't like the deception - so played along with the story her cousin had been fed by Nick. The truth would devastate Annie. In the meantime, whilst Ariella was away, Nick planned to look after the bookstore and would be in the shop most of half term. Although Annie felt concerned about her grandmother, she was also grateful for the opportunity to see Luna. Nick was planning to return early on Monday morning, and Annie intended to get a lift with him so she could spend the day with her best friend.

'I've been thinking...do you reckon we *should* meet Oscar on Halloween? Not sure it's a good idea, what with everything that has been happening?' Annie suggested quietly, worried that one of her dads, or her brother, might overhear their plans.

'I know what you mean...but Oscar isn't like his dad. He's different...' Luna said sounding uneasy, worried that she didn't sound very convincing. However, she was determined to give Oscar a chance, despite what the Le Fais said about the Blackthorn family. Regardless of all the awful things his dad had supposedly done, in her mind, Oscar was as much of a victim in all of this as the Le Fais were.

'Well, I suppose he has always been okay to me. I mean, I know my brother hates him, but my brother seems to hate lots of people. Think he hates me most of the time.' Annie giggled, trying to lighten the tone of the conversation.

'Annie, we can always come back if he turns out to be a...'

'Yeah. I guess we can. Listen, I better go. Maybe, speak tomorrow? If not, see you on Monday. You sure your dad won't mind me coming over?'

'Course not. Anyway, he'll be at work most of the day.'

'Okay, I better go. See you Monday.'

'See you Monday Annie. Bye.'

After Luna hung up, she smiled to herself, pleased that she would be spending time with Annie on Monday, but also that their plans to meet Oscar and his friends on Halloween were still going ahead. Luna thought about her time with nang in the afternoon and how she had learned to direct her powers, discovering her capabilities. However, Luna felt that there was still much more to discover and learn. She thought about her mum, Aggie, and wondered about her powers. Were they the same as Luna's? When did she discover what she could do? How did she feel about it? Did she feel like Luna? Excited. Apprehensive. Alive, even reborn. As she pondered on this, Luna felt a pang of sadness, hit by the realisation that she would never be able to ask her mum any of those questions. She would never be able to talk to her about everything she had recently discovered about herself. Lost in her thoughts, Luna realised that with everything that had been going on, she hadn't thought about her mum as much as usual. Her stomach sank. Was she forgetting her mum? Luna started to fret that if she didn't make every effort to keep her mum in her mind, she might start to fade away and be nothing more than a faint memory. Or worse, it would be as though she had never existed. Luna clutched the amulet and closed her eyes, wondering if she would still be able to feel her mum – as she usually did when holding the magical object and thinking about her. Luna closed her eyes and whispered, 'I love you mum', as she said this her dad walked through from the sitting room.

'You okay love? I know it's been a tough day,' he said gently, his face looked slightly pained as though he was keeping something bottled up inside, something he needed to let out.

'Yeah…what do you mean by tough day?' Luna eyed her dad searchingly, suddenly thinking that Nick or nang must have told him about Ariella, 'You know then?'

'Yes. I know about Ariella…sorry love.' Neil paused, reflecting on all the secrecy Luna had been at the centre of. He felt guilty and wanted to make it up to her. 'I suppose it's about time we had a chat,' he said, determined to make things right.

Neil walked through to the kitchen and beckoned Luna to follow. She wondered what he was about to tell her. Hoping it might shed light on why her mum had been so intent on keeping everything about her identity a secret, surely it couldn't just be because she didn't want to be a witch or didn't want *her* to be one. There must be more to it – Luna had a sense that nang wasn't telling her everything, only offering her a slither of the detail. Luna sat down at the kitchen table while Neil silently made them both a hot drink.

'I heard you and Nick talking when he dropped Annie off,' Luna admitted, testing him, hoping it would provoke him to say more, tell her the truth.

'Yes, I realised that when you stormed out. I don't blame you. It wasn't fair to keep everything from you…I should've told you sooner…Must be a shock to find out your parents are witches.'

On hearing this, Luna took a moment to register his words.

'Parents? Parents?' Luna was flummoxed, and stared at her

dad in disbelief, wondering if she had misheard him.

'Yes…Nick said you knew?' Neil had a sudden look of panic on his face, as he registered Luna's expression.

'Knew that *mum* was a witch. You said parents, not *parent*?'

'Ahh. Christ, Luna. I'm so sorry love. I thought you knew.' Neil rubbed his hands over his face, looking uncomfortable, thinking he had now added to Luna's confusion and frustration, 'Sorry, love. It's both of us.'

'But, how? *You*…you're nothing like the Le Fais.'

'Well not anymore, but I was…That was a long time ago.'

'What do you mean? Did mum stop you? Was it her? Why are there so many secrets?' Luna's head started spinning and she glared at her dad expectantly, wanting answers.

'I lost my powers Luna. That's what happened,' Neil said quietly; Luna sensed there was regret in his voice.

'What do you mean? How? What happened?'

'I suppose I better tell you from the beginning,' Neil sighed, poured their drinks, then walked over to the table, sat down opposite Luna and stared into his cup, as though he was regressing back in time, recalling long hidden memories.

'I met your mum in Leicester when we were in our 20s. She hadn't left Lindull long really. We mixed in the same circles, with other witches. Me and your mum hit it off straight away and it wasn't long before we were dating. We got married pretty quickly after that. We were a good fit.' Neil remembered fondly, reliving the moments he recounted, his face softened by his love for Aggie. Luna pulled a face at the romantic suggestion, and gave a shudder, which made Neil chuckle, momentarily distracting him from his memories.

'We were so happy Luna…I was working as a mechanic. Your mum was trying to make a living working as a psychic. Though it was tough on her at times. But…it was what she wanted to do…That's how she met Adam…when things started to change.'

'Adam? Who's that?' Luna asked, leaning into her dad's story.

'He was another witch. He was a bit like your mum. Well, in some ways…He did readings for people and was a good psychic, but didn't really have anything else to offer as a witch. He couldn't really do the stuff that your mum and I did...'

'Was this before you had me?' Luna interjected, trying to understand how she was placed in this unravelling story.

'Yes, it was before you came along. We hadn't been married long...Your mum gave Adam a lot of help. He was a good friend. Or so we thought...' Neil cut himself off, as though it was starting to get too painful to continue. He furrowed his brow, his expression becoming more wounded.

'What happened dad?'

'Your mum read for a lot of people, she had a lot of clients, but he didn't. And you see, typical Aggie felt sorry for him. He was good, but not like your mum. She started passing some of her clients over to him. This helped him a lot. It really increased his popularity too. But the more popular he got, the bigger his ego got. You would call him a bragger, and he was. He got to the point where his psychic abilities weren't enough for him. He wanted to be more powerful, and it got out of control...' Neil stopped again, looking pensive. Luna wondered if he was going to continue, but waited patiently, without prompting him. Neil took a long sip from his cup and continued.

'I remember coming back from work and your mum was distraught. Wouldn't stop crying. Turns out Adam had been threatening her. He was after something she'd had since she was a child, something Liz had given to her...'

'The amulet. This amulet?' Luna lifted the magical pendant out from underneath her top, where, until now, it had gone unnoticed by her dad. As he cast his eyes on the precious amulet, his faced turned pale and he gulped.

'How did you? I thought she'd taken it back! How did you? Do you know what that thing can do Luna! It's not meant for anyone to wear!' Neil stood up, about to step forward to pull it from her neck when she stopped him.

'No dad. It's fine. I'm its keeper. It was meant for me. It's okay. It's better I wear it than not.' Luna sounded strangely calm. Neil took a step back and sank into the kitchen chair, looking agitated.

'It's all happening again. Luna, you need to return it to the faye. It's not safe. You're my baby. If anything was to happen to you...I'd...' Neil pleaded with Luna, but she had other ideas.

'Nang said it would cause more trouble returning it,' Luna said assertively.

'Nang knows you have it? Who else knows? I can't believe Liz hasn't told me what's going on.'

'Don't blame her! She's just trying to help...besides, I had it all along. It was in the 'goth' box. I've had it since mum died.'

'She kept it...she said she'd returned it. Said that it was all over.' Neil said in disbelief.

'She couldn't dad...I think she just hid it away. Kept it safe.'

'This is why your mum didn't want you to know about us. She didn't want this for you cos of everything that happened. If I'd known it was in that box, I wouldn't have let you have it.'

'Dad, it's okay. It's safer with me wearing it. It'll protect me. It must have protected mum?'

Neil paused, glanced at Luna, then stared down at the kitchen table. He was suddenly transported back to the past again.

'Yes. It did protect her...But it didn't protect me,' Neil lamented.

'What do you mean?' Luna looked concerned and probed her dad for more information.

'Your mum had told Adam about the amulet. She trusted him. We both did at first. But when he started wanting more power, well, he changed. He thought that getting his hands on the amulet would give him what he wanted...thought it would make him more powerful than any witch he knew. He started threatening and bullying her. He was relentless Luna. He wouldn't leave her alone. So, in the end, I went to confront him. I went to see him one night.' Neil paused giving a heavy sigh, and Luna could see he was struggling, 'I couldn't take it anymore Luna. Your mum was a mess...'

'What happened dad?'

'We got into an argument. He started threatening me. Said he

would do everything in his power to get the amulet, including…
Well, I couldn't let him, so I cursed him…I hexed him, there and
then. Let my temper get the better of me. I was at breaking point
Luna.' Neil put his head in his hands and fell silent.

'What happened then?' Luna asked softly, feeling her dad's
anguish as he relived it.

'I don't know really. When I hexed him, it somehow bounced
back…Back onto me. Serves me right really…I didn't realise at
first…though, at the time, I remember thinking that he didn't
seem bothered by what I had done…it was strange, cos he
seemed unaffected by it, like he knew he was invincible. I
thought he must have good protection around him, but I didn't
realise what had actually happened at first.'

'What do you mean, dad?'

'When I hexed him, I intended for it to strip him of his powers.
We call it the death curse, not because it takes a life, but because
it kills a witch's powers; removes every last one. Some witches
would rather die than lose their powers…it's the same thing
really,' Neil paused, took a deep breath, then continued, 'when
I got back, I told your mum what I'd done to Adam. She didn't
hold it against me.…we just started increasing our protection,
but I just couldn't do anything, my will was too weak, and I
got easily distracted. Every time I tried to do any magic; my
head went blank, like a thick fog was filling up my mind. Then
as days followed, I started noticing I couldn't do other things
anymore…that's when I realised. The hex had bounced onto me
and stripped *my* powers. They'd all gone.'

Luna slowly stood up, walked over to her dad and put her
arms around his shoulders; he started to weep.

'I'm so sorry dad. That's awful.' Luna leaned into him, feeling
his deep sadness and regret.

'It gets worse…The hex hadn't just bounced back onto me, it
somehow transferred all *my* powers directly to him…he didn't
get the amulet, but he got the next best thing. He seemed to
lose interest in the amulet after that, but was a different witch,
a really powerful one. Then one day, he just disappeared. Never

knew what happened to him. We were just relieved it was all over. Then you came along and took our minds off everything. It was when you arrived into our world that your mum swore, she would never use her powers again and would give you a very different life. I wasn't sure at first, but I loved her, so went along with whatever she wanted.' Neil turned to look at Luna affectionately and wiped his eyes.

'I'm so sorry dad. It must have been really hard.' Luna paused reflecting on what he had just shared with her. Everything was starting to make sense. Although they'd kept everything from her, she no longer felt angry or resentful about it, 'Thanks for telling me. It can't have been easy.' Luna thought about what Annie had said to her the day before - that things happen when the moment is right. Perhaps she wasn't meant to know before.

'Is that why you never talk about mum? Why, any time I try to bring her up you change the subject? I thought you blamed me for something. Like I had done something wrong.'

'No, never. Would never blame anything on you...I just wanted to protect you. That's all...You're so like your mum... It's hard talking about her cos when I think about her, I have to accept she isn't here anymore,' her dad said pensively, his voice trailing off as though he had been transported somewhere else. They both remained silent for some time, gathering their thoughts. Neil took a long deep breath and stood up, trying to lift himself out of his sombre mood.

'Are you okay Luna? It's a lot for you to take in,' Neil looked at his daughter tenderly, 'I'm sorry I didn't talk to you sooner. I hope you understand. I never meant to hurt you. Everything has always been about protecting you. Your mum only ever wanted the best for you. She loved you more than anything. More than her own life.'

'It's okay dad. Everything will be okay now. I'm just glad it's all out in the open...I love you dad,' Luna said affectionately, giving Neil a long hug.

'I'm going to get an early night. Lots to get my head round. Love you.' Luna yawned, then slowly made her way to the kitchen door.

'Okay, love. See you in the morning.' Neil gave a weak smile and carried his cup to the sink.

There was still an unsettled feeling lingering, it was as though there was still some unfinished business. Whilst Luna thought there were no more secrets, she would be sadly mistaken. The past always has a habit of returning when we least expect it. Neil's past was waiting in the wings, but no one, including Luna, had any idea what was coming and when it would strike.

CHAPTER 14: THE FAIRY ELM

The next morning Luna decided to make the most of her day. She wanted to go back to Lindull woods and search out some of the locations marked on the map nang had given to her. Luna felt more confident, and this time she knew what to expect. Moreover, being able to communicate with the animals and trees of the woodland, along with her new fine-tuned powers to assist her, Luna thought she was now better placed to meet any challenges head on.

Luna planned to be out most of the day, giving herself time to explore Lindull woods properly. In preparation, she packed a small rucksack of essential supplies, including: - the Le Fai map, something to drink and eat, a torch - just in case it started getting dark - and a pen and notepad - so she could write down any observations for next time. Before leaving the house, she left her dad a note on the kitchen table.

'Dad,
I've gone out for a walk to the shops
and will pop to nang's on the way back.
Will stay at nang's for lunch, but back for tea.
Love, Luna xx'

Luna thought it was best not to tell her dad exactly where she was going and what she was up to. He would only worry and probably stop her. Luna was convinced he would believe her little white lie.

After exiting the house, Luna made her way to the shortcut near her house which led to one of the entrances to Lindull woods. As Luna sped up, she spotted Jack randomly sitting on the ground, using his hands to move around small piles of dirt, shaping them into tiny mounds – she found this curious.

'Hello stranger. Where have you been?' Luna said enthusiastically, pleased to see him, wondering if he would join her on her trek into the woods.

'I've been around; it's you who hasn't,' Jack joked, then looked at the bag on her back.

'Where you going? Running away?' Jack stood up and walked up to Luna, wiping the dirt off his hands onto the sides of his trousers.

'No silly. I'm going back into Lindull woods. Not been since we went...maybe you would like to come too?' Luna locked eyes with Jack, willing him to say yes.

'Spose I've got nothing better to do.' Jack sounded nonchalant, but Luna could tell that he was secretly pleased she invited him.

'Don't run off this time. It's not cool to be chicken,' Luna mocked Jack, then smiled affectionately at him.

'*You* were the chicken. Not *me*. *You* vanished and left me,' Jack gibed her back maintaining the friendly banter.

Before they set off into the entrance of the woods, they stood around chatting. Luna informed Jack about what had happened since they last met – telling him all about the lessons in magic nang had given her. Luna decided that sharing stuff with Jack was somehow okay, and didn't breach her promise to her grandmother not to brag about her magical abilities. Despite Jack's proneness to sarcasm, Luna felt comfortable confiding in him. Jack was less involved than Annie, as a non-witch, making it easier overall - Luna didn't feel there were any immediate risks in discussing details with Jack.

'You get weirder Luna,' Jack jested, smirking, 'seriously though, that's impressive you can do all that stuff. Why don't you show me?'

'Maybe later,' Luna said heading into the woods with an increased pace. She wanted to get going, feeling they had already delayed things by stopping to chat. Luna took the map out from her bag and opened it up.

'Right. Shall we head to the same spot again. The portal marked 'X'? Or should we go somewhere else?' Luna examined the map, feeling like she was spoilt for choice.

'Well last time we headed in that direction for that portal,' Jack said pointing at the portal marked 'X' on the map, 'we ended up getting separated. Maybe we need to try somewhere else,' Jack suggested sensibly.

'Yeah, okay.' Luna looked at the map again, pausing to think, 'I would like to find the faye. So maybe we should head over to the fairy elm tree.'

'I guess...' Jack didn't sound too keen, Luna flashed him a quizzical look, wondering what was causing his sudden reluctance.

'You're not worried, are you?' Luna asked, hoping he wasn't going to back out.

'Nah, its fine. Just, dunno. Spose cos we got separated last time. But, sure it'll be fine this time. Come on let's go,' Jack agreed, shrugging off any hesitancy.

They used the map to guide them further into the woods, however, it wasn't too long before Luna started wondering if it would be better to ditch the map and ask the trees for directions, given how helpful they had been last time. Luna was finding the map difficult to follow.

'Jack, can you help with this map. I just find the directions so confusing,' Luna moaned thrusting the map over to him, however, he somehow failed to take it, and it landed on the ground.

'It's okay. I'll hold it,' Luna snapped as she bent down and snatched up the map from the ground. However, as she stood back up, Jack was nowhere to be seen.

'What the..?' Luna said under her breath looking all around

her.

'It's not funny Jack. Where are you? Come on I want to get going,' Luna called, sounding irritated, suspecting that Jack was just pranking her.

'Jack? Jack...Oh never mind. Looks like I'm on my own again,' Luna sighed, then rolled up the map and stuffed it into her bag, deciding that the trees would be better guides than the old map. Luna studied the wooded area directly around her, wondering if she should speak to one of the trees directly or just call out to them all in hope one of them would answer. As she pondered on this, she heard a hissing sound by her feet and immediately looked down to see an adder winding around the undergrowth. Luna admired the scaled reptile as he gravitated towards her, using his forked tongue to taste the air around where she stood.

'Have we met before?' Luna asked the familiar looking snake, as he continued to linger near her feet.

'Yeessssssss...Missssss...we have...sssssss...when you were here before, with the boy...sssss,' the adder replied.

'Not today, he has ditched me.' Luna gave a deep sigh.

'His lossss....Missssss,' the adder was now winding around her feet and lifting his scaly elongated body up towards her legs.

Maybe you can help me. I'm looking for the fairy elm tree. Do you know where I can find it?' Luna asked tentatively.

'I'm afraid not...ssssss...I am sorry...ssssss...why not ask the treesss...sssss... we will meet again Missssss,' he said, then slithered off and disappeared into the woods. Luna took the snake's advice.

'Hello...trees? Erm, any trees want to talk to me?' Luna reluctantly called out.

'Hello? Trees, excuse me? Oh, this is hopeless.'

As Luna almost gave up hope, a deep-toned voice answered back, 'And what can we do for you?'

Luna looked around, trying to distinguish where the voice was coming from as it was difficult to pinpoint.

'Look up,' the voice continued.

'Look up where? You're all round me.' Luna said sounding

slightly frustrated.

'In front of you.'

'In front of me?' Luna looked directly in front of her at a tall tree, which was laden with conker husks, fat and ready to fall. 'Oh, the conker tree,' Luna quietly concluded.

'Thank you for answering me. Can you help me find the fairy elm?' Luna asked.

'The fairy elm? I am not sure I can help you, but perhaps the others can,' the tall conker tree replied.

'The fairy elm is where the sun sets, beyond the water,' another voice interjected, however, Luna was unsure which tree had spoken – or if it even was a tree.

'Maybe I do need the map...the sun rises in the east and sets in the west. I have no idea where west is,' Luna complained to herself, unaware that someone was listening.

'I do,' came another, familiar voice.

'I'm behind you,' the voice continued, sounding amused. Luna spun around to see Oscar Blackthorn standing smiling at her, with a crow on his shoulder; this was the last person she expected to see, and certainly *not* with a bird using him as a perch.

'Oh, Oscar. Where did *you* come from?' Luna startled, then quickly pushed her hair behind her ears.

'What are *you* doing here Luna Le Fai?'

'For the record it's actually Luna Woods, *not* Le Fai.'

'Nah, you're definitely a Le Fai...you never answered my question.'

'You never answered *my* question, and I asked first.' Luna was mildly irritated; Oscar's sense of self-importance grated on her.

'Fair enough.' Oscar shrugged, 'I'm always in here. But not seen you here before, so that's why I asked. Who were you talking to?' Oscar probed, looking at her curiously.

'Erm, just the...the trees,' Luna said uneasily, worrying she would sound unbelievable and even ridiculous.

'You can speak to them too...hmm, something I can't do... that's pretty cool to be honest.' Oscar sounded genuinely impressed.

'Thanks…I was just looking around,' Luna said vaguely, unsure if she should tell him too much about her plans in Lindull woods.

'Looking around for what exactly? I only ask cos, well, I could help you. I know these woods pretty well…north is that way, east there, south there, and west over there. I heard you saying something about west, so that would be in that direction,' Oscar explained helpfully, suddenly less superior in his manner – it was his softer side Luna couldn't help but warm to.

'Thanks…do you want to come with me?' Luna asked reluctantly; part of her wondered if this was a bad idea but felt like giving him a chance.

'Sure. Oh, this is my friend, Leon,' Oscar said, turning to the crow who was busy preening his black glossy feathers, which looked purple iridescent as the sunlight caught his plumage.

'Hello, Leon.' Luna said amiably, greeting the crow.

'Hello. Caw, Caw. I have seen you before. Caw, caw. Are you Oscar's friend? Caw, caw.' Leon replied, tilting his jet-black head, and staring at her with his dark ominous looking eyes.

'I guess we're friends?' Luna said cautiously, looking at Oscar for affirmation of their friendship.

'That's right Leon. I'm actually friends with a Le Fai, so it seems. Just don't tell my dad, he'll be sure to go mental if he finds out.' Oscar said jokingly, then scowled.

'If you're friends with Oscar, then you're my friend too. Caw, caw.' Leon said indicating his loyalty to the young Blackthorn.

'You never actually said where we're going?' Oscar said quizzically, looking at her narrowing his eyes.

'Okay, I guess we're friends, so I can trust you, *right*?' Luna asked hopefully, looking at him searchingly.

'Believe me, it's not in my interests to hang round with a Le Fai. You can trust me.' Oscar looked back at her earnestly, then arched his eyebrows.

'Okay, well, I'm looking for the fairy elm tree. Do you know where that is? Supposed to be west of here? Over the water?'

'The fairy elm? Urgh, such a Le Fai thing to ask.' Oscar shook his head condescendingly, teasing Luna, 'I don't know where the fairies are, but, I know where some elm trees are in that direction, which happen to be over the brook. We could try there?'

'Well, I also have this.' Luna reached for the bag on her back and pulled out the map, opened it out and showed Oscar where the fairy elm was located.

'Oh, yeah, I know where that is. This way,' Oscar instructed, starting to head westward. Luna followed him and tried to map out where they were going, making mental notes of memorable features of the wooded landscape. As they disappeared further into the trees Oscar started to make conversation.

'So, who gave you that map?'

'My nan gave it to me.'

'Ahh. It'll be one of the old witch's maps from years ago. No one uses those maps anymore. Nice to have though, I guess. Probably been in your family for years. Don't see many Le Fais round the woods these days, well apart from you.'

'Yeah, nan thought I'd like it....How far is this tree?' Luna said sounding a little impatient. Oscar stopped and looked at her furrowing his brow.

'It's not far now. We're nearly at the brook. Once we get over that, it's only a couple of minutes away.' Oscar started walking again, Luna continued to follow him.

'How did you make friends with Leon then. Does he live in the woods?'

'Nah, not really. He does come out here, but he lives with me most of the time. He's my companion.'

'Companion?'

'You know. Like a witch's companion, like companion creature?'

'I've no idea what that is,' Luna admitted, feeling embarrassed at her limited understanding of witch terminology. Oscar looked at her and again furrowed his brow.

'You see, I only just learned I was a witch. My mum and

dad never told me. They didn't want me to know. Then my mum died, and we moved here, and well I accidently found out. There's a lot I don't know, I guess.'

'Sorry about your mum...That must have been hard...Why didn't they tell you?' Oscar surprised Luna by how sympathetic he sounded.

'It's complicated, but it's all out in the open now...My nan has been helping me.'

'I had no idea. Sorry I assumed you would know what I meant. Witches usually have companion creatures, well not always, but most of us do. They usually help us in some way. So, I can send Leon to look for things, people, places. But he's my mate too. I talk to him about stuff that I probably don't talk to anyone else about,' Oscar explained, nudging his head affectionately towards Leon, who cawed back to reciprocate the sentiment.

'Does that mean all witches can talk to animals? I thought only some of us could?'

'Nooo, not *everyone* can talk to animals. Not everyone is like us,' Oscar said smiling at Luna, then blushed and flicked his hair back out of his eyes.

'So, do you choose your companion creature? How does it work?'

'Sorta, well, they find you, or so I've been told. My mum said that companion creatures are like our soul companions. Creatures that keep returning to us from our past lives, so we have known them before. Like it's fate, you can't escape it.' Oscar suddenly glanced at Luna and caught her eye, then they both quickly looked away.

'My nan has a cat called Mau-Mau. I guess he's her companion,' Luna said thinking how much she loved her grandmother's feline friend, secretly wishing he was her companion. As she continued to walk on, thinking about Mau-Mau, Luna was so distracted by her thoughts she didn't see a raised knot of tree roots, which were bunched up on the floor of the woodland. Her foot caught the roots causing her to trip and fall forward, twisting her ankle in the process. This startled Luna and was visibly painful - she winced as she tried to stand up.

'Shame I didn't film it. That was a pretty spectacular fall,' Oscar jested, but soon realised Luna had actually hurt her ankle. 'You okay?' he asked, as she limped towards him.

'Do I look okay?' Luna said sarcastically, still wincing as she moved, trying not to put pressure on her ankle. Oscar looked at her and then started rubbing his hands together. Luna looked puzzled and frowned at him, wondering why he was now kneeling and hovering his hands around her injury. As he continued to move his hands around the area of her swollen ankle and foot, Luna felt a rush of heat through her twisted limb. She looked down to see what Oscar was doing and witnessed a bright blue light radiating around the injury - it appeared to be emanating from his hands. After a few moments, he moved away and stood up, still looking down at her ankle, holding his head to one side as though he was assessing it.

'Try walking on it now. It should be fine,' Oscar instructed. Luna gaped at him still trying to make sense of what she had just witnessed.

'Walk on it. Go on,' Oscar urged her. Luna reluctantly put her foot forward and slowly leaned into her step; she looked up at Oscar in amazement as it felt completely back to normal, as though it had never been injured.

'How did you do that?!' Luna astounded, now able to walk with ease.

'I can heal.' Oscar gave a coy smile.

'Wow...my ankle feels great,' Luna said cheerfully, lifting her foot and rotating it.

'You might be able to do it too. You should give it a go,' Oscar suggested encouragingly.

'I wouldn't know where to start,' Luna said sounding prematurely defeated.

'You ever played with energy balls?'

'No. Energy balls?'

'Rub your hands together. Watch me,' Oscar directed and started vigorously rubbing his hands together. Luna reluctantly copied him, focusing her mind as her grandmother had taught her, and quickly felt her hands grow warm as the friction built up between them.

'Now slowly pull your hands apart and create a ball with the energy,' Oscar said moving his hands apart to reveal a pink tinted light which grew as his hands were pulled further apart. He rolled the pink-illuminated energy into the shape and size of a tennis ball, then passed it from one hand to another. After watching him closely, Luna slowly pulled her hands apart to reveal green coloured energy, which she shaped into a small ball, holding it in her hands closely examining it.

'This is amazing. I never knew I could do this. What kind of energy is it? Where does it come from?' Luna said, mesmerised by her sphere of green glowing light.

'It's from you. It's your energy. You can put your will into it, to send things out. Watch.' Oscar rested the tennis ball sized sphere of energy on the flat of his hand and stared at it, as though he was concentrating as hard as he could. As he focused on it, the ball turned from a pink colour to a bright yellow illuminated sphere of light. Oscar then looked at Luna and hurled the energy ball at her; it hurtled at speed and hit her directly in the stomach, dissolving into her body as it made contact. As it did, Luna started laughing and felt a heightened sense of happiness.

'What was that?' Luna giggled, feeling euphoric.

'It's a giggle ball. Feels good, doesn't it? It won't last much longer.' Oscar smiled, then continued, 'You try. Send me something. Just don't hex me,' he said smiling sarcastically. Luna kept her energy ball on the flat of her palm and gazed at it concentrating, using her will to fill the illuminating sphere with her intention. As she focused, the ball grew and radiated a beautiful indigo light; Luna looked at Oscar and directed the ball at his head hitting him in the middle of his brow, dissolving as it made contact.

'Can you hear me?' Luna's voice echoed in Oscar's head as she communicated with him telepathically.

'That's smart. Your telepathy ball. Nice one,' Oscar replied without speaking.

'It worked!' Luna communicated back.

'Not bad for your first try Le Fai,' Oscar said, now speaking directly to Luna as the energy ball spell started to wear off.

'I've so much to learn. What else can you teach me?' Luna enthused.

'Steady on Le Fai. Thought you wanted to find this elm tree,' Oscar said, reminding her of her original plans.

'Yeah, I do, I just want to learn.'

'Plenty of time for that. Come on let's get going,' Oscar said walking ahead.

Luna and Oscar continued to talk, heading in the direction of the brook. As they walked on, Luna marvelled at the beauty of her surroundings, taking in the different autumnal colours and textures highlighted by the rays of sun which burst through small openings between the branches above. Whilst peaceful, the air was filled with the sounds of different birds chirping and chattering to each other; Luna smiled to herself, thinking how at home she felt wandering through Lindull woods. It wasn't long before they reached the brook, which was wide, but shallow, flowing over an uneven bed of rocks, and earth. The sun danced on the water like silvery ribbons, in a display of magical elegance, highlighting the quick flow of the brook.

'Here we are. Once we have crossed the brook, we're pretty much there.' Oscar pointed over the water towards some tall trees. Luna was not paying attention but was mesmerised by the water and walked closer to the edge of the bank, peering into the brook. As she gazed admiringly at the mirror like quality of the water, she heard a gentle voice, which sounded like a whisper rising up in front of her.

'I flow to the south, but was born in the north, I call to all creatures to follow my voice, but none of you hear me, just the undines of Trelorth. My sadness it lingers, it never subsides and flows with the water right before your eyes. I wish you could sooth me, and answer my call, alas I still weep into night fall.'

'I hear you,' Luna whispered back, which was met with a moment of silence.

'You hear me sweet one, why I cannot believe it, I thought all hope had gone, but your voice I have to admit it.'

'You're beautiful. I was looking at how the sun reflects off you, and it looks so magical.'

'Why thank you sweet one, what a wonderful treat, for you to tell me I make your heart skip a beat.'

'Do you know anything about the fairies of the elm?'

'Why of course sweet one, they live over yonder, by the magnificent elm, why not have a wander and ask for Aurora the Queen of the faye. But be careful sweet one, they don't like betrayal, so if they tell you a secret or bestow you a gift, keep your word and honour their ways.'

'How do I call them?'

'Talk to the elm and ask their permission, and if they believe you, they will help you on your mission.'

Oscar was standing behind Luna listening to her but couldn't hear the words of the brook; it seems he did not share her ability to communicate with water.

'Luna, are you talking to one of the trees?'

Luna turned to face him and said, 'No, I'm talking to the brook...We need to talk to the elm tree'. Then returned her attention to the water.

'Thank you. I really appreciate your help,' Luna spoke softly to the brook.

'Thank you sweet one, now mind your way, look after yourself and have a good day.'

Luna thanked the water again, and made her way over the brook, using the natural rocks through which it flowed, as stepping stones. Oscar followed her, with Leon whispering in his ear as they crossed; Luna could not hear exactly what was being said but she felt curious about their private conversation.

After crossing the water, Oscar led the way towards a small cluster of trees, and there before them stood a tall, thick-trunked elm tree, with gnarled bark. Oscar stood next to the tree and slapped his hand against its bark, 'Here he is!'

'Tell your friend not to do that. And, I am not a *he*, I am not a *she*. I am just *me*,' the elm asserted, sounding less friendly and more dominant than the other trees Luna had spoken to.

'The tree didn't like that,' Luna gibed Oscar and flashed a wry smile at him.

'Now what do you want human?' the tree stated, its tone stern.

'Sorry. I'm Luna Le Fai...'

'You said you were Luna Woods,' Oscar interrupted sarcastically, provoking Luna to scowl at him. She then turned back to the elm tree.

'My family have had a long history with the faye of the elm,' Luna said pulling out the amulet, 'see I have this. I'm its keeper and my mum, Aggie Le Fai was the keeper before me, and Liz Le Fai before her.'

'I see. Who is the other one with you? Another Le Fai?' the elm enquired.

'No, he's my friend though.' Luna quickly glanced back at Oscar and smiled.

'Only you Le Fai are permitted to enter the fairy elm. As keeper of the amulet, you can call Aurora, Queen of the faye, whenever you wish. She will always hear you, wherever you are. Why not try it now Le Fai?' the elm tree instructed.

'I just call her name?' Luna asked uncertainly.

'Yes, Le Fai,' the elm tree confirmed.

'Okay.' Luna turned back to Oscar, 'I'm going to call the Queen of the fairies.'

'Aurora, Queen of the faye, please, are you there?' Luna wasn't sure if she was saying it correctly, but thought she would give it a shot. Everything went silent, the birds seemed to temporarily quieten their chatter; the air turned cold, and even Oscar noticed and started shivering. Suddenly Luna felt the amulet grow hot and it started to glow indigo, then suddenly in front of the elm, appeared a tall, elegantly dressed human-like being.

'You called. Which Le Fai are you?' the fairy said sounding

authoritative; Luna found her slightly intimidating.

'I'm Luna. Luna Le Fai, daughter of Aggie Le Fai, and granddaughter of Liz Le Fai. And you're Aurora, Queen of the faye?' Luna spoke uneasily but tried to keep her nerve.

'Yes, I am she. And you are the keeper of the amulet. And who is this other one?' Aurora said coldly pointing at Oscar, giving him an icy stare.

'He's my friend, Oscar.'

'He can't see me, but he hears me.' Aurora determined, then spoke directly to Oscar, 'child, you're not permitted into the fairy realm with any Le Fai, regardless of being a friend. You carry that crow, who sees too much. He has been here before, and *you* child, *you* have been here before.' As Aurora spoke, Oscar scanned around trying to locate the voice to no avail.

'She's in front of you Oscar,' Luna said helpfully. Oscar turned to face in that direction and spoke directly to Aurora.

'I don't mean any harm. Neither does Leon.' Oscar gestured to the crow who was still perched on his shoulder.

'Very well,' Aurora said dismissively, then looked directly at Luna again.

'Luna Le Fai, if you need me, wherever you are. Call to me and I will be of assistance.'

'Thank you…I wanted to ask you something.'

'Yes.'

'You said I was allowed to visit the fairy realm, your fairy realm. How do I do this? Should I call upon you?'

'Child, I do not think you are ready for my world just yet. But, when you are, place the crystal of the amulet against the trunk of the elm and the portal will appear.' Aurora waved her hand in a circular motion, causing a tear in the woodland to appear, which grew into a more visible opening. A swirling purple and silver light emerged as the opening expanded to reveal a completely different world. Luna gazed on into the portal, keeping her distance. The scene inside the fairy realm depicted an indigo sky and a rich, luscious multicoloured landscape. 'Remember, you must *not* bring anyone unpermitted into the realm, they would not survive the journey into our world. Your world, Luna.'

'My world?'

'Yes. You have our blood as well as human blood. But you have a few things to learn first. You will know when you are ready.'

'I wanted to ask you about the amulet, if I may?'

'You may.'

'There are others in my world who want it. My nan, Liz Le Fai, has made it clear to me that it must stay with me. That if others take it, it would cause problems.'

'Yes, you're forbidden under faye law to allow anyone else to wear the amulet. It must only be worn by its keeper. Many others, not just humans, have tried to take the amulet without success. If they were to convince you to give it to them, this would not only break our trust with you and your family, but the consequences to my world and yours would be catastrophic.'

'What do you mean? What would happen?'

'The amulet chooses its keeper wisely. It only chooses those who will use it for good, who will respect it as a being in its own right, who are already part of it. Those who desire to wear the amulet, who have not been chosen, only want it for the power it can offer them. The path they take, will always be in conflict with the greater good. Were they to wear the amulet, as their power increases, they will desire more; however, their desires will never be fully satisfied. Their hunger for power will increase and they will seek control over everything in their world and beyond. This will lead to mass conflict on a phenomenal scale, and eventually they will destroy everything in their path, until they're left with nothing. There will be nothing left. And once they face this reality, they'll see no other option but to end their own existence. So, you see. This amulet might seem attractive to many, but it's of no benefit to *anyone* but the keeper. By protecting the amulet, you're protecting all of us.'

Luna looked on intently at Aurora, realising the seriousness of her role as the keeper of the amulet. As she reflected on it, she panicked, suddenly terrified of it getting into the wrong hands. Luna had to quickly reason with herself, reminding herself of what her grandmother had said. She would have to be the one to hand it over, willingly, it could not be taken from her by force.

'As keeper of the amulet I promise to look after it...I really do,' Luna said earnestly, clutching the amulet in her fist.

Aurora nodded, then turned and walked towards the elm, disappearing from Luna's view, as though she had never been there. Luna turned back to Oscar looking serious faced.

'You heard all of that Oscar. You heard about the amulet, and what it means if anyone else wears it, didn't you?' she said quietly, meeting his eyes. Oscar glanced down at the ground, uncomfortable with the eye contact. He didn't answer her, but she could tell he was thinking about it. She continued to look at Oscar as his gaze still lingered on the woodland floor. She didn't want to say anything about his dad, she didn't think she needed to, given his reaction.

Luna and Oscar remained silent as they headed back towards the brook, and through the woodland, both lost in their own thoughts. Luna wondered if Oscar would still want to be friends with her - if he really was genuine. Part of her was concerned that his true intention might be to retrieve the amulet for his dad. She hoped that Aurora's warning was enough to make him think about the consequences of taking the magical object. Even if Oscar wasn't part of his dad's plans, perhaps he could stop his dad pursuing it. Although Luna had reservations about Oscar, she still couldn't help but like him, and felt a connection, the same connection she felt with Annie, and Jack for that matter. She wanted to be his friend, and give him a chance, because everyone deserves a chance, don't they?

CHAPTER 15: JACK

Luna awoke early on Monday morning and laid in bed thinking about her time in Lindull woods the day before. She wondered what Oscar actually thought about Aurora's warning but hoped he would somehow discourage his dad from pursuing the amulet. When they had parted on Sunday, Oscar seemed distant, as though he was mulling things over. Although they still agreed to meet on Halloween, the atmosphere between them was tense as they went their separate ways. Luna was now concerned that Oscar might feel resentful towards her and no longer want to be friends. This bothered Luna. However, she wasn't sure why it troubled her as much as it did and put it to the back of her mind.

Luna's thoughts quickly turned to Annie. She wondered how much detail she should share with her cousin, remembering she needed to tread carefully given Annie was unaware that Ariella had been hexed, inflicted by the coma curse. As Luna remained in bed working this out in her head, she was startled by three loud knocks on the front door. She glanced at her bedside clock, surprised at the time. Luna had been so distracted by her thoughts, it was already ten o'clock. In haste Luna jumped out of bed, quickly pulled off her pyjamas, and threw on her clothes from the day before, which were scattered on her bedroom floor. She then galloped down the stairs, speeded to the front door and opened it to find Annie standing there looking disgruntled.

'You took ages. I didn't think you were in,' Annie moaned impatiently, walking straight into the house, looking tired.

'Sorry, I was still in bed,' Luna admitted guiltily.

'Wish I was. Dad had me up at seven. Been at the shop since eight.' Anne said yawning, then scowled and rubbed her eyes.

'Do you want a drink?' Luna asked in a friendly way, trying to lift Annie's mood, then started walking to the kitchen with Annie sauntering behind.

'Yeah, just some water…did you get up to much yesterday?' Annie asked as she leaned into the kitchen table, using it as a rest.

'I saw Oscar,' Luna said quietly, trying to sound casual.

'Oscar? Where? How?' Annie was interested but there was a smidge of irritability in her voice.

'I went in the woods to see if I could find the fairy elm, and well, I met him in there…It wasn't planned. He was just there… He helped me find the elm tree,' Luna explained, trying her best to emphasise the chance nature of her encounter with Oscar, as she sensed Annie did not approve.

'Oh. I see.' Annie sounded slightly jealous and disappointed that she hadn't been there.

'You know, he's okay…I think…Like, I think we can trust him. He's like us,' Luna said warily, trying to convince Annie, who looked at her cousin suspiciously, wondering why Luna seemed so taken with Oscar.

'Do you fancy him Luna?' Annie asked bluntly. This caused Luna to turn red and fidget with her hands.

'No! No way! Why would you think that!?' Luna blasted, irritated by Annie's suggestion.

'Okay. If you say so…Anyway, I've been thinking about Halloween. Are you sure it's a good idea to meet him? I mean, what with his dad and the amulet…I'm hoping you haven't told Oscar about it. That you have it, the amulet?' As Annie asked this question, Luna blushed again looking uncomfortable and turned away to walk to the kitchen cupboard to retrieve a glass. Luna then slowly walked to the tap and filled the glass, avoiding answering Annie's question.

'You have. Haven't you!' Annie sounded angry.

'Yes, but he does know how much trouble it would cause

everyone if the amulet was taken from me. Aurora told us, and he seemed to take it all in. Annie, he won't do anything. He can't anyway. It's not like I would give it to him! I wouldn't even give it to you, or anyone!'

'What's that supposed to mean? I'm not important enough to be trusted with it, am I not?' Annie snapped, turning away from Luna, then petulantly folded her arms.

'No! It's not that! I just need to make sure I'm the only one who handles it. I do trust you. I really do…why are you being so unreasonable about all of this?' Luna complained, trying to get Annie to look at her. Both stood there at opposite ends of the kitchen, in silence, until Annie caved.

'Sorry. I'm just worried you'll forget me and soon it'll be all Oscar,' Annie said childishly, slowly unfolding her arms and turning back to face Luna.

'Never. You're my best friend Annie. I wouldn't do that to you. He's a friend, well I think he is, but not like *you*!' Luna said earnestly, then walked over to her cousin and gave her a hug.

'Sorry. I'm being silly. You're my best friend too,' Annie said softening.

'Let's go out. We should try to find Jack,' Luna suddenly suggested.

'Jack? Is that the boy you told me about? The mysterious one?' Annie asked inquisitively.

'Well, I wouldn't call him mysterious…he's an odd one. But he's funny. You'll like him. Trouble is, I never know when he's going to show up.'

Luna and Annie decided to head out in search of Jack. As they walked down Hubble Road, Luna heard the familiar greeting, 'Luna! Oi, over here!' It was Jack. Luna found it strange how he always seemed to appear out of nowhere; it was almost as if he knew when she thought about him and wanted to see him. Luna looked around in the direction of his voice and saw Jack standing on the opposite side of the road waving over at her. She waved back and then beckoned him to come across. He crossed the road and walked towards her and Annie.

'So that's Jack. Not how I imagined him,' Annie whispered to Luna, looking Jack up and down.

'Yeah, this is Jack.' Luna lifted her head in his direction as a way of introduction as he approached.

'You must be Luna's friend?' Jack said looking at Annie grinning.

'Yeah. Hi. I'm Annie.'

'Another Le Fai. Luna told me about you. What you both up to?' Jack wondered, looking from Luna to Annie.

'We were looking for you…You ditched me again, when we went into the woods. What happened?' Luna asked, arching her eyebrows at him.

'You disappeared, not me, so I left,' Jack retorted sharply. Luna frowned and gave him a serious look, wondering what had actually happened, but decided it was pointless pursuing it, given Jack rarely gave her straight answers.

'Why don't you come with me and Annie to town, or we could go back to my house. No point going into the woods,' Luna said widening her eyes at Jack, with a hint of sarcasm in her voice as she mentioned Lindull woods.

'I don't mind,' Jack replied shrugging his shoulders, seemingly happy to follow Luna's lead.

The three of them continued to walk down Hubble Road, with Luna explaining what had happened in the woods with Oscar the day before. As usual, Jack made several sarcastic remarks about Luna being a witch; this irritated Annie, however, she kept her feelings to herself. By the time they made their way onto Main Road into town, Luna had got to the part where Aurora had appeared to her; Jack and Annie listened intently as she told them what Aurora had said about the amulet.

'I didn't realise it was really *that* serious…That's a big responsibility Luna,' Annie said sounding serious-minded.

'Yeah, and I think Oscar must have taken it all in. I mean, how could he not. I just hope he finds a way of stopping his dad wanting it. Maybe if his dad realises how dangerous it is…' Luna innocently suggested.

'Are you serious Luna?' Jack interjected bluntly.

'What do you mean?' Luna stopped in her tracks and looked at Jack offended by his question.

'Well, think about it. His dad has probably heard it all before. But why would it stop him? He'll believe what he wants to, if he wants it that much,' Jack said in a matter-of-fact way.

'He's right Luna. Some people won't let anything stop them, if they really want something,' Annie said quietly in agreement with Jack. Luna's face suddenly drained of colour as the burden of being the keeper of the amulet weighed heavy on her.

'What am I going to do,' Luna said quietly, sounding worried.

'Well, you said no one can take it from you. You have to give it to them, right? So, you just have to do what your nan said. Don't give it to anyone,' Jack suggested, sounding practical.

'Not even me,' Annie said showing her agreement. Luna smiled nervously, then walked on quietly, deep in thought, with Jack and Annie making small talk next to her, feeling guilty about forcing Luna to think about her new responsibilities as keeper of the amulet.

As they continued down Main Road, three push bikes flew between them and almost knocked Luna and Annie over. Luna shouted after them, 'Oi! What you doing! Idiots!' Following her blast of anger, one of the bikes came to a sudden halt - the brakes squealing - and headed back towards Luna. It was Oscar Blackthorn.

'Sorry. Didn't realise it was you,' Oscar said apologetically, as he stopped the bike in front of Luna.

'You nearly took us out!' Luna scolded, glaring at him.

'Sorry, we were in a rush. Just with Ace and Tom. They'll be there at Halloween… where are you off to?' Oscar asked Luna, and then looked Annie up and down, which made her feel uncomfortable.

'Not sure. Might go to town… Oh this is Jack,' Luna said to Oscar, then turned to look at Jack, but he had disappeared.

Luna was puzzled and caught Annie's eye who seemed equally confused.

'Who's Jack?' Oscar said sounding a bit baffled, glancing around.

'I told you he was like this didn't I? One minute he's here and the next he's…gone.' Luna rolled her eyes and sighed, then tried to figure out how he had managed to vanish without anyone noticing.

'I didn't even see him go. Where could he have gone?' Annie said searching her head for rational explanations.

'Listen, I've got to catch up with my mates. See you tomorrow…8pm.' Oscar smiled at Luna, then took off on his bike, disappearing into the distance. Luna noticed that this time Oscar sounded much more upbeat about meeting up, which was quite different from how he was when they parted ways on Sunday.

Annie and Luna were still wondering where Jack had got to, distracting them from their brief encounter with Oscar.

'Should we look for Jack?' Annie asked, still baffled by his disappearing act.

'No point, he always does this. He'll appear again as quickly as he vanished. He's so weird. But, you've met him now.' Luna shrugged and they both continued to walk in the direction of town, with Annie asking to stop off at her grandmother's bookstore to collect something.

They walked into the book shop, which was unlocked, despite the closed sign hanging in the door. Annie made her way towards the back of the shop.

'I just need to pop upstairs. Won't be long,' Annie said, rushing into the back room and up the stairs which led to the top of the building – a space Luna had already been acquainted with weeks earlier. As Luna waited for Annie, she browsed through some of the books which were randomly ordered. As she examined the different book titles, Luna felt a sudden change in temperature and an icy presence next to her; she glanced to the side of her and saw the same old woman she had seen the first time she went into 'Ariella's Books'.

'Your mum would be very proud of you Luna. You're doing a wonderful job as the amulet's keeper. But you must be careful, there's danger on its way,' she whispered. However, before Luna could reply, the mysterious woman turned and headed into the back of the shop. Luna started to follow her but could not see where she had gone; then Annie came rushing down the stairs.

'Sorry, forgot my money. For town,' Annie said and wondered why Luna seemed so distant and distracted.

'Who *is* that woman? The one who works here?' Luna asked, staring past Annie into the back of the shop.

'Which one? No one else works here. My dad is here alone... Oh but look who is back,' Annie said pointing at the shop door, which Jack was peeping through from outside. Luna and Annie left the shop and greeted their friend, then asked him where he had got to.

'I didn't like those bikes. Spooked me,' Jack said vaguely. Luna made a face and shook her head looking at Annie, 'Told you. No point asking him, cos you won't get more than that.'

Annie, Luna, and Jack continued to stand outside the shop. They were about to set off into town, as originally planned, when Annie started to ask Luna about the woman she had seen in her grandmother's shop.

'What were you on about before, you know, about the person in nan's? Was someone there then?' Anna asked curiously.

'Well yeah, when you went upstairs, she just appeared out of nowhere. Spoke to me then walked into the back and...I dunno, she was gone. I couldn't see where she went, then you came down,' Luna said ponderingly.

'What did she look like?' Annie asked curiously, wondering who it could be.
'I told you about her before Annie. Remember? She looks like your nan. I asked you if it was Raven, and you said it couldn't be,' Luna replied, furrowing her brow. Annie went quiet, her face

indicating she was thinking it over, when she suddenly widened her eyes and gaped at Luna, with her mouth open.

'What's up?' Luna asked urgently.

'Maybe you're right Luna.' Annie confirmed, then pulled on Luna's arm, urging her to head back into the book shop. Jack stayed outside and sat on the curb as the other two rushed inside.

'Dad! Dad!' Annie called running through to the back of the shop and up the stairs with Luna dashing behind.

'What's wrong?' Nick asked as he opened the door of the room - where Luna had seen him once before, a time she had tried to put to the back of her mind.

'Dad, are there any pictures of Raven here?' Annie said, pushing her way past him and into the room.

'Of Raven? Well, yes, somewhere.' As Nick said this, Annie was already grabbing her nan's photo albums, which were kept on a shelf with various books and other miscellaneous items. Annie sat down on the brown two-seater leather sofa and dropped three photo albums on the seat next to her. She started to frantically turn the pages of the albums, quickly scanning the photos, examining them for any trace of her great aunt Raven.

'Aha! Here. Look,' Annie said, quickly standing up and thrusting a photo album in Luna's face.

'Is this the person you saw?' Annie asked excitedly pointing at the picture. Luna carefully examined the photograph, which was of a younger woman than the one she had seen, but there was a clear resemblance.

'Sorta. I think so. She's younger than the person I saw,' Luna said slowly, as she scrutinised the photograph. Annie snatched the photo album back and put it down on the floor and picked up another one searching through it.

'Annie, why are you looking for a photo of Raven?' Nick sounded puzzled.

'It's just, Luna spoke to an old lady downstairs, and she looked like Raven. I'm sure it was her,' Annie said still flicking through the photo albums but was starting to feel defeated; there didn't appear to be any of their aunt in her later years. Nick glanced at Luna and Annie, took out his mobile phone and started looking through it, as though he was searching for something. He stopped and showed Luna his phone. On the screen was a picture of a memorial service sheet, and on it was a photo of Raven, which was identical to the mysterious woman Luna had now spoken to on two separate occasions.

'Is this who you spoke to?' Nick asked Luna gently. She nodded – there was no doubt in her mind that it was Raven.

'It's not unusual for witches to be able to talk to the dead. I too see Raven from time to time, but she has never spoken to me. My mum often talks to her.' As Nick said this, Luna remembered the first time she saw Ariella through the book shop door and how she looked as though she was talking to someone out of view. Luna wondered if this had been Raven. She remembered how odd she found it. But now it seemed so incredibly normal to her.

'Luna, I knew it! This is awesome!' Annie trilled, then had a sudden thought, 'Oh. We left Jack downstairs. We'd better go and find him.'

'He'll be okay. I told you what he's like. He's probably not even there now,' Luna said nonchalantly.

'Jack?' Nick asked slowly, as though the name was familiar to him.

'He's a friend of mine. We sometimes hang out. Annie met him today.' Luna explained. Nick looked back at Annie and then at Luna.

'So where is he now?' Nick seemed curious.

'Outside. Did you want to meet him? He's okay dad,' Annie said dryly, arching her eyebrows, thinking her dad was probably being overprotective about her hanging out with a boy he hadn't yet met.

'Show me,' Nick said and left the room, with Annie and Luna following him, wondering what the urgency was to meet Jack. They walked down the stairs, still trailing after Nick as he proceeded to the door at the front of the shop. He stood gazing out; Jack looked back and smiled. Annie pulled a silly face behind her dad, quietly giggling to herself at the private joke. Luna was more interested in Nick, as he continued to stare out of the shop in Jack's direction but without saying anything.

'It's Jack,' Nick quietly muttered to himself, then opened the door and approached the boy, looking to make sure no one else was about.

'Jack Rogers. Do you remember me? It's Nick. Do you remember? Nick Le Fai,' Nick said gently, looking directly at Jack. Jack looked back at Nick, as though he had been hit by a distant memory of something he had long forgotten. Panic was now etched on Jack's pale face, and he started looking around as though he didn't know where he was or what was happening. As though he was waking from a deep sleep and had been lost in a dream.

'It's okay Jack. You're safe. You just forgot, that's all…I'm Annie's dad. Luna is Aggie's daughter. You know Aggie, you remember Aggie?' Nick's voice was gentle. Jack suddenly looked less anxious and glanced over at Luna.

'She looks just like Aggie. Maybe that's why you spoke to her. But it's not Aggie,' Nick explained softly.

'Do you remember hanging out with me and Aggie? We used to hang around the back of this book shop. Remember?'

'Yes. Yes. I do now. I remember now. But you left me.'

'We grew up Jack.'

'I didn't,' Jack said sounding disappointed, looking down at himself with a sad expression on his face, then stared at his feet.

'I know. I'm sorry Jack…do you remember what happened?' Nick asked warmly, leaning into him.

'No, not really… I remember something…I remember we were standing in the road, and then, you and Aggie shouted, and then nothing. Nothing at all. Everything went blank,' Jack said solemnly, still staring at his feet. Annie and Luna were still behind Nick and Jack, quietly listening.

'We tried to stop it happening, but we couldn't. It happened so quickly. I'm so sorry Jack,' Nick lamented, sighing regretfully at not being able to save his friend.

'I died…didn't I? That car hit me. I didn't see it coming.' Jack slumped down on the path as though the memory of his death had exhausted him. Nick slowly crouched down and sat next to him.

'Aggie never really got over it. Neither did I…I'm so sorry Jack.' Nick stared at the road.

'I kept coming back here cos it felt familiar…I even took Luna up the back steps and…' Jack paused looking deep in thought for a few moments, then continued, 'Well, we hid in the cupboard and listened in on you,' Jack said guiltily. Nick looked back at Luna, and crumpled his brow slightly, and Annie simultaneously gave her a pointed look.

'What do you mean?' Nick asked uneasily.

'A bit ago. I can't remember when. Everyday seems to run into another. I don't know when, but I told Luna you were witches. I couldn't remember how I knew, but I just knew. She didn't know about it…it wasn't her idea to come here. It was me. I'm sorry.' As Jack made this confession, Nick sighed and looked back at Luna. She felt guilty and held her head down in shame.

'I think I know when you were here with Luna, Jack. I was talking to mum and Suzie about the amulet, and I remember when I left the room, I felt something. I felt a presence. It reminded me of you. I almost went back to check…but I thought it was probably nothing.'

'I'm so sorry.' Luna's little voice came from behind Nick and Jack, her head still hanging down.

'Why would you do that?! How could you?' Annie fumed, glaring at Luna in disbelief at her friend's behaviour.

'Annie. Enough,' Nick asserted, giving his daughter a stern look.

'It was before I was friends with you. I had no idea about anything then. Didn't even know I was a witch. I'm so, so sorry. I understand if you don't want anything to do with me again.' Luna started to quietly weep. Annie looked away, but as she heard her friend cry, she couldn't help but turn back to comfort her.

'Oh, it's okay. Just don't do anything like that again,' Annie sighed resignedly, pulling Luna towards her.

'Jack, you don't have to stay here. There's somewhere better for you now,' Nick said gently, his attention back on his old friend.

'No. I'm not ready. I'm not ready...I feel like there's something keeping me here,' Jack said uncertainly, trying to work out what it was.

Nick continued to sit with Jack in silence, with Annie and Luna standing behind him thinking about their friend, trying to wrap their heads around what they had just learned about Jack. That he was, like Raven, no longer part of the physical world. He was a spirit, a ghost. One in the literal sense, but also, a ghost from Nick's and Aggie's childhood; of a time in the past, a time in which he was still suspended, even lost, unwilling to move on. Luna wondered what it was that kept him here. She wondered if he had parents, still living, or siblings, who still clung to his memory. Luna wondered if the connection she felt with Jack was because of her mum – maybe he felt that connection too. As she reflected on this, another question entered her head. If it is only witches who see the dead - what does that make Annie?

CHAPTER 16:
FIGHTING, SPELLS, AND A GRAVEYARD

Luna and Annie left Nick with Jack outside the book shop, wondering if there was going to be an attempt made to move Jack's spirit on to somewhere else, to a place away from this physical plane. Luna was curious about this; she had never considered the possibility of people being more than their physical body – until recently of course. It had become clear, very quickly, that life has a habit of making you question everything and may even force you to rethink reality entirely as you once knew it– *'whatever that even means?'* Luna thought to herself. She and Annie sat at Ariella's reading table in the back room of the book shop waiting for Nick.

'Do you know where spirits go?' Luna asked pensively, thinking about her own mother.

'I don't know exactly, well I'm still alive, obvs…but my nan tells me that our souls can break off and go in different places… it's a bit confusing…part of us may choose to stay, but then other parts might travel to different dimensions,' Annie said thoughtfully, recalling her grandmother's explanation.

'Have you ever seen spirits before?' Luna asked quietly.

'I didn't think I could…I'm not supposed to be able to…I'm not a witch.'

'You don't know that though, do you? Maybe you *are* Annie.'

'I don't know.'

'Does it scare you?' Luna asked gently, glancing across at Annie, who avoided eye contact.

'Maybe…a bit…I guess I never thought it was a possibility. I mean, when you're told something, and then turns out things are different, it's kinda unsettling. If you know what I mean?' Annie said reflectively, rubbing her index finger on her chin.

'Yeah. I know exactly what you mean,' Luna said, thinking about her own situation, and whilst different, she was faced with the same sense of unsettling uncertainty.

'Are you going to talk to your parents about it?' Luna asked, wondering if her dads knew, or at the very least had some answers for Annie.

'Yeah, I will…not sure what they know about my biological parents though. They've never told me…but I never wanted to know…but maybe I do now.'

'Are you and Arthur *both* adopted?'

'Yeah, but we have different biological parents, well, I think, but I'm not sure now. We don't talk about that stuff. I don't even know if he has spoken to our dads about it. I mean, they're our parents whatever, so, well, not even thought about having biological parents.'

'Of course. I get that…Does Arthur have powers?'

'Yeah, recently, they've started. But he was always told it would happen. They never said any of that to me, just told me it didn't matter if I wasn't a witch. So. Well, I'm guessing, maybe they didn't know.'

'Hmmm…maybe not,' Luna said pensively and then went silent as they both finished up their drinks. Suddenly Nick came in, but without Jack. Luna looked behind him to see if Jack was following, but there was no sign of him. Nick pulled a chair up to the table where Luna and Annie were sitting.

'Has he gone. Moved on somewhere?' Annie asked sensitively.

'No. He doesn't want to,' Nick said looking at Luna, giving her the feeling that Jack's refusal to go was something to do with her.

'Why doesn't he want to go?' Annie asked looking at Luna, then back at her dad, having the same suspicions.

'He doesn't want to leave Luna…Thinks she…needs him,' Nick sighed and continued, 'Luna, he told me about the amulet.'

'He did? What else did he tell you?' Luna said avoiding eye contact with him, worried that Jack might have also told Nick about her and Annie's association with Oscar Blackthorn.

'Just that you're the keeper of the amulet,' Nick said smiling gently at Luna. He could see the worry on her face, so he attempted to reassure her.

'It's okay. You're not in trouble. You are the keeper. It's just how it was meant to be. We just have to make sure we keep each other safe, and everything will be okay.' Nick looked deep into Luna's eyes to register how important it was for her to take this role seriously and be committed as the amulet's keeper.

'I know. I know how important it is. I know I can do this. You can trust me. Honestly…If mum did it. I can,' Luna said certainly, maintaining eye contact with Nick. He smiled at Luna and nodded his head to acknowledge his confidence in what she was asserting. Nick then stood up and turned to Annie.

'Annie. We need to talk later. But, you two have got the rest of the afternoon, so don't feel you have to hang around here with me. I've got plenty to be getting on with. Annie, dad will be here about four, so make sure you're back around then. Oh, and Luna, before I forget, I think your dad is bringing you to us tomorrow for the family gathering. I told him to get to us for five…Annie said something about you having a sleep over at yours after? That's fine with me and Daniel. But just checking your dad is okay with it?' Nick said to Luna, which caught her by surprise, given Annie hadn't even told her about this part of the plan. Luna surreptitiously glanced at Annie wondering when she was going to tell her that bit.

'Er, yeah, yeah, he's cool with it,' Luna lied trying her best to sound convincing. Annie gave a little triumphant smile and quickly glanced at Luna.

'The family party will be over by seven, so we could be back before eight,' Annie determined, which prompted Nick to respond.

'Does it matter if we don't finish by seven? That's very precise Annie. It finishes when it finishes,' Nick said suspiciously, giving Annie a warning look.

'I know. Just saying cos we've got plans for a film and popcorn at Luna's.' Annie said smiling sweetly at her dad, who instantly seemed satisfied with her explanation. Luna grinned to herself, impressed by how easy it was for Annie to manipulate her dad.

Luna and Annie left the bookstore, and while keeping an eye out for Jack, just in case he showed himself, they headed in the direction of the town centre, chatting on the way. As they got nearer to town they decided to stop in the park and headed to sit on the swings. Luna had never been in this park before and wondered if they would see anyone from school; maybe it was another opportunity for 'normal' watching she thought to herself.

'How are we going to sneak out? We need to plan this carefully.' Annie said thoughtfully, which surprised Luna, given her sudden interest in meeting Oscar and his friends in the woods.

'You seem keen. Thought you didn't think it was a good idea?' Luna said suspiciously.

'I didn't say that. I said we just need to be careful. Anyway, like you said, Oscar is probably okay. So, well, we'll be okay won't we. And his friends will be with him – I think that's what he said – Tom and Ace.' Annie said shifting her eyes around.

'Sure. When did you decide about the sleep over? You never mentioned it this morning. In fact, you didn't seem keen at all.' Luna looked at Annie searchingly.

'Oh, I was just grumpy this morning…I asked dad before, when I went up for my purse…good idea though, isn't it?' Annie smiled at Luna, looking pleased with herself. Luna grinned and nodded in agreement, feeling more excited than ever about their evening plans for Halloween. They just needed to figure out how they were going to avoid arousing Luna's dad's suspicions and make their way into the woods unnoticed. As Luna and

Annie continued to chat and pull together a foolproof plan, Luna spotted a crow perched up high on the branch of a tall rowan tree, opposite the swings. The crow looked at her and tilted its head as though it was listening and observing her. She got up off the swing and approached the bird.

'Is that you Leon?' Luna called up to the crow.

'Yes, Le Fai, it is. Caw. Caw. Oscar is on his way. Caw caw,' Leon replied then flew off out of the park.

Luna turned to walk back towards Annie and sat back down on the swing next to her friend; Annie wondered what she had been doing.

'Oscar is on his way.' Luna said, relaying the crow's message. Annie looked on confused by her friend's unexpected announcement.

'Oscar? How do you know? Can you sense him?' Annie asked curiously, looking at Luna searchingly. Then almost immediately, three push bikes, with Oscar in the lead, and his friends Ace and Tom not far behind, raced into the park, riding straight up to the swings.

'What are you doing here Le Fai. Can't get away from you,' Oscar said sounding cocky, turning to his friends who laughed mockingly, looking Luna and Annie up and down.

'I think you'll find *we* were here before *you*,' Luna scoffed, matching Oscar's swagger.

'Ooh Le Fai. Listen to you,' Tom sneered at Luna. Oscar looked back and eyed his friend daggers to silence him.

'Shut up Tom...Luna and Annie are alright. Even if they *are* Le Fais.' Oscar felt the need to defend them but still wanted to maintain some sense of authority.

'I just saw Leon. He said you were coming,' Luna remarked, leaving Annie wondering who her cousin was talking about. Oscar looked up and cupped his hands around his mouth to make a caw like call. After doing this a few times Leon flew over and down from somewhere outside of the park and landed on Oscar's shoulder.

'Do you two still reckon you'll be okay for tomorrow night?'

Oscar asked as he stroked Leon.

'Yes, we have a plan.' Annie replied confidently.

'Good. Should be fun...just don't bring your brother Annie.' Oscar turned to his friends and laughed, then back to Annie, 'You probably know that though,' Oscar snorted, the self-importance returning. Luna could see why her family did not like the Blackthorns, but she knew there was more to Oscar than this, so chose to ignore his displays of arrogance, suspecting it was all bravado for his friends.

'Are you going to introduce us to your mates then?' Annie asked, eyeing his two friends.

'This is Tom.' Oscar casually gestured to his friend who was shorter than him, with mousy coloured hair tied back in a ponytail. Like Oscar he was dressed entirely in black – this seemed to be a trend with all three of them. Tom seemed to take the introduction in his stride and simply nodded, as way of a greeting Luna and Annie.

'And this is Ace. They're in your year.' Oscar said. Ace had long brown straight hair, and a friendly face.

They smiled over at Luna and Annie, 'Sup. Oscar hasn't shut up about you...'

Oscar quickly stopped Ace before they could go any further. 'Sooo, what you been up to?' but before Luna and Annie had a chance to respond to Oscar's question, they were interrupted.

'Look at this. The freaks all together, and one of them has even brought his pet bird,' came a sneering voice from behind Luna and Annie, who were both still perched on the swings. Oscar and his friends were visibly uncomfortable but quickly tried to hide it with a physical display of confidence, as they moved in closer, glaring ahead.

'What do you want Billy?' Oscar spat, looking through Luna and Annie, who became aware that there was not just one, but others standing behind them. Luna quickly glanced back to see a year ten boy, with four others standing behind him; she recognised one of the faces – it was Emily from school. Emily, the girl she made fly across the school canteen. Luna gulped and felt her stomach do somersaults, then directed Annie to look behind her, by flashing her a side glance. Annie peeped back, then after registering Emily's presence, quickly turned away.

'See that Woods girl who dissed me is with them,' Emily gobbed. Luna's heart raced and Annie closed her eyes wishing them away.

'Which one's that Emily? Or should I say WITCH,' the other girl said smugly, leading the rest of their gang to laugh disdainfully. Luna could see Oscar's knuckles turn white as he tightened his grip on the handlebar of his bike. Annie looked angry and shot up off the swing, then turned around to face the girl who made the remark.

'What did you say,' Annie asserted, stepping forward aggressively. This incensed Emily and her friend, who swiftly moved in towards Annie, to intimidate her. The girl then leaned in, she was so close, that Annie could feel her warm breath on her face.

'Wanna say that again,' the girl warned vehemently. This action sparked something in Luna who swung around and advanced towards her. Emily looked anxious and gave her friend a worried look.

'Leave it Scarlet. They're not worth it,' Emily appealed to her friend. However, Scarlet chose to ignore her advice and continued to antagonise Annie and Luna.

'What ya gonna do girl? You might have spooked Emily but takes more to scare me,' Scarlet sneered, then smugly turned her head to face her friends, to revel in her assumed victory. However, as she turned back to face Annie and Luna, she suddenly found herself hovering a few meters off the floor, looking down to see a stern-faced Luna glaring up at her. Luna used her hands to conduct Scarlet's movements as she remained elevated above the ground, moving her back and forth, then stopping and keeping her suspended in the air. Annie, Oscar, Tom, and Ace stared up at Scarlet and started laughing.

'Are you going to apologise?' Luna called up.

'I'm sorry. I'm sorry,' Scarlet said sounding panicked, with her friends motionlessly staring up at her from below.

'You gonna leave us alone,' Luna instructed assertively.

Yes. Yes...sorry,' Scarlet said quickly, the terror still audible in her voice. Luna gently brought the girl back down, until she had two feet on the ground. As soon as she realised that she was no longer suspended in the air, Scarlet ran behind her friends, with Emily quickly offering her comfort. Luna and Annie turned to face Oscar, however, as they did, a guttural raw came from Emily who rounded in on them, with her gang of friends following suit. The group piled in on the unsuspected witches, who found fists frantically pounding against their bodies from every direction – it was like watching a pack of lions descending on their prey. One of the boys pulled an unsuspecting Oscar off his bike and launched it at Tom, who was trying to push another one of the boys off him, while Ace felt the force of the bike land on him instead. Emily had targeted Luna and grabbed her hair pulling it as she kicked her hard in the legs; Annie somehow managed to crawl her way out of the pile on and grabbed Emily by the torso to pull her off Luna. As Luna was freed from the attack she moved into the sideline and started centring herself, then rubbed her hands together to create energy balls. Oscar was defending himself against one of the other boys pushing him hard into the floor leaving him dazed on the ground. As Oscar got away, he saw what Luna was doing and joined her, creating balls of energy to increase their defence against the gang's attack. Luna and Oscar began hurling balls of bright white and blue light into the fighting bodies, aiming to calm the aggression. As the spheres of light flew through the air they dissolved into the unknowing casualties, bringing calm and healing energy, gradually causing the fighting to slow down and stop. Now there were bodies lying still and silent on the ground; no longer angry, no longer injured, but at peace.

'Let's send in some giggle balls,' Luna suggested, smiling at Oscar, who grinned back and started rubbing his hands together to create bright yellow balls of light, which he then directed at the others. As Luna and Oscar threw in more giggle balls, each of their targets sat up and started laughing uncontrollably; looking at each other in a state of euphoria. They were no longer enemies on a battlefield; they were temporarily transformed into friends.

'We need to get them away from each other before the magic wears off,' Oscar said in haste, as he ran towards his friends and Annie, ushering them away and out of the park. He called back, 'Luna, send in a few more peace balls to give us time to get out.' In response Luna started creating several energy balls of white light and hurled them at the others as she backed out of the park to follow her friends. Oscar, Tom, and Ace cycled ahead, with Annie perched on the handlebars of Ace's bike. Luna ran after them. Annie looked behind to see her cousin galloping towards them and shouted at the others to stop for Luna.

'Luna, come on!' Annie called urging her friend to catch up. As Luna reached them, she hung her head down and rested her hands on the tops of her legs, panting and out of breath.

'Might be a good witch, but you're not very fit,' Oscar said sarcastically, then smiled at Luna, who slowly looked up. Whilst she wanted to scold Oscar, she couldn't help but laugh, as they all did.

'Seriously. That was a good call Luna. You got us out of there without a scratch,' Oscar said sounding proud of his friend.

'Yeah, that was awesome Luna,' Ace agreed.

'Never thought I'd say that about a Le Fai,' Oscar joked.

'Yeah, reckon you've got competition bro,' Tom mocked Oscar, who responded with an instant frown, however, he then couldn't help but beam at Luna and Annie.

'Who would have thought the Le Fais would be so much fun...why don't you come with us to St Paul's?' Oscar urged Luna and Annie, then looked at Ace and Tom for their approval.

'St Pauls?' Luna enquired, unsure of where or what exactly that referred to.

'The church Luna,' Annie interjected quietly. Luna grimaced, wondering why Oscar would want to go to church.

'The graveyard at St Pauls,' Oscar confirmed, then stared at Luna as though she should've guessed.

'Spose,' Luna said, looking at Annie to gauge if she thought it was a good idea.

'Yeah, sure, I guess we've got time. What do you do there?' Annie said warily.

'It's one of our hangouts. Less likely to get bothered there. Those lot in the park never go near the graveyard,' Oscar scoffed, with Tom interjecting, 'Cos they're a bunch of wusses.' This provoked Oscar and Ace to laugh haughtily.

Oscar led the way towards St Paul's graveyard, with Luna on the back of his bike, and Annie on the front of Ace's handlebars. The trek didn't take much time, and as they approached the gated graveyard, Annie and Luna jumped off the bikes. Luna noticed a car parked up outside the church. She was surprised to see her maths teacher Mr Porter, sitting in the driver's seat. Oscar and the others pushed their bikes around the other side of the graveyard and hid them in a cluster of bushes, while Luna and Annie waited by the gate.

'Have you seen Mr Porter's there?' Luna pointed to the red car, where Mr Porter's head was faced downward, as though he was doing something on his phone. As the girls watched, he looked up and smiled, instantly recognising his pupils, and gave them a friendly wave, prompting Luna and Annie to wave back. Oscar and the others reappeared behind them, and Luna watched Mr Porter's expression change, becoming more serious as he spotted Oscar, Tom and Ace. Luna looked back at Oscar, who was visibly uncomfortable and started nervously scratching the back of his neck – he didn't seem to know what to do with his hands so took out his phone and started looking through it. Mr Porter then started his engine, waving to Luna and Annie, but then glared disapprovingly at Oscar as he drove off – Oscar was still on his phone.

'What was all that about?' Luna asked Oscar after Mr Porter had driven off.

'What do you mean?' Oscar said defensively, putting his phone away, and readjusting his hair off his face.

'Mr Porter gave you proper evils,' Luna said curiously, wondering what had caused the tension, remembering all the mysterious interactions between them at school.

'Don't know what you're on about. Anyway, come on let's go,' Oscar said trying to move the conversation on, and walked into the graveyard through the old, rusty iron gate which was hanging off one of the hinges making it difficult to open and close. Luna and Annie followed behind the others into the graveyard and looked at each other bemused, not sure how to interpret the frostiness between Oscar and Mr Porter. As the others went ahead, passing several rows of graves, Annie and Luna quietly chatted amongst themselves.

'That was weird,' Luna said uneasily.

'Yeah...Oh no, just thought. What if Mr Porter tells Suzie he saw us with a Blackthorn,' Annie said anxiously.

'I don't think he would do that. He's not like that. We can trust him, Annie,' Luna said convincingly, reassuring her friend.

Annie and Luna caught up with the others, who had stopped near a cluster of trees which were set back slightly from the graves, out of view. Oscar stood in front of them all, looking like the gang leader in his black zipped up hoodie, black jeans, and black lace-up army style boots. He was taller than the others, which emphasised his sense of authority, as he began giving instructions.

'Luna, Annie, I reckon it's time we taught you some proper magic...Blackthorn magic,' Oscar said dramatically, lifting his head up, signifying his leadership. Luna couldn't help but roll her eyes, and snort, which Oscar immediately spotted and challenged.

'Le Fai, what was that for? You said you want to learn, so we'll teach you,' Oscar said conceitedly, then looked at Tom and Ace who nodded agreeingly.

'What do you mean by Blackthorn magic?' Luna asked sneeringly, trying to thwart Oscar's arrogant tone.

'Time for a bit of necromancy Le Fai,' Oscar said giving a superior smile. Luna did not know what necromancy was, and thought it sounded strange. However, she didn't want to look unknowledgeable, so just looked at him and didn't respond.

'He's just trying to sound clever. He only means talking to spirits,' Annie said boldly, tutting and giving him a pointed look.

'Not just talking to them. Let's do a bit of summoning and manipulating spirit,' Oscar contended, sounding increasingly like his dad. Luna glared at him, thinking the manipulation part sounded cruel and unnecessary.

'I'm not doing that. How does that help us? Sounds like a bad idea,' Luna scolded, as though she was chastising a younger child. Oscar looked awkward and could see his friends giggling at him.

'It's not as bad as it sounds. We've just brought our pendulums to see whose about. We sometimes find local spirits and ask if they want to help us. We don't make them do anything they don't want to,' Ace admitted, trying to break the illusion set by Oscar.

'Alright Ace,' Oscar said, worried his friend would make him look stupid, then continued, 'when we find a spirit who wants to help us, we might draw them into things, like this.' Oscar reached into his pocket and pulled out a few crystals which included a silver and black obsidian pendulum, and two clear quartz stones.

'Oh. I've done that before,' Luna said nonchalantly, 'my nan taught me.'

'Oh right, well, spose, you know what you're doing. Won't need my help then,' Oscar said petulantly, disappointed that he wouldn't be able to take the lead.

'But I haven't used a pendulum,' Luna admitted.

'Well, I haven't done either,' Annie said awkwardly.

'But she has spoken to spirits,' Luna interjected, to boost Annie's confidence and image.

'Okay. Well, I'll call them in first. I just need you all to form a circle around me and hold hands. DO NOT break the circle,' Oscar decisively instructed, looking at Luna and Annie to make sure they understood his directions.

The four friends stood around Oscar holding each other's hands, waiting for him to give further instructions.

'Close your eyes and clear your minds. Bring your will to a golden protective ball of light and hold it around us all. This will protect us,' Oscar said, directing his words at Luna and Annie in particular. As they concentrated, a golden sphere of light appeared and surrounded the friends. As the light illuminated their magic circle, Oscar took his pendulum from his pocket, then focused his gaze on it and spoke in a commanding tone. 'Spirits of air, spirits of earth, spirits of water, and of fire, we call upon you to join us. Come not those who wish to cause harm, or those filled with uncontrollable sorrow, we only permit those who come in peace...' Oscar paused, trying to remember what to say next, which spoiled the ceremonial effect.

'And don't want to disrupt the calm?' Tom suggested, quietly, attempting not to unsettle the flow of the summoning spell.

'Yeah, that'll do...and don't want to disrupt the calm,' Oscar continued, momentarily coming out of character. Annie and Luna started giggling quietly, which prompted a warning look from Oscar.

'I can see why his dad likes to call himself a sorcerer. So dramatic,' Luna whispered to Annie trying not to laugh out loud.

'He's definitely not a poet,' Annie sniggered back in a hushed tone.

Oscar continued to focus his attention on the pendulum as it started to vigorously swing back and forth, and then, at speed, it started to swing in a circular motion. As this happened, Luna felt the amulet grow hot, almost burning her skin, causing her to grimace. Oscar saw Luna's pained expression and urged her not to let go of the others' hands.

'Luna! Don't let go! Don't break the circle!' he asserted.

'It's the amulet. It's burning me,' Luna said her face grimacing from the pain it was causing. As she looked down at the amulet, which was underneath her jumper, she could see it glowing red through her top. Suddenly there was an audible voice, which they all heard. But for Luna this was recognisable. A voice she hadn't heard for a long time. A voice that made Luna catch her breath and filled her with an intense feeling of love, that was so overwhelming she no longer felt the amulet burning into her chest. It was her mum's voice.

'Danger is coming my sweet. Do *not* let go of the amulet. Your life depends on it. They all depend on you. I love you.' After Luna's mother's soft voice uttered those words, everything went deadly quiet, and the pendulum stopped moving. The protective golden light which had encased them, suddenly dissolved. The five friends looked at each other, with Oscar and Annie clearly aware of which spirit they had summoned. They looked at Luna uneasily, with Oscar being the first to speak.

'You okay Luna? I'm sorry. I didn't mean that to happen. I didn't think we'd bring your mum through,' Oscar said gently, which prompted Annie to turn to Luna and rub her arm affectionately. Luna didn't speak, but gazed ahead, then clutched the amulet through her top. After that, no one spoke, but decided in silence to stop what they were doing and leave the graveyard.

They soon set off, heading in different directions - Annie and Luna one way, and Oscar, Tom, and Ace taking another route. However, as they parted, Oscar turned back, pushed his bike to Luna and hugged her, which took the others by surprise. As he pulled away from the embrace, he smiled and spoke.

'Mates, yeah?' Luna smiled back and nodded; he continued. 'See you tomorrow. And Luna. Thanks for not judging me.'

'Judging you?' Luna asked uncertainly.

'For being a Blackthorn...You're not how I thought you'd be. You're really decent. You're a real friend Luna,' Oscar said, appearing not to care how the others would view his admission. He smiled and mounted his bike to head off.

As Luna and Annie headed away from the graveyard Luna thought about Oscar, and their serendipitous friendship. Behind Oscar's smiles and friendly gestures, Luna could sense that there was still some hesitancy. Luna wondered if the conflict between the Blackthorns and the Le Fais, and simultaneously his sudden friendship with her and Annie, was making him confused, making him feel at odds with everything he had been brought up to believe. Afterall, the Blackthorns' hatred of the Le Fais seemed to be deeply embedded in Oscar's family identity. It was something that would always be there, always reminding him that the Le Fais could never be his true friends.

CHAPTER 17:
IMPORTANT LESSONS

It was the early hours of Halloween morning and Luna had been awake for most of the night; she had been reflecting on events of the day, as well as working out how she and Annie could leave the house that evening and head to Lindull woods, without raising suspicion. Today would be one of the most memorable days of Luna's life, however, she did not yet know it. As Luna drifted into that liminal space between being asleep and awake, her thoughts stumbled on to her mum's memorable words, *'Without darkness, there wouldn't be light. There's nothing to be scared of. Darkness, like the light, is our friend.'* Luna did not know why these words kept playing through her mind; she wondered if it meant something – connected to what had been happening recently. As she pondered this, Luna thought about hearing her mum's voice that afternoon in the graveyard. She was reminded how much she missed her mum and how much she still needed her. Luna thought about the warning she had given her. She then remembered what Raven had also said in the book shop – prophesying imminent danger. What did they mean? Was it about the amulet? Was Todd Blackthorn going to try to take the amulet from her? Luna was suddenly struck by panic, but tried to shake the feeling, shifting her focus on to the checkered pattern on her bedding, using it to help clear her mind of any worry, until those feelings gradually dissolved and Luna drifted off to sleep.

However, it wasn't long before she was awake again; disturbed by a tapping coming from her bedroom window. Luna opened her eyes and sighed, irritated that it was still dark. She looked at her clock and it was only 3am. Luna took a deep breath and closed her eyes again, hoping she would get back to sleep. However, the tapping started again causing her to open her eyes once more. Tap, tap, tap, it went. Then stopped. Luna closed her eyes. Tap, tap, tap on the window again. Luna pulled her pillow over her head to block out the sound, thinking it must just be something blowing against her window, producing the repeated tapping. However, it got louder. TAP, TAP, TAP, TAP, TAP. It was now relentless. Luna jumped out of bed huffing, stormed over to the window and pulled open her curtains to see what was making the din. As she looked through her window into the darkness she gasped when two small black eyes and a slightly curved black beak peered at her from outside.

'Leon?' Luna whispered to herself. She then heard a voice from outside.

'Luna. Come down.' It was Oscar. She opened her window and leaned out, scanning the garden so see where he was, then spotted him looking up at her directly below her window.

'Come down,' he repeated, motioning his arm to direct her.

'It's 3am! What are you doing here? How did you even know where I live? How did you even get in? You're going to wake everyone.' Luna complained, trying not to raise her voice above a whisper.

'Come down Luna,' Oscar called, keeping his voice at a low but audible level. Luna sighed resignedly, giving in to his persistence.

'Okay. I'm coming. Just be quiet,' Luna said sharply, then closed the curtains and put her hoodie on over her pyjamas. She crept out of her room, closing the door behind her. Then slowly tiptoed down the stairs, slipped on her trainers, and went into the kitchen leaving quietly by the back door. As she walked into the back garden, she shuddered at the temperature difference and could see her warm breath as it created a mist in the cold air. Luna approached Oscar, frowning, however, he seemed cheerful and looked amused at how dishevelled and grumpy she appeared.

'Look like you have just rolled out of bed,' Oscar mocked Luna, grinning.

'Ha.Ha. Very funny. What are you doing here?' Luna complained, scowling.

'Come with me and Leon...Thought we could do some magic,' he said sounding bright and lively as though it was the middle of the day.

'What, at this time? You're crazy.' Luna tutted and turned to head back into the house.

'I can teach you how to fly,' Oscar offered. Luna stopped in her tracks, then turned back to face him.

'To fly?' she said slowly, her eyes suddenly lighting up.

'You heard me Le Fai,' Oscar said, the familiar cockiness detectable in his voice.

'I suppose that sounds like it could be fun,' Luna considered, trying not to sound too eager, even though she was jumping up and down with excitement inside her head. Oscar gave her a self-assured smile, smug in his presumed knowledge that she was always going to go with him.

They made their way through the side gate of the garden and headed towards the woods, via the entrance at the back of Luna's Street. As they walked into Lindull woods, Luna suddenly felt apprehensive; it was so dark, she couldn't make out her surroundings. Oscar could see that she was feeling uneasy.

'You're not wimping out on me, are you?' he asked narrowing his eyes at her.

'No,' Luna lied, sounding snappy. 'It's just a bit dark. Can't see where I'm going.' Oscar looked at her, his dark eyes somehow twinkling, and started rubbing his hands together. As the friction built up, he pulled his hands apart to reveal a bright white light, which he shaped into a ball. Oscar directed the illuminated sphere above their heads, which lit the path in front of them.

'See. Who needs a torch when you have magic,' Oscar said as

they continued walking further into the woods.

'Where are we going?' Luna asked, trying to see if they were walking in a familiar direction.

'Not far. A few more minutes and you'll see,' Oscar said vaguely, and kept walking, confident in his surroundings, which Luna found enviable. It was clear that he had a detailed knowledge of how the woods mapped out. They walked for ten minutes when Oscar suddenly stopped.

'Here will do,' Oscar said. As Luna scanned her surroundings, she realised they were standing in a clearing between two large oak trees, which were opposite each other. Oscar began rubbing his hands together, in the usual way, to create another sphere of light which he shaped into the size of a football. He then propelled it about two meters directly above them. Luna looked up at the ball of energy as it radiated light.

'Now get that light down,' Oscar directed assertively. Luna started to concentrate on the light, using her will to draw it down into her hands. As she proceeded with this method of retrieval, Oscar started shaking his head, and tutted.

'You Le Fais are always taking short cuts,' Oscar said sarcastically, then continued 'I don't want you to get it like that. I want you to go up and get it, like this.' Oscar then started to glide up into the air with ease, as though it was second nature to him. Luna gazed at him in admiration as he gracefully retrieved the sphere of light and gently glided back down, landing lightly on the ground.

'How did you do that?!' Luna said in awe, her mouth hanging open slightly.

'My will, Le Fai. I wanted it and I got it,' Oscar said confidently, tossing the light back into the sky, then locking eyes with Luna. This made Luna feel uncomfortable, causing her to quickly divert her eyes away from his gaze.

'Okay. I'll give it a go.' Luna sounded reluctant, but then took a deep breath, gearing herself up. 'Okay. So, I just need to will it. Okay. I'm going to try.'

'Think about how you make the energy balls. You direct your

will into them. You need to will your body to move where you want it to. Simple,' Oscar said, with a shred of that self-assuredness which Luna found quite irritating.

'Okay.' Luna sounded determined, and concentrated as hard as she could, directing her will. After a few moments, Luna started moving up into the sky, which startled her, making her lose focus and fall to the ground.

'Try again. Just focus on what you want. Ignore everything else. Nothing bad will happen to you. Might take a few tries,' Oscar instructed. Luna made another attempt to elevate her body into the air. As she focused, and directed her will, she started to lift off the ground, not as smoothly as Oscar, but the harder she concentrated the higher she went, and the more fluid her ascension was.

'Catch this!' Oscar called up as he threw a golden sphere towards Luna, which she caught and hurled back. As Luna relaxed, it started to become effortless; she was able to fly in different directions, with Oscar watching from below.

'Alright smarty pants,' Oscar joked, rising up to join her mid-air.

'It's easy once you get the knack of it...Come with me.' Oscar grabbed Luna's hand and guided her up above the trees. They were now hovering high above Lindull woods, looking down on the tops of the trees which were illuminated by the light of the moon.

'This is amazing Oscar.'

As she beamed at her newly acquired skill, Leon flew up to join them and whispered in Oscar's ear. Luna wasn't sure what he had said, but it seemed to influence Oscar's course of action.

'Okay. Let's go down. This way.' Oscar pulled on Luna's arm to follow him as he changed direction and they re-entered Lindull Woods in a different place from where they originated, landing on the ground.

'Right. No time to waste. I think I'll teach you something a bit different now. Enough Le Fai white magic. Now for some proper magic. Magic, Blackthorn style,' Oscar instructed arrogantly, lifting his head slightly reflecting his feeling of superiority.

'Blackthorn style? That doesn't sound good,' Luna said sardonically, flashing him a disapproving look.

'Sometimes being all love and light isn't going to do you any good Le Fai.'

'What does that mean.' Luna sounded irritated at his gibe at her family.

'Nothing...just think you need to arm yourself sometimes,' Oscar said vaguely, looking shifty. Luna scowled and narrowed her eyes at him mistrustfully.

'Why do I need to arm myself Oscar?' Luna asked defensively and folded her arms; she couldn't help but think he knew something she didn't.

'My dad taught me to prepare for the unexpected, and I think that's good advice. Anything could happen.' Oscar said matter-of-factly.

'Okay...what do you want to teach me,' Luna said resignedly, unfolding her arms.

'I'm going to teach you how to hex.' Oscar stated, the haughty tone returning.

'I don't think that's a good idea. I don't want to hurt anybody,' Luna said warily.

'Well sometimes, it might be a life or death situation. It might be your only option.' Oscar sounded serious.

'You're scaring me now Oscar.' Luna was worried and retreated slightly, taking a few steps away from him.

'No. Sorry. I didn't mean to scare you,' Oscar said slowly, moving towards her, his face softening, struck by the realisation that he may have made it sound worse than it was.

'You don't have to use any of it...I just think you should know. Just let me show you?'

'Okay. But I'm not going to use any of it. It's just in case. Right?'

'Right. Just in case,' Oscar smiled cooly, looking relieved, and took a few steps back, then continued to issue instructions to Luna. 'Stand away from me, over by that tree.' He pointed to a tree a couple of metres or so from him. Luna walked over, standing away from Oscar, unsure what to expect.

'I'm going to show you the paralysis hex. Leon is going to assist me. Now don't get worried when you see it. Leon will be fine. It'll wear off after a few moments. And, well, I know how to reverse it. It just temporarily freezes your target. Gives you thinking time,' Oscar explained, Luna listening intently.

'So, if someone was trying to attack you, you could use it on them, then get away?' Luna asked reluctantly.

'Yes, exactly,' Oscar confirmed with a broad grin. 'Now remember not to get scared.' Oscar gave her a condescending look, and she scowled back.

'Just get on with it,' Luna said impatiently.

'Okay. You ready?'

Luna nodded and Oscar proceeded to hold his hands out, with his palms facing Leon, who was perched in the tree above. Almost instantly, Luna witnessed a flash of light leave the palms of his hands and fly towards Leon. As it made contact, it caused the crow to fall to the ground with a thud.

'Leon!' Luna screamed, and instinctively moved forward to see if he was okay. Oscar turned and held his hand up towards Luna, which physically stopped her in her tracks. Her feet fixed to the ground.

'I told you not to get scared! Stay there! It could be dangerous. It could bounce on to you; that's why I told you to step back,' Oscar warned, sounding irritated, still holding her in place.

'Why can't I move my feet?' Luna sounded panicked.

'Sorry. Just needed to keep you away.' Oscar said releasing her by moving his hand out of the way. As he did this, Leon started to move and suddenly got up and flew up back into the tree from which he fell. This came as a relief to Luna.

'Can you teach me how to do that…and the thing you just did to me?' Luna asked, blushing, feeling embarrassed about her sudden change of mind after being so opposed to learning to hex. Oscar flashed a smug smile, looking somewhat triumphant, but thought it was better not to gloat too much.

'One thing at a time Le Fai. Let's start with the paralysis

hex. Reckon you're ready?' Oscar asked, lowering his head and looking at her directly in the eyes.

'Yes. What do I do?'

'I want you to use your will again, but this time direct your threat at Leon. Visualise what you want to happen, as though it has already happened. Direct it from your eyes, or your hands like I did. I only used my hands so you could see what I was doing, but you don't need to.'

Luna started to concentrate on Leon, her eyes fixed on him. After a few moments, he fell to the ground. There was a moment of panic in her face, after seeing him fall, but told herself he would be okay.

'Sorry Leon,' Luna said guiltily.

'Awesome Luna. You did that really well. So well, I think it's time to do it to me.' Oscar said bravely.

'You? I'm not doing it to you! What if it goes wrong?' Luna said anxiously.

'Nah you'll be fine...I trust you.' Oscar smiled at her, and continued, 'Might take a bit more effort, but reckon you're up for it. Go on Luna. I believe in you,' Oscar said genuinely.

Luna let out a long controlled sigh and began staring at Oscar, directing her will at him until he suddenly dropped to the floor, completely still. Luna covered her eyes and peeped out, hoping he would move. Then after what seemed like forever, he jumped up and started clapping.

'Well done, Luna. Honestly. That was awesome. There's so much you can do. Whatever you want. Really. Anything. Just direct your will. You gotta command it.'

Luna beamed at Oscar, amazed at her capabilities, and how quickly she was able to learn her craft. Oscar went to walk towards her, when Luna stopped him in his tracks, his legs suddenly unable to move forward. This took him by surprise, causing him to frown at first, but then they both just started laughing which broke the spell.

'Thank you, Oscar. You've taught me so much.' Luna beamed, proud of herself.

Oscar took out his phone to check the time. 'You should probably get back before your dad wakes up,' he suggested, as he put his phone away. They then both headed back by foot to exit the woods, chatting along the way.

'It's your birthday, isn't it?' Luna asked, suddenly remembering.

'Yeah. My dad was made up I was born on Halloween...just a shame he still doesn't feel like that,' Oscar said quietly.

'What do you mean? Do you not get on?' Luna enquired reluctantly, worried this might somehow be triggering for Oscar.

'We do. Well, sometimes. But it's hard to live up to his expectations.' Oscar paused, reflecting on what he had just shared with Luna, wondering if he had over shared. 'Sorry, you don't need to hear this. Not even sure why I'm telling you.' Oscar looked at Luna ponderingly, as though he was trying to figure out their evolving friendship.

'I don't mind. You can talk to me.' Luna caught his eye and smiled gently, which caused Oscar's pale face to flush red, however, it was too dark for Luna to notice, much to his relief.

'Thanks.' Oscar stopped and pulled his head back to look directly at Luna, then chuckled, shaking his head, 'What am I doing being friends with a Le Fai. My dad's right about one thing. Expect the unexpected.'

'The last month has been full of surprises as far as I'm concerned. So, yeah, one thing your dad is probably right about.' Luna smiled resignedly, and they carried on walking.

'Not sure if anyone has said this to you, but you need to be careful who you do things in front of. Don't let every witch know how powerful you are. Keep stuff to yourself,' Oscar said, then continued, 'other witches might get jealous and find ways of weakening your powers. It's better if they think they're more powerful than you.'

'My nan pretty much said the same thing...I suppose your dad has a reputation for that?' Luna said without thinking but quickly cringed as she realised this would hit a nerve.

'What do you mean by that? You don't even know him.' Oscar sounded troubled by her remark.

'I just mean, he's got this reputation, you know.' Luna wanted to sugar-coat it, but she was just digging herself into a deeper hole.

'No, I don't know what you mean. Just because you Le Fais are different from us, doesn't mean you're right and we're wrong. There isn't such a thing. We're all capable of being good and bad. There's no black and white Luna…I'm not like him anyway.' Oscar sounded hurt, which made Luna regret her initial flippancy.

'Sorry. I didn't think,' Luna said guiltily, avoiding looking at him.

'It's okay. I just get sick of having to defend my family all the time,' Oscar said bitterly, then paused to reflect on things, and continued, now trying to lighten the mood, 'I guess you *are* a Le Fai, so I shouldn't expect any less,' Oscar joked, his eyes twinkling with mischief; he then gently elbowed Luna in the ribs. She reciprocated by elbowing him back, and then smiled making eye contact with him. They both looked away, quickly, and continued walking in silence for a few minutes before Luna started up their conversation again.

'I would just fly everywhere if I could!' Luna fantasied.

'Don't tell anyone you can do that! That's our secret,' Oscar warned looking serious as he turned his head to look at her.

'Why not? Can't all witches fly?' Luna asked.

'No! No, they can't. You have to be a powerful witch to do that…well we're the lucky ones. I say lucky. I think sometimes being able to do all this stuff is more of a burden…'

'What d'you mean? How can it be a burden!'

'It doesn't matter…you'll figure it out…But anyway, you did really well. But it's our secret. I mean it Luna, don't tell *anyone* else. Not even Annie.' Oscar said soberingly. Luna furrowed her brow, thinking this was yet another secret she had to keep from Annie. Luna was starting to feel uncomfortable about all the secrecy.

'I mean it. You need to keep quiet...we're different from the others Luna. Really different. In time you'll see,' Oscar said cryptically, which left Luna wondering what he meant.

As they made their way out of the woods, Oscar said goodbye and Luna headed home, hoping to get back into her bedroom before her dad woke up. Luna thought about Oscar's warning to keep her abilities a secret because sharing this may put her in further danger. She then thought about the first time she encountered Oscar's dad, and how his stare had caused her to collapse, now realising that he must have deliberately targeted her, no doubt because she's a Le Fai. Luna wondered how Oscar could be so different from his dad, and how long their friendship would be allowed to continue, given the conflict between the two families. This really troubled her. Each time she met him, the thought of not being friends seemed to weigh heavier on her. Luna was no longer sure if the connection she felt with Oscar was the same one, she had with Annie – she was starting to feel confused about her feelings. However, Luna did her best to push it out of her head, trying not to dwell on it. It would be some time before she would understand what it was that connected her and Oscar, and her feelings would inevitably complicate things.

CHAPTER 18: THE LE FAI FAMILY GATHERING

Luna had managed to get back home and into her room without disturbing her dad. By the time she settled back into bed it was 6am. Luna was so exhausted after spending most of the night awake, and galivanting around Lindull woods, as soon her head hit the pillow, she fell straight asleep. It was 11am before she woke up. Her dad had already left the house for work and wasn't due back until 2pm. Luna got out of bed, had a shower, and got dressed, ready for the family gathering later that afternoon. She was excited about seeing Annie and meeting up with the rest of her family and speculated about who would be there. Luna wondered if she would see Mr Porter and Suzie, who she had recently discovered were dating each other. She really liked Mr Porter, or Frank, as she was told to call him out of school. Luna still couldn't believe how everything seemed to be coming together so very perfectly, despite the threats made to her family by Todd Blackthorn in his pursuit of the amulet.

Luna took her time to eat breakfast and then went upstairs to get out the fold up bed for Annie, who would be staying there that night for a sleepover. After making up Annie's bed, Luna took out the 'goth' box and unlocked it. She sat on the edge of her bed and browsed through the contents, stopping to examine one of the rings which had a purple stone embedded in it. Luna wasn't sure why she was suddenly drawn to it but felt compelled to take it from the box. As she studied the ring, she wondered why it had been placed in the wooden container. Then, without much thought, she stuffed the ring in her pocket, locked the box and hid it under her bed in its usual spot. Luna headed back downstairs, making sure she still had the amulet safely around her neck, mindful of the consequences of misplacing it.

As the day went on, Luna became impatient about going to Annie's, wishing time would go faster. Just after 2pm her dad returned from work and popped into the sitting room to speak to Luna. He seemed unaware of her adventures in the early hours of the morning with Oscar but remarked on how tired she looked.

'Sure you're okay to go to Annie's? You look knackered Luna.'

'I'm fine. I just didn't sleep too well. I'm really looking forward to it.' Luna sounded slightly put out by her dad's observation, 'I'm guessing you haven't been to one of these Le Fai family things before?' she asked tentatively.

'Er, no love. Well, you know why,' Neil answered, sounding uneasy.

'I guess,' Luna paused for thought, 'will they be doing magic do you think?'

'What makes you think that? I doubt it. Well not with you kids about,' Neil said dismissively.

'Us kids can do magic you know. We're not babies,' Luna said petulantly, suddenly realising she had perhaps said too much.

'I know *exactly* what young witches get up to. I was one once you know,' Neil remarked, giving her a perceptive look, then left the room.

'I'm making something to eat before I get ready. Do you want anything?' he called back as he walked to the kitchen.

'No, I've eaten. Are we going soon then?' Luna shouted through to him, sounding impatient.

'In about an hour or so. Not long love.'

Luna sighed and sank back into the chair, tapping her foot impatiently on the floor wishing time away. Then the doorbell rang.

'Can you get that love,' Neil shouted through as he made

himself something to eat. Luna reluctantly got up out of the chair and sauntered to the front door, opening it to see Annie and her dad, Daniel, standing there.

'Annie! What are you doing here?'

'We were at the book shop and wondered if you and your dad wanted a lift back with us?' Daniel said, then continued, 'we'll bring you all back after.'

'Come in. I'll ask dad,' Luna said, eager to get off.

Annie and Daniel walked into the hallway and Luna hurried towards the kitchen to get her dad. Neil followed Luna back through and greeted Annie and Daniel.

'Hi, Daniel, isn't it? I'm Neil…I've met Nick.'

'Nice to meet you. Nick said you'd talked,' Daniel said perceptively, meeting Neil's eyes and giving an affirmative nod.

'We're on our way back from the shop. Did you want a lift?' Daniel asked.

'I've just got back from work, but if you want to go Luna, then you can go ahead now, I'll follow soon when I'm ready. I've got your address,' Neil said.

Without saying anything Luna swiftly grabbed her jacket and pulled on her trainers and followed Annie and Daniel out of the door. She then looked back and briefly waved goodbye to her dad.

On the way to Annie's house the girls chatted in hushed tones, planning their secret expedition later that evening. Daniel looked surreptitiously in the driver's mirror trying to figure out the reason for their secrecy. He watched closely, making note, but did not say anything to them as they continued to whisper and giggle. On arrival, Annie and Luna jumped out of the car and ran into the house, greeted by the boisterous boxer, who Luna affectionately remembered from her last visit. Nick guided the wagging dog into the kitchen out of the way and welcomed Luna.

'How are you?' Nick asked looking pleased to see her.

'Yeah. Good.' Luna sounded genuinely happy.

'Have you seen Jack?' Nick asked, his tone more serious.

'No. Not at all,' Luna said, leading Nick to furrow his brow momentarily.

'Maybe he has moved on. I'm sure he's okay,' Nick said reassuringly, however, part of him couldn't help but worry about his old friend, 'anyway, lots happening tonight. Two new people to formally initiate into the Le Fai family.' Nick changed the subject, now beaming at Luna.

'Two?' Luna asked, suspecting one might be her, but wasn't sure who the other one was.

'Your dad and Frank,' Nick explained, then winked.

'What about me?' Luna asked, looking a bit disheartened. Nick and Daniel both glanced at each other then smiled reassuringly at Luna.

'You're already one of us. No doubting that. We'll of course give you a formal welcome, of sorts, in the circle later on, but you have Le Fai blood, so it's different,' Nick explained, ensuring Luna knew she had a place in the Le Fai family.

'Your dad never got the chance before...and well Frank... well that's not for me to announce. Not yet anyway,' Nick said mysteriously, keeping Luna and Annie in suspense, leading the friends to quickly glance at each other wondering what the news could be.

'Why don't you two set the back room up for later. Annie should know what she's doing,' Nick directed, then headed back to the kitchen where he was preparing some food for the family guests.

Annie led Luna into a large room at the back of the house. On entering the room, Luna observed that the wall directly opposite the door was lined with books – there were so many, it was like walking into a library. As Luna glanced around the room, she noticed there was some sort of altar against the wall on the side of the room opposite a large picture window, which looked out onto an open lawn. Next to the window, there was a solid oak desk, with objects scattered on top, which Luna thought must be work-related, including a laptop, a pile of books, a pen, and black diary. Annie saw Luna looking at the desk.

'It's my dad's office. Well, sort of. It's a bit like an office. A bit like a library, and where they do other stuff,' Annie explained, widening her eyes.

'Other stuff?' Luna asked curiously.

'They sometimes hold their magic circle here. They don't involve me or Arthur. Say we're too young,' Annie tutted, then continued, 'I've listened in a few times, and it sounds a bit dull really. Not like the stuff you and Oscar did at the park,' Annie delighted, her eyes twinkling.

'Oh yeah,' Luna said awkwardly, hoping Annie wouldn't start probing her about all the magic her and Oscar did in Lindull woods. Luna hated keeping so many secrets from Annie; she felt guilty and disloyal.

Luna walked over to the altar and eyed the different magical objects placed on it. She was instantly drawn to the centre piece, which was a statue of a fairy – Luna thought it looked rather like Aurora, Queen of the elm, with the same elegant, yet authoritative appearance. Several crystals surrounded the statue, along with a few stones which had different symbols painted on them. She recognised a couple of the symbols, which she had seen before tattooed on Todd Blackthorn's fingers. Her eyes then drifted to a thick white candle; there was one positioned on each corner of the altar.

'It's a protection altar,' Annie explained, approaching Luna, who continued to examine it.

'Protection? From what?' Luna asked, having never knowingly seen a witch's altar before.

'My dads say it's to keep us all safe, from any psychic threats. The statue is of the great fairy mother Morgan Le Fai.'

'What are those?' Luna asked pointing to the stones which had painted symbols on them.

'Witch runes. They each correspond to the different element. So, the harvest rune, for earth, in the north, flight for air in the east, the sun in the south, representing fire, and waves for water in the west.' Annie reeled this off as though it was second nature to her, reminding Luna how much she had to learn.

'Oscar's dad had the sun and harvest ones tattooed on his fingers. He has a lot of tattoos. A bit like my mum.' Luna seemed to momentarily drift off into her thoughts, thinking about her mum, finding it peculiar that a man so dark and dangerous, like Todd Blackthorn, could evoke memories of her mother.

'Yeah, he's actually a tattoo artist, so probs why he has so many. But, he's nothing like your mum.'

'Spose not. I think they must've known each other. I mean, I'm sure they did. Remember he said something about me being like my mum?' Luna paused, reflecting on her encounter with Todd Blackthorn in the shopping mall, and thought about how uncomfortable he made her feel. 'I can't imagine they got on. They probably hated each other...not like me and Oscar. But I guess Oscar is okay, right?' Luna was overthinking things again, something she had a habit of doing.

'Right. He's nothing like his dad.' Annie smiled at her reassuringly.

The friends carried on chatting as they tidied the back room, pushing the desk back, and removing any clutter or personal belongings. Daniel came in and lit the candles on the alter, then placed a couple of lit incense sticks next to the great fairy mother statue, and ushered Luna and Annie out to help transport some of the nibbles Nick had been preparing in the kitchen, through to the dining room. It wasn't long before everything was ready, and guests started arriving. Whilst Luna was excited about meeting some of the family members she hadn't yet been introduced to, she was a little nervous about mixing with new people.

The first to arrive was Suzie, however, Frank was not with her.

'Oh, where's Frank?' Daniel asked sounding surprised at his absence, as he greeted Suzie with a hug and a kiss on the cheek.

'He's running a tad late. He had some things to see to, so we've had to come separately. But he won't be long,' Suzie said sighing – Luna could detect a trace of worry in her voice.

'Suzie, you've met Luna I believe?' Daniel gestured to her, smiling.

'Yes, yes, I have. A couple of times now,' Suzie replied, her eyes crinkling as she smiled at Luna. Suzie walked through to the dining room to talk to Nick, as more family members arrived and were directed through to join the others.

Luna and Annie awkwardly stood in the dining room as everyone chatted. After some time, Luna started to wonder where her dad was, given the flow of guests seemed to have stopped, but there was still no sign of him. Then the doorbell rang. Daniel rushed through to answer the door. When he re-entered the room, a few moments later, Luna expected to see her dad, but it was Frank, who everyone affectionately welcomed – it was clear everyone liked him as much as she did. Frank spotted Luna straight away, acknowledging her with a friendly wave before approaching Suzie and giving her an affectionate kiss. Luna kept wondering where her dad was and felt concerned that he wasn't going to make it in time. She looked at the door, anxiously biting her lip. Frank noticed her worried state and walked across to talk to her.

'You okay Luna?' Frank asked gently.

'Yeah, just wondering where my dad has got to.'

'Sure he won't be long,' Frank said reassuringly, then excused himself, 'try not to worry. I've just got to pop to the car, back in a minute.' he said quickly leaving the room. As he exited the dining room, Nick came over with two women who looked about the same age as him – in their early to mid-40s.

'Luna, this is Jayne, and this is Glenda,' Nick said, the two women nodded at Luna but didn't say anything.

'Nice to meet you,' Luna said politely, not knowing where to look, as an uncomfortable silence followed.

'They're Raven's other daughters. Suzie's older sisters. They're twins, though not identical.' Nick smiled at his cousins, who again did not speak, but smiled back. There was another awkward silence; Luna didn't know how to make conversation with them but was saved by Suzie who came over and started chatting separately to Nick and her sisters. They soon walked away in the direction of the table of food.

'That was weird.' Luna whispered to Annie.

'Yeah, they're a bit strange. Never heard them say much,' Annie said quietly, confirming Luna's thoughts.

'Who are those people over there?' Luna asked Annie subtly pointing to an older woman, who was about the same age as her nan, and two slightly older teenagers.

'That's great aunt Lily...Oh and those two are annoying. It's Jamie and Olivia. They're stuck up. They're Izzy's kids.' Annie pointed to a tall slender woman who was standing by the table alone, grazing on the food.

'Oh, and here's Arthur,' Annie said sounding annoyed, as Arthur approached them. She then talked directly to her brother, 'Where were you when we were working our butts off? Slacking off as usual.'

Arthur screwed his face up and gave his sister a dirty look, 'None of your business.' He then turned to Luna and looked at her searchingly, which made her feel uneasy.

'Hope you two listened to what I said about Blackthorn. Make sure you keep away from him. Told you he's trouble. A little bird tells me you've been hanging around with him, messing about in the park with some idiots from school,' Arthur said accusingly, now directing his attention at Luna *and* Annie, who both looked away sheepishly.

'I've not told our dads. Yet. But if I find out you've been hanging out with him again. I will. Then you will be in trouble.'

'We don't! Anyway, shut up. I can tell dad plenty of stuff about you,' Annie threatened, sounding defensive. Arthur shook his head pompously then walked over to Olivia and Jamie and started chatting to them in an animated and friendly way – he was like a completely different person from the one Annie and Luna had just spoken to.

'He does my head in. He's such a loser,' Annie complained, narrowing her eyes, then giving her brother daggers.

Luna thought about what Arthur said, and whilst she felt a strong connection to Oscar, she was still not sure if she could trust him.

'Just ignore Arthur. Oscar's alright. My brother just hates him cos he's a Blackthorn. But we know he's different, don't we?'

'Yeah, sure,' Luna said unconvincingly, suddenly taken in by that little voice of doubt in the back of her mind. Annie did not seem to notice the uncertainty in Luna's voice and continued to talk about the night ahead.

As they chatted, Nick walked over to them, looking disappointed.

'I'm really sorry Luna, your dad just messaged. He can't make it. Said he had to sort something out. He was a bit vague, but asked if we can drop you back after. That's fine with us. He'll just have to be formally welcomed into the family another time. There's always time for that.' Nick put his arm around Luna's shoulders seeing she was upset. As Nick comforted Luna, the doorbell rang again, and Daniel hurried through to answer it.

'Listen. Today is an important day for you. Everyone gets to meet you.' Nick squeezed her shoulders gently, flashed Luna and Annie an intuitive smile, and followed Daniel, who could be heard greeting the new arrivals in the hallway. The jovial tones of the Le Fais, which echoed around the room, reminded Luna that today was indeed an important time for her.

Nick, Daniel and two older looking men entered the room. One looked distinguished, dressed in a long black tailcoat, with a black top hat. He walked with a black cane which he gripped firmly in his hand, supporting him as he limped across the room. In contrast, the other man looked dishevelled and wore a pair of brown corduroy trousers, with what looked like a piece of twine instead of a belt, holding them in place around his waist. He also wore a blue t-shirt, which was creased and had several tears in it. His hair was long, silvery white and tied back in a ponytail, and he had a long white braided beard which hung down to just below his chest. Luna thought he looked rather like the wizards depicted in children's books and films. Luna leaned into Annie and enquired about the mysterious arrivals.

'Who are they?' Luna probed, trying to keep her voice low.

'Oh. The one with the hat is Azreal and the other one with the beard is Uriel. More twins! They're probably the oldest Le Fais here. I don't know how old, but I think they must be over 100,' Annie said quietly.

'100! I mean they look old, but not that old!'

'They're the youngest brothers of our great granny. You know, Seraphina.'

'Really. Wow. I can't believe how well they look.' Luna suddenly remembered her experience of meeting Seraphina at her nan's house and recalled drawing her great grandmother's spirit in and out of the mirror. Luna's thoughts were quickly interrupted by Nick as he gathered all his relatives together, directing them into the back room Annie and Luna had prepared earlier.

'Thank you everyone for coming, and although some of us can't be here today we know that they're here in spirit. Halloween is always a special day for us. A day when the veil is thin; when those who have passed on walk more freely across this earthly plane. It's a time for us to pay our respects to our Le Fai ancestors who gave us life, and passed onto us their wisdom, customs, and magic. We're lucky and privileged to be Le Fais and must continue to show our gratitude for the blessings our ancestors bestowed on us. But today, we've even more to be thankful for. We've two members of the Le Fai family to welcome in. Luna and Frank.' As Nick uttered their names, everyone turned to Luna and Frank in turn and raised a glass. Luna blushed and looked coyly at everyone, whilst Frank smiled confidently and kissed Suzie on the head, who looked back at him adoringly. Nick continued, 'As members of our family you're guaranteed the loyalty, love, and protection of the Le Fais, which we will declare before our great fairy mother Morgan Le Fai. Can we raise our glasses to that.' Everyone cheered, and once again acknowledged Luna and Frank by raising their glasses.

'Luna, the daughter of my dear cousin Aggie, is a special member of our family. After our time has gone on this earthly plane, Luna will be revered in our family as one of the great Le Fai matriarchs. We must offer our love and protection to Luna, who has been chosen as the keeper of the Le Fai witch amulet.' Nick paused for thought and everyone turned to Luna and started clapping. As the clapping died down, Nick continued, 'As keeper of the amulet, Luna has the responsibility of ensuring it does not get into the wrong hands. A duty I know she will be able to fulfil. But, and this is important, we must protect her and ensure that her job as its keeper is made as easy and safe as possible. We all know that there are other witches, outside of our family, who want that amulet.' Nick's tone was now serious and sobering. Arthur caught Luna's eye and gave a warning look, which unnerved her, causing her to glance down at the floor.

'Let's make another toast to Luna. Our new matriarch!' Nick bellowed, with the others following suit. Luna felt a smile creep up on her face, but still felt awkward at the attention, and didn't really understand what a matriarch was.

'Now, we have some more news.' Nick turned to Suzie and Frank smiling affectionately. Suzie beamed back at him then gazed at Frank, her eyes filled with love.

'Don't keep us in suspense!' Daniel called out jovially.

'Suzie, would you like to tell everyone?' Nick asked gently, causing her to blush.

'Well, last week Frank asked me to marry him, and I said YES!' Suzie wrapped her arms around Frank and they both kissed, which caused the room to erupt in whooping and celebratory cries. Luna and Annie glanced at each other and raised their eyebrows, then looked giddy at the happy news.

'Frank, you will soon be an official Le Fai, and we welcome you in. I know how happy you make Suzie. After everything she has been through, she deserves that happiness. And you know that as a husband of a Le Fai, you will take *our* name as your own.' Nick looked at Frank who nodded in agreement.

'Now, I would like us to put our glasses down and form a circle,' Nick instructed, with everyone following his lead and forming a circle by holding hands.

'Let us close our eyes and offer our thanks to our great fairy mother Morgan Le Fai for her blood that runs through our veins and the magic she has gifted us with. Mother Morgan, blood of our blood, mother of our mothers, we call upon you to offer your love and protection to Luna and Frank as we formally welcome them in.' As Nick fell silent, Luna felt the ground shake beneath her feet, and the room went cold; she could feel her skin prickle up as the icy air brushed against it. She slowly opened her eyes and saw a beautiful green illuminated figure floating in the middle of the circle. The mysterious spectre resembled the fairy Queen Aurora. Luna looked on in wonder, as Nick continued to speak.

'Mother Morgan your presence confirms your acceptance of our new family members. We thank you. In love, and respect, we promise to honour your name and magic. So be it.' As Nick uttered those last three words, the others repeated, 'So be it'. Suddenly the spirit of the great fairy mother Morgan disappeared, and for a few minutes everyone apart from Luna held their heads down with their eyes closed. Nick then raised up his hands, which signalled everyone to let go of each other. 'Luna, Frank, welcome.' Nick radiated his delight at his family members, and everyone once again cheered and clapped at Luna's and Frank's initiation into the Le Fai family.

Luna and Annie hugged each other and continued to talk over their plans for the night ahead. However, as their discussion progressed, Luna started to get a sick feeling bubble up in her stomach, brought on by a nervousness which was difficult to dismiss. Luna considered what Nick said about her responsibility as keeper of the amulet, and the importance of protecting the magical object. She started to feel guilty about being friends with Oscar and suddenly panicked that this friendship would only complicate things. Perhaps make her more vulnerable to Todd Blackthorn. As Luna battled with these thoughts, she considered cancelling their plans to meet up with Oscar that evening. Luna felt torn. But she liked Oscar. He'd shared so much with her. He wasn't like his dad. He was different. He was just like her. Everything would be okay. It had to be. Luna managed to force her doubts to the back of her mind.

It wasn't long before the celebrations came to an end, and it was time for Luna and Annie to head back into Lindull. Annie was so eager to get going she had persistently pestered her parents every ten minutes or so, in the last hour, urging them to wrap up the celebrations quickly. On the way out of Annie's, Daniel gently probed his daughter and Luna about their plans; it was evident he had some scepticism about the nature of the sleepover.

'I'm assuming you're both going to watch a film. You wouldn't be planning anything else, would you?' Daniel gave his daughter a warning look, but Annie quickly averted her eyes away from him.

'I told you what we're doing. What else could we even do? Luna's dad is going to be there! Gawd,' Annie moaned shaking her head signalling her irritation.

'Okay, well, be careful, and don't do anything stupid.' Daniel tried to make eye contact with Annie again, but she continued to avoid his gaze and rushed into the car with Luna behind. They both put on their seatbelts and talked quietly.

'Whatever you do, don't let dad look in your eyes if he asks you about something you don't want to tell him. He'll know what you're thinking.'

'What? Like he can read minds?'

'Yeah, he can. It's annoying. But he has to *really* look into your eyes.' Annie mimicked her dad's intrusive glare, then crossed her eyes and pulled a goofy face, causing Luna to chuckle at her friend's slapstick humour.

It wasn't long before they reached Luna's house. As the car pulled up outside, Luna noticed all the lights were off, which, for a moment, she thought was strange. Daniel peered at the house through his windscreen and frowned concernedly.

'Hmm, maybe he's not back. I might come in with you.' Daniel sounded somewhat worried.

'Er, no. It's okay. We'll call you if there's a problem,' Luna said uneasily, ensuring she avoided making eye contact with Daniel.

'Well, let me watch you go in. I can hang around for a bit. When you get in just wave and let me know it's okay for me to go. I guess he might've fallen asleep.'

'Yeah, maybe. He has a habit of falling asleep on the sofa,' Luna lied, still avoiding eye contact.

The friends hopped out of the car and ran over to the house. Luna had to use her key to unlock the door, which made her think her dad must be out. As they entered the house and closed the door behind them, Luna called out for her dad, but there was no answer. Then Annie spotted a note next to the phone in the hallway and read it out.

'Sorry Luna, I had to go out.

Be back later.

Love dad'.

'Wonder where he is?' Luna paused, then thought he had probably gone to help nang, assuming it must have something to do with Ariella.

'Just wave through the window to let your dad know everything is okay. I think I know where he is,' Luna said. Annie walked through to the sitting room and waved at her dad, signalling him to head home. They watched him drive off down Hubble Road.

'Well, it looks like it might be easier than we thought. Let's go before my dad gets back,' Luna said with a hint of triumph in her voice.

CHAPTER 19:
CAREFUL WHO
YOU TRUST

Luna and Annie headed out of the house, with Luna locking the door behind them. She was pleased that her dad was out, but hadn't considered that he may very well return home before they got back. Luna hadn't thought that far ahead, as she was too focused on spending time with her friends in Lindull woods over the next couple of hours. As they looked down Hubble Road, standing a few meters away, they saw a recognisable figure standing silently watching them. It was Jack - the boy they had only recently learned was a ghost. A ghost suspended in adolescence, perhaps forever. Luna and Annie approached him, and he grinned, pleased to be reunited with his friends.

'You okay Jack? I'm sorry I didn't know,' Luna said tenderly, finding it difficult to use the right words. Jack gazed down pensively at his feet; Luna could feel a sadness about his presence.

'I'm okay…I forgot what happened…but I do remember now. I remember…everything,' Jack said wearily. Luna felt it wasn't the time to ask questions about what exactly *did* happen to him.

'We're going to Lindull woods. Do you want to come with us?' Annie asked, trying to involve him in their plans.

'I don't think I can. Something stops me. Every time I tried to go with Luna, I just ended up back where I started…maybe I'm bound to certain spaces, like near where I…' Jack cut himself off, but Luna and Annie knew exactly what he was referring to. He was referring to his death. Luna paused, as she mulled something over in her head.

'You *can* come with us. I know a way. But you have to trust me.' Luna looked earnestly at Jack, who nodded to agree to whatever she was proposing.

'Okay. My nang taught me how to draw spirits into objects. I can draw *you* into the amulet.'

'Is that wise Luna? I mean, you don't know if it's okay to do it with that.' Annie dissuaded Luna, concerned that her idea could backfire in some way. Annie then pulled a brass pendulum out of her pocket.

'Why do you have a pendulum? I didn't think you used them?' Luna asked sounding puzzled.

'I just have one. Okay,' Annie said defensively, then continued, 'use it instead of the amulet,' and passed Luna the pendulum.

'Okay, Jack. Do you think you want to try? For me to draw you into the pendulum? I think it might help us cross whatever barrier it is you can't cross,' Luna explained, sounding confident.

'I'm ready.' Jack put his head down and Luna started to concentrate, using her will to draw him into the pendulum. After a few moments, Jack's spirit began to shift its shape forming a whirling vortex, becoming longer and thinner as he was sucked into the pendulum.

'It worked!' Annie elated, giving two excited claps with her hands.

Luna put the pendulum in her pocket, and they continued towards the entrance of Lindull woods on Cashmere Road, where they were due to meet Oscar at 8pm. Cashmere Road was further away than Luna and Annie had anticipated. Luna looked at her watch as they speed-walked to their destination.

'Hope he's still there. It's after eight now.' Luna fretted, increasing her pace with Annie half running to keep up.

'Slow down a bit. Why the rush. He'll be there. Sure of it,' Annie said trying to calm Luna who now seemed a little jittery.

'Sorry. You're right.' Luna took a deep breath and steadied her pace but was still walking faster than she normally would.

'Are you going to get Jack out when we get to the woods?'

'I will. But I'll wait a bit…I don't even know what we're doing, or where we're actually going when we get in there.' Luna shrugged and upped her pace again.

It was twenty past eight by the time they got there, and Oscar was waiting by the entrance with Leon on his shoulder. Leon bowed his head slightly, acknowledging Luna and Annie. Behind Oscar, further into the entrance of the woods, stood Tom and Ace. Luna noticed Oscar seemed distracted and a little agitated.

'Let's get going. Almost thought you weren't coming,' Oscar moaned, then caught Luna's eye, smiled vaguely, but quickly looked away. Luna couldn't help but think he had things on his mind, but she wasn't sure what.

'Sorry. We didn't realise what time it was,' Luna explained guiltily, sounding a little puffed from speed-walking. It had been less than twenty-four hours earlier that Oscar and Luna were doing magic in the woods. The day had been so long, it was as if that time they had spent together in the woods had been days ago. Luna wondered if she would be using any of her new magical skills tonight but then remembered what Oscar had stressed to her about not sharing too much with others - like being able to fly.

'How are we meant to see where we're going,' Annie complained, trying to make out her surroundings as they continued to walk forward into the darkness.

Oscar gave Luna a side glance and gently elbowed her, 'Your turn,' he urged. Luna started rubbing her hands together and created a sphere of white light, which she directed above their heads.

'Thanks Luna,' Annie said looking up at the light which lit the path ahead.

'Where are we going Oscar?' Luna asked, not familiar with the area of the woodland they were walking in.

'Just a little further,' Oscar said vaguely.

'What are we doing? You said magic?' Annie asked, impatiently curious.

'Haven't decided yet,' Oscar said loftily. Luna screwed her face up at how overassertive he sounded – she really wished he would drop the bravado.

'*You* haven't decided? Who put *you* in charge?' Luna said emphatically, directing a stern look at Oscar, causing him to tut at her.

'We're *all* equal, Oscar,' Luna stated patronisingly as they walked together, the others looking on.

'No, we're not.' Oscar remarked bluntly. 'You're an idiot if you think we're all equal.'

'Well, we should be.' Luna said rolling her eyes.

'Maybe we should. But we're *not*,' Oscar stated matter-of-factly, shrugged, then ran ahead. Moments later he hurled a bright red energy ball at Luna and shouted 'Catch!' She caught it and threw it to Annie, who passed it to Tom, then to Ace. This continued for some time as they trekked further into the dark woods. The game suddenly ended when Oscar lobbed the ball into the ground, staring at it as it dissolved into the earth. He looked around, thinking in silence. All that could be heard was the rush of wind blowing through the trees and the intermittent solitary hoot from an owl.

'What about some target practice,' Tom suggested, creating an energy ball and hurling it at one of the broad oak trees in front of him.

'Yeah okay...But let's make it interesting. Let's target each other,' Oscar said, giving a smug smile.

'Will it hurt though?' Annie worried, wincing slightly.

'Why would it hurt? Don't be lame. Come on Le Fai...Luna you can be on my team,' Oscar said presumptuously.

'No. I'll be on Annie's. Reckon we can manage against you three,' Luna asserted, then turned to Annie who looked doubtful about her friend's confident assertion.

'Luna, I can't do magic. I won't be able to do much,' Annie whispered in Luna's ear.

'I think you can. You just don't *believe* you can…You can see spirits, can't you. Well, maybe you're a witch too. Just try. I can help you.' Luna was careful to keep her voice low so the others couldn't hear, and looked directly into Annie's eyes, urging her to give it a go.

'Okay, but can we not do it in front of them at first. I don't want them knowing I can't do magic.' Annie whispered back.

'Are you two going to take all day?' Oscar said impatiently, wondering what they were talking about. He didn't seem to like the secrecy and felt excluded.

'Hold on Oscar. Can you three go back there, behind those trees?' Luna pointed to three tall trees further back in the distance.

'Over there? Why?' Oscar asked suspiciously, screwing his face up. He was inclined to reject her request but then softened, 'Okay then.'

'Thanks. Make sure you get right behind them,' she gestured to the trees. 'We'll call you when we're ready.' Luna said, then turned to Annie and pulled on her arm directing her behind the big oak in front of them.

'No tricks though. I know how sneaky you Le Fais are,' Oscar shouted back as he led Tom and Ace towards the trees in the near distance in the opposite direction from Annie and Luna.

Luna peeped out from the oak to check that the others were out of view, then turned back to talk to Annie. 'Okay. Right, first you need to watch me,' Luna instructed as she began rubbing her hands together, focusing her will in on the yellow sphere of illuminated light which emerged from between her palms. Luna cupped it in her hands and smiled.

'What do I do?' Annie asked examining the ball.

'Concentrate. Rub your hands together and use your will to make it happen. Tell yourself that you're making a ball of energy, picture it in your head. You need to block everything out around you. Really focus. Go on. I *know* you can do it.' Luna watched as Annie focused her mind. She rubbed her hands together and as she pulled them apart a small glimmer of purple light shone from her palms but quickly faded.

'See told you! Do it again. You just need to concentrate a bit more…I knew you were a witch Annie Le Fai!' Luna sounded giddy but tried to calm herself in case it distracted Annie.

'Okay. Give me a minute.' Annie concentrated, and after a few moments of rubbing her hands together, a distinctive glow of yellow light grew from between her palms. Luna beamed at her friend.

'You did it! You did it!' Luna had to lower her voice, realising she was probably audible to the others.

'OMG I did it,' Annie said, amazed at herself as she held the yellow sphere of light in the palm of her hand.

'Do you think the colours mean anything?' Annie said sounding enchanted by her magic ball of light.

'I guess. What did you feel when you made that one?' Luna asked.

'Happy. Happy that I'm doing magic with my best friend. I couldn't think of a better person to discover I'm a witch with.' Annie was so overjoyed she had tears in her eyes, and Luna realised how important this was for her, given that for Annie's whole life she didn't think she was a witch. Luna smiled and pulled out a pink glowing sphere of light and passed it to Annie.

'Pink for love. Cos you're my best friend. You're like my sister Annie.' Luna beamed and gave Annie a hug.

'I think we're ready, aren't we?' Luna determined, then continued 'right. Watch Oscar cos he's sneaky. But we can be sneaky too.' She grinned and gave a villainous laugh causing Annie to giggle.

'Just follow my lead. Get your weapons ready soldier,' Luna said jokingly. Annie saluted her friend, then started frantically rubbing her hands together. They both slowly crept out from behind the tree, looking around in case the others were planning on taking them by surprise.

'Come out, come out, wherever you are,' Luna said attempting to lure out the others for the friendly battle. However, they did not answer. Luna and Annie moved in closer to the trees where

Oscar, Tom, and Ace had been waiting out. Luna called again. But nothing. And again. But still nothing.

'Stop messing about,' Luna called, starting to worry they'd abandoned her and Annie in the dark woods. She turned to Annie and sounding slightly concerned, asked, 'Where are they?' Then suddenly, just as Annie shrugged her shoulders, flying spheres of light bombarded her and Luna; they came hurtling from different directions. Some were hurled from the trees above and others from somewhere deep within the woods. Oscar's attack strategy had completely taken Luna and Annie by surprise; in haste they retaliated, quickly producing energy balls and propelling them haphazardly in any direction. But still the opposition's attacks came thick and fast, with Luna and Annie unable to navigate where their friends were hiding. Then they heard Oscar's disembodied voice.

'You Le Fais are so lame,' Oscar shouted from above them. Luna looked up and spotted him in the tree.

'You're so sneaky!' Luna called up merrily continuing the battle banter.

'Watch out Le Fai!' Oscar laughed, looking directly at Luna, then hurled a large pink ball at her which took her off her feet, making her gasp. Annie observed the interaction. Her mouth fell open and she gaped at Luna in disbelief.

'OMG Luna. Did you see that?' Annie exclaimed, her eyes wide. Luna looked dazed as she got up, not really knowing what had hit her. Annie stared at Oscar as he started to climb down the tree, still gobsmacked.

'What's your problem, Annie Le Fai. What are you staring at?' Oscar said defensively.

'Nothing. Nothing at all.' Annie smiled smugly. Luna had come around from Oscar's bomb and rounded in on him.

'Oscar! No need to do that! Knocking me over like that!' Luna snapped, marching towards him, causing him to take a few steps back and laugh nervously.

'All is fair in...' Oscar was cut off by Annie.

'In *love* and war were you going to say Oscar...maybe just love,'

Annie teased, then started laughing, as Tom and Ace approached none the wiser.

Luna and Oscar turned to Annie and glared at her, both simultaneously screwing up their faces and saying, 'What are you talking about?' Ace and Tom looked puzzled, unaware of Annie's conclusion that Oscar had a crush on Luna, and that he had unintentionally hit her with a love bomb.

The gang continued through the woods, occasionally stopping to play a game with energy balls, and climb trees - something Oscar seemed particularly good at. Unbeknown to the others, apart from Luna, Oscar was using his flying powers to gain height up various trees. Luna kept this to herself, remembering what Oscar had said to her earlier that day in Lindull woods.

They all chatted, as they continued walking, until Luna thought she had better check the time. When she looked at her watch it was already 10pm.

'The time! Annie we better head back. My dad will be home by now,' Luna panicked.

'I don't even know where we are?' Annie worried, concerned it would take them ages to get back.

Luna, Annie, Tom, and Ace noticed Oscar was checking his mobile phone surreptitiously, quickly putting it away when he saw them looking. Oscar's mood suddenly changed, and he looked grumpy and distracted - like he was when Luna and Annie met him at the entrance to the woods on Cashmere Road earlier on.

'What's up with you bro?' Tom asked, furrowing his brow at his friend's changed mood.

'Nothing,' Oscar said, frowning.

'I don't mind walking them back dude if you and Tom are staying out.' Ace offered, thinking that Oscar seemed irritated.

'No...it's okay. I'll take them back. You two wait here for me. Yeah.' Oscar directed, looking at his friends pointedly, emphasising his order for them to remain there. They both nodded, and Oscar led Annie and Luna away.

Oscar remained silent for some time as Luna and Annie followed him through the darkened woodland. He seemed distracted, as though he was mulling things over in his head. Luna wondered what was wrong and speculated that it must be something to do with a message he received on his phone.

'You're quiet Oscar...You okay?' Luna asked tentatively. Annie hung back a bit to let them talk, sensing it might be a private conversation.

'Yeah...I'm fine.' Oscar turned to look at Luna; his face softened again, and he continued lowering his voice, 'Don't forget all that stuff I taught you earlier today...the paralysis hex...and flying.'

'I'm hardly going to forget it,' Luna said in a slightly jokey tone.

'I mean it Luna.' Oscar stared at her, his face stern, holding his gaze to indicate the seriousness of what he was saying, his eyes seemed to look darker and menacing. 'You don't know when you're going to need it,' he said slowly, his voice trailing off.

'Okay. Okay....About earlier. What do you think Annie meant?' Luna asked cautiously.

'What d'ya mean?' Oscar avoided looking at her.

'When she said something about love...' Luna looked down at her feet, not really sure why she was even asking him about it.

'Don't know,' Oscar lied, then looked Luna dead in the eyes. He couldn't keep his feelings back. They both stopped walking and gazed at each other. Annie looked on, then stopped, feeling awkward, so averted her eyes.

'I really like you Luna...Didn't realise how much.' Oscar's face softened, he continued to gaze at her tenderly.

'I like you too, Oscar.' Luna felt butterflies in her stomach and could feel her heart starting to race – but it wasn't because she was scared or angry, it was something else. Oscar smiled gently, and they both slowly leaned into each other. As their faces moved closer, they were abruptly interrupted by a voice Luna did not expect to hear. It was Mr Porter. Oscar pulled away from

Luna, and they all looked at their teacher who watched on, his face expressionless.

'Well. So here you are, altogether. Up to no good,' Mr Porter said disapprovingly, his voice laced with disdain.

'Oh crap,' Annie said under her breath, 'did my dads send you? We're really, really, sorry. Honestly. Please don't tell them. I promise we're going home now.' Annie panicked, as she moved in closer, worried she and Luna had been caught out in their plans.

'Be quiet Annie,' Mr Porter commanded, coldly. This took Annie by surprise, causing her to gape at him. Luna furrowed her brow, wondering what had caused his sudden change in character. Oscar looked down at his feet and didn't react. He just kept quiet.

'I should've known better than to trust you to follow simple instructions.' Mr Porter leered at Oscar. 'Look up when I talk to you boy,' Mr Porter demanded, glaring at him contemptuously. Oscar slowly lifted his head to face Mr Porter, breathing nervously.

'Thought you could outsmart me, did you? Idiot. Like your father. An idiot.' Mr Porter spat on the floor in front of Oscar's feet. Oscar clenched his fists, the anger starting to rise inside him. Mr Porter observed this display of resentment and started to laugh malevolently. He then raised his hand towards Oscar, causing the boy to swiftly rise up off the ground. As Oscar hovered in the air, Mr Porter, drew his fingers together as though he was gripping something. Oscar started to choke.

'For your stupidity. Do *not* try to outwit me. It will not end well for *you*,' Mr Porter spat, then brutally plunged Oscar to the ground, leaving him gasping for air. Annie started crying and shaking, and Luna pulled her cousin into her body to comfort and shield her from their fierce teacher. Luna was trying to get her head around what was happening, but knew she had to remain calm, and not provoke him too much.

'I'm sorry. Luna. I'm sorry,' Oscar cried, laying on the floor.

'Sorry doesn't cut it. Do you want to tell your little girlfriend what you are really like Oscar? Do you want to shatter her illusion or shall I?' Mr Porter was enjoying the pain this was causing Oscar.

'Luna, I'm sorry. I had no choice...he was going to kill my family...he...I was going to tell you...I just...' Oscar sat up and buried his head in his hands, as Mr Porter interrupted his apology.

'Shut up. Pathetic child,' Mr Porter scolded, then turned to Luna; his once soft and amiable eyes were now cold and empty.

'I tasked Oscar to befriend you. Make you think he liked you. It didn't start well though, did it Oscar? Fighting with the Le Fai brat in the canteen at school, and then finally when you actually buck up the courage to lure Luna in, you only end up making a mess of it. I'm afraid you don't even get full marks for effort, as your attempts were utterly useless. You have caused me other problems. Your fun and games in the park left another mess for me to sort out. So many mistakes Oscar. Tut. Tut. But I had my other plan. I started at the bottom with Suzie Le Fai. I even got engaged to her! Engaged to a Le Fai! Me?! What was I thinking.' Mr Porter started laughing maniacally, and Annie started to weep again. He continued, 'This is all your fault Oscar. Because of you, things are going to be messier than I intended. You have made things very difficult.' Mr Porter sighed, then paused, and turned his attention to Luna.

'Luna. You. Know. What. I. Want. Don't you,' the words left Mr Porter's mouth slowly and cut through Luna like sharp shards of ice.

'Yes. Yes, I do,' Luna said quietly, now terrified of where this encounter was going, and where it would end.

CHAPTER 20: A LESSON IN TERROR

Mr Porter moved in closer to Luna and although her instinct was to retreat, she tried not to show any weakness and stood her ground.

'I want that amulet from around your neck,' Mr Porter commanded in a sinister whisper.

'Take it from me then,' Luna spat back, testing him.

'Luna!' Annie cried in fear.

'Nice try Luna. Of course, you know I cannot simply take the amulet from you. This is why I instructed that idiot Oscar to get it for me. There would be no need to force anything. If he'd done his job properly you would have willingly passed it over.' Mr Porter shot Oscar a deadly look, then returned his attention to Luna, taking a few steps away, using the open space between the trees, as his stage, continuing his monologue of terror.

'Luna, do you remember that day Oscar spoke to you at school, when he gave the sob story about being different from his dad, about getting caught in the middle of the fighting, boo, hoo... well he didn't mean any of it Luna. He was following my orders. I told him to say that to make you feel sorry for him. It worked. I thought things were going to plan. I could see I was also gaining your trust, making you think I actually cared. You're as stupid as him.' Mr Porter turned back to Oscar and spat on the floor in his direction. 'When did it all start falling apart Oscar? When did you start liking her Oscar? Things didn't have to be like this...But you decided you knew better. Thought you could double cross me, didn't you. Teaching her tricks in the woods to take me on. When did you plan to tell her? Or *did* you? I don't think you ever did. Something stopped you, Oscar. Part of you wanted her to give me the amulet, didn't you. See her fail as its keeper. Part of you hates her Oscar. Hates her for being a Le Fai,' Mr Porter said coldly, directing his contempt at all of them.

'That's not true! I was going to tell her, tonight…but then…' Oscar called out, frustrated and deflated.

'But. Then. What? Oh, wait, I decided to speed things up, didn't I. Idiot boy.' Luna was still holding Annie, who had stopped crying, but clung onto her cousin in fear. Luna remained still. Listening, wondering what to do next.

'I had another minor problem. Ariella. I had to find a way to quieten her. She knew who I was, and what I wanted. Silly woman even invited me to her shop to talk to me, to confront me. You see she had a vision, a prophetic vision warning her about me. But rather than telling *you*, Luna. The foolish woman approached me first. I had to shut her up, stop her from causing further issues. So that's why she is. Well. Incapacitated.' Mr Porter bellowed a vindictive laugh. Annie looked distraught.

'What have you done!' Annie screamed, Luna hushed her and whispered 'It's okay. She'll be okay. She's with my nan. She'll be okay. I promise.'

'Stop whispering!' Mr Porter ordered, sounding deranged, and continued with his taunts. 'Then I thought. How can I get to you Luna. Ahh, yes, of course, your father. I had the perfect opportunity this afternoon when you left him *alone*. It was like a gift from the gods.' He paused, his eyes reflecting his contempt, 'the text message to Nick, and the note I left for you, seemed to work a treat. You are all so gullible, so trusting.' He stared coldly at Luna, her brow furrowed as his gaze shadowed her face. Her heart started racing and she felt sick in the pit of her stomach.

'What have you done to him?' Luna breathed rapidly, feeling her despair being replaced with anger.

'Let's just say he won't forget my visit any time soon. He's in safe keeping for now. But. There's one condition. And I think you know what that is Luna. Don't you,' Mr Porter said smugly.

'Don't give it to him Luna!' Oscar shouted, Mr Porter turned swiftly, and directed an attack at the Blackthorn boy, striking him with a lightning bolt flash which fired out from his hands, hitting Oscar's leg, causing it to break. Oscar groaned as he lay wounded on the ground, his face contorted with pain. Luna's anger continued to rise, as she watched her friend writhe in agony.

'Tut. Tut. You're quite stupid Oscar. You need to learn to keep your mouth shut…Now Luna. If you want to see your dad again, you know what to do.' Luna glared at him; her eyes suddenly dark, filled with rage.

'No. I won't.' Luna's voice was quivering from the anger.

'No. No? Noooo!' Mr Porter suddenly held his hand in the direction of Annie and used his will to scoop her up in the air. He then did the same to Oscar, hovering him and Annie side by side, manipulating their limbs like a torturous puppet master.

'Is that still a *NO* Luna?' Luna watched on in terror as Mr Porter continued to torture her friends, mid-air, twisting their limbs in different directions. It was too painful to watch.

'Three lives might be lost tonight, Luna, if you don't play ball. Now be a good girl and pass me the amulet,' Mr Porter demanded, as he performed a squeezing action with his hand, which caused Oscar and Annie to choke. Luna closed her eyes and went to take the amulet from around her neck. As she touched the magical object, it started to grow hot, and glow. The ground began to shake, taking Mr Porter by surprise, causing him to lose his magical grip on Oscar and Annie, who came crashing down landing on the floor of the woodland. As Mr Porter was distracted by the tremors which continued to unsteady him, Oscar took his opportunity and dragged himself out of his torturer's view, urging Annie to move to safety with him. Suddenly the ground stopped shaking and, in the clearing, near to where Mr Porter had been conducting his orchestra of terror, a magnificent indigo light appeared. As it grew brighter and expanded, a beautiful white light radiated from the centre and an iridescent figure emerged. It was Aggie, Luna's mum.

'Luna do *not* give him the amulet,' Aggie ordered, then turned her attention to Mr Porter, using an invisible force to hold him away from her daughter.

'You will *not* take the amulet. You will *not* harm my family or Luna's friends.' Mr Porter stared up at Aggie, the superiority that once dominated his expression was suddenly replaced with fear, as Aggie directed more powerful magic towards him, freezing him on the spot. The others looked on at the human statue, which seemed devoid of any life.

Luna instinctively ran towards her mum, entering the light which surrounded her, and embraced the illuminated figure.

'Mum! Mum! I've missed you so much,' Luna cried. Aggie lifted her daughter's face and spoke gently to her.

'I never left you sweet. A part of me is in the amulet you wear; it carries a part of you too, and all of those who were its keeper before us. We're bound to the amulet forever.' Luna pulled away, fearful of what that meant.

'I don't understand. I'm going to be trapped in it?'

'No, no. Part of your spirit lives on in the amulet and will serve the keepers who come after us. It's our energy, as pure love, that drives its power and acts to protect our family. The witch amulet was only ever meant for those with Le Fai blood, and only those chosen as the true matriarchs. It connects us directly to our ancestry in the fairy realm. You're its keeper, you *are* the amulet, as I am, and our mothers before us.' Aggie raised her translucent arm, gesturing for Luna to look at the light which radiated around her. As Luna gazed into the light, she saw many faces appear, some she recognised, including nang, Seraphina, and even her own face, but others were unfamiliar to her. 'These are all the Le Fai matriarchs who are bound to the amulet,' Aggie paused, gazing lovingly at her daughter, then continued. 'No one but the keeper must have control of the amulet. It will not let that happen. *We* must not let it happen.' Aggie smiled wistfully and stroked Luna's hair.

'I failed. I failed didn't I. I nearly gave it away.' Luna hung her head down in disappointment at her perceived moment of weakness.

'No, you did not fail. You showed Annie and Oscar that you care about them, that you're a true friend. You were never going to give it to him. It's not that easy. I tried to return it to the fairy realm, but it would not let me, so I hid it away in my old box, but it always called to me. I understand now that we cannot escape our destiny, and our destiny is as its keeper.'

'What will happen to Mr Porter?' Luna looked on at the frozen figure, who she once thought was a kind-hearted teacher, but now revealed to be a manipulative monster.

'That's not Mr Porter. There's no such person.' Aggie suddenly waved her hand, and his face began to transform into another person, someone Luna did not recognise.

'Mr Porter was a persona he adopted, and shape-shifted into. This man is Adam. Adam and I were once friends. He once tried to take the amulet before. This is the person who took your dad's powers.' Aggie's voice saddened.

'Him?! Dad told me about him! All this time he still wanted it!'

'Now he must be taken to the fairy realm where they will deal with him. He's too much of a threat here in this world.'

'What will they do to him?'

'They'll bind him and imprison him there.'

'Bind him?'

'Bind him to Aurora's ring. The ring you're carrying in your pocket.' Luna slowly pulled out the ring she had taken from the 'goth' box and held it between her fingers to examine it, the purple stone seemed to twinkle as it caught the moonlight.

'This ring. How did I...' Luna continued to gaze at it.

'The fraction of your spirit which is bound to the amulet, knew it would be needed. It told you to bring it here tonight.' Luna looked confused, as she didn't quite understand what her mum meant. Then suddenly, once more the ground started to shake, but this time Aurora appeared. The queen of the fairy elm approached Luna and requested the ring, placing it on her own finger. Luna observed as Aurora drew Mr Porter into the magical object. She watched as his body shifted shape into a whirling vortex which vanished as he was sucked into the stone of the ring. The fairy queen acknowledged Luna and Aggie with a graceful nod of her head and then faded away.

'He has gone now. He can't harm anyone anymore. But you mustn't be complacent. There'll always be others who want the amulet. Call upon it when you need to. You will learn how to truly unlock its powers over time. You've only just started your journey sweet. There are many battles you'll need to fight in this physical lifetime. You can't escape your fate.' Aggie explained; Luna wondered what she meant, and for a moment worried about what her future held, anticipating many challenges ahead. Then her thoughts drifted to her dad.

'What about dad? We need to get help. We need to find him!' Luna fretted, suddenly remembering what Mr Porter had told her.

'Your dad is in safe hands Luna. The others are with him,' Aggie said reassuringly.

'Others?' Luna sounded confused.

'Your nang, Nick, and Daniel,' Aggie confirmed, then paused to look at Luna, 'I love you, Luna. Remember I'm always with you. In the amulet, but more so in your heart.' Aggie placed her luminous hand onto Luna's chest, smiled, and as Luna closed her eyes feeling her mother's love, Aggie drifted away. Luna opened her eyes and stood there for a moment looking at the now empty spot where her mum had been standing. Annie slowly walked over to Luna and put her arm around her.

'Are you okay Luna?' Annie asked gently.

'Yes...I guess,' Luna sounded distant, lost in her thoughts.

'It's going to be okay. You heard your mum.' Annie said tenderly, gently pulling Luna towards her.

Luna then turned to look at Oscar who remained on the ground, using his arms to keep his body upright, whilst his legs were stretched out in front of him.

'We need to get you help. Get you home,' Luna said sounding worried, watching his pained expression.

'I'll be okay Luna...Leon has gone to find Ace and Tom for help.' Oscar groaned, the pain audible. Luna walked over to Oscar and knelt next to his broken leg, then placed her hands over the break. As her hands covered the damaged limb, a blue healing light emitted from her palms and permeated the injury. Oscar slowly moved his once broken leg and the agony that showed on his face disappeared.

'Luna...thank you...I didn't deserve that. I didn't expect you to do that...after everything I've done. I'm so sorry. I really am.' Oscar held his head down, avoiding eye contact because of the guilt he felt.

'It's okay. I understand.' Luna paused, thinking about what had happened, 'Oscar. It's okay. You didn't do what he asked in the end, did you. I understand now why you taught me all that stuff. You didn't want to give him the amulet. Something stopped you. Because we're friends, right?' Luna smiled at Oscar, who looked at her regretfully, but seemed grateful for her compassion and understanding. Annie, however, looked on at Oscar in disgust, and could not keep her feelings to herself.

'You're as bad as Mr Porter! You're a typical Blackthorn. Self-centred. A traitor. A coward. A true enemy of *my* family. My brother was right about you. You're nothing but trouble.' Annie continued to glare at him with contempt. Luna felt differently, and did not approve of Annie's scorn.

'Annie!' Luna scolded.

'Don't fall for it Luna. He's not the person we thought. He's not our friend.' Oscar didn't say anything, he just accepted Annie's vitriol. Luna went quiet, not knowing what to say, feeling torn between her sense of loyalty to Annie and her growing feelings for Oscar. There was an uncomfortable silence, which was interrupted by the arrival of Ace and Tom, who came running over with Leon flying next to them. Oscar stood up and walked towards them.

'What happened dude? Are you all okay?' Ace asked sounding fretful.

'Everything's alright mate. Come on. Let's go.' Oscar started walking away from Luna and Annie but briefly turned back to look at Luna, his dark eyes meeting hers.

'See you around Luna Le Fai,' he said quietly, with a trace of sadness in his voice. Luna did not speak but gazed back at him, her eyes soft but overflowing with sorrow. As he disappeared into the woods with Ace and Tom, Annie hugged Luna, recognising how affected her cousin was by Oscar's departure. However, she did not regret forcing it, believing that Oscar would only bring further problems for Luna and the rest of the Le Fais. Although in many ways, it felt like her friendship with Oscar had come to an end, something deep inside Luna knew that it was not yet over. That Oscar Blackthorn and his family, in one way or another, would always be part of her life.

'We better get home. But I don't know where we are,' Annie said uneasily, worried at the thought at being stranded in the woods overnight. Luna raised a ball of light above their heads to help them see better. Then, through the undergrowth, Luna heard the familiar hissing of a snake, it was the adder she had encountered on two previous occasions in Lindull woods. It circled Luna's feet and she bent down to pick it up, holding its head up towards her face.

'Urgh...I hate snakes.' Annie shuddered, moving away from Luna.

'I am not too keen on humans...sssssss...,' the adder hissed. Unlike Luna, Annie was unable to hear the snake talk, but Luna gave a wry smile as the adder gibed her cousin.

'You're back again. You seem to follow me around here a lot. Shouldn't you be hibernating?' Luna asked, looking at its reptilian face.

'I am not like other adders...sssss...I have been waiting for you my friend...sssss,' the snake replied affectionately.

'Well, maybe you can help us get out of here?' Luna suggested, still holding the snake in her hands.

'Yessss...anything for my friend Luna Le Fai...sssss...put me down and I will lead the way...sssss,' the snake confirmed. Luna gently placed him on the ground, and he slithered through the woodland, with Luna watching intently, followed by Annie who was careful not to get too close to the adder.

It wasn't long before Luna and Annie were at the edge of the woodland, near to the entrance close to the back of Luna's house. The adder raised its head up towards Luna and spoke.

'Take me with you…sssss…it was only a matter of time before you found me…ssss.'

Luna wasn't sure why, but she instinctively picked up the adder, following the snake's request.

'And what should I call you?'

'Hisssssssss whatever you wish…sssssss.'

'How about Zak?' Luna suggested uncertainly. Annie screwed her face up.

'Zak? Nah.' Annie paused to think, then continued, 'How about Sebastian. Sebastian the snake?' Annie suggested. Luna furrowed her brow, then thought about it.

'Sebastian…Sebastian…Yeah, okay. Sebastian!' Luna said merrily, allowing the adder to slide into the deep pocket of her hooded top.

They continued to walk towards Hubble Road, when Annie stopped and gently slapped her forehead, as she had a sudden thought.

'Jack! We forgot about Jack. We left him in the pendulum.'

'Oh, I forgot. Poor Jack. We better get him out.' Luna reached into the pocket of her jeans to retrieve the pendulum; however, it didn't appear to be there. Now in a state of panic, she frantically searched through both pockets, checking multiple times. But it was no good. The pendulum had gone. Jack could be anywhere, and Luna was concerned that they may never get him back.

CHAPTER 21: UNEXPECTED ENDINGS

'Oh my god, I've lost it. How are we going to get Jack back?' Luna sounded distressed, wondering when it had fallen out of her pocket, worried that it could be anywhere in the expanse of woodland. She went to head back to the woods when Annie stopped her.

'There's no point now Luna. Would take you ages in the dark. We really need to get back.'

'But what about Jack? We've left him trapped in that pendulum!' Luna fretted.

'I don't know. We can ask my dad. He'll know. But I just think...I know this sounds bad, but we can't do anything right now, can we.' Annie said uncertainly.

Luna flopped down and sat on the curb, then buried her head in her hands, riddled with guilt about misplacing the pendulum. Annie sat next to her and tried to reassure her.

'It's not your fault. I'm sure there's something that can be done to find him. But we can't do anything now, can we? We need to get back.' There was a sense of urgency in Annie's voice to move on. Luna resigned herself to the fact that looking for the pendulum now would be futile, and she stood up.

They both walked towards Luna's in silence. When they approached the house, the lights were on, and Daniel's car was parked outside. They ran into the house and Daniel hugged

Annie, relieved to see her. Luna continued at a fast pace, and raced into the sitting room, calling for her dad, hoping he would be there. But he was not.

'Luna, he's not here,' Daniel said gently, trying not to raise too much concern.

'Where is he? Is he alright?' Luna fretted. Daniel could hear the anxiety in her voice, so approached her, then put his arm around her to offer some comfort.

'He will be. He has been taken to your nan's to recover. We found him upstairs, unconscious.'

'Unconscious? What happened to him? It was Mr Porter. He did it!' Luna sounded frantic.

'Yes, we know. We know everything. It has been a difficult night for all of us.' Daniel looked at Annie and Luna solemnly.

'When I left you here, I didn't go straight away. I drove a little further down the road and parked up so you couldn't see me. Something didn't feel right so I stuck around...I watched you both leave and was about to follow you, but then I saw you talking to that spirit, Jack, I believe. So, I held back. I saw you start walking towards the end of the street, then I got out of my car to follow you, when I spotted Frank coming from the cut at the back of your house. I didn't know what was happening. Wondered why he was here. Something felt off. So, I walked further towards your house to try to get a closer look, to see what he was doing. He looked in your front window and disappeared again. I then walked up to your house, and as I got outside, I felt something. I had a vision of your dad trapped inside, upstairs in one of the bedrooms. So, I called Nick, and he came straight over. He got the spare key from your nan's and when we got in, we found him. We just took him straight to her house. We knew she would know what to do. That's when she told us it was Frank. That he, did, everything. She also said that you would both be okay, and someone should come back here to meet you.' Daniel gave a long sigh, then continued, 'I'm going to take you both to Liz's now.'

'Dad...Is nan going to be okay?' Annie asked sounding worried about her grandmother Ariella, her voice quivering.

'Yes, yes, she'll be absolutely fine. There's nothing for you to worry about. I promise.' Daniel sounded genuine, which gave Annie some comfort. He once again pulled her into a warm embrace, allowing her to feel the love and safety of her dad. This silenced all the intrusive thoughts which had been making her worry about her grandmother.

'We need to get Luna to her nan's so she can see her dad. So, she can see he's going to be okay.' Daniel looked Luna in the eyes earnestly, then smiled.

'Everything will be okay now girls,' Daniel said, and started heading towards the door, which signalled to them it was time to go.

Daniel, Annie, and Luna headed out of the house, turning the lights off, then locking the door behind them. They all got into Daniel's car and headed towards Luna's grandmother's house on Main Road. When they arrived, Luna was relieved the door was unlocked so she ran straight in with the others slowly following behind.

'Dad? Where's dad?' Luna called, sounding distressed. Her nan walked through from the sitting room and stood in the doorway, hugging Luna as she approached.

'Your dad is okay. He hasn't been awake long. I gave him an antidote to reverse the spell, it seems to have worked,' nang said, sounding positive.

'Can I see him? Is he in there?' Luna pointed urgently into the sitting room.

'Yes, but be gentle with him. He's still a bit sleepy.' Luna walked into the sitting room, not knowing what to expect, worried that there was something they were hiding from her. She was relieved to see her dad looked as he should. Neil shuffled himself up into a sitting position, looking a bit stiff and sleepy. Despite her grandmother telling her to be gentle, Luna threw her arms around him, and held onto him as though she didn't want to let go, feeling that if she did, she might lose him forever.

'I'm okay Luna. I'm okay love. You can put me down,' her dad said sounding like her embrace was suffocating him. Luna released her grip and pulled away.

'I feel like this is all my fault. I should've waited for you, instead of going off with Annie to the family party, then this wouldn't have happened.'

'No love, it's not your fault, you have nothing to feel bad about.'

'What did he do? What happened?'

'I don't remember much...The doorbell rang, and your teacher was at the door. He asked if he could come in. Had something important to tell me. Well, I panicked, worried something had happened to you. I let him in and then I just remember turning round to walk to the sitting room, and, well, the next thing I'm waking up on nang's sofa,' Neil said sounding confused. Nang re-entered the room, stood behind Luna and placed her hand on her granddaughter's shoulder.

'Mr Porter used a sleeping curse. I'm surprised he didn't use the coma curse, but he must have had his reasons. The sleeping curse isn't as long lasting. But it can be unpredictable, so I gave him the antidote just to be sure. I think Mr Porter had other plans for your dad.' Nang paused, carefully thinking about her words, then continued, 'The most important thing is that your dad is okay now. And you and Annie are okay. That's all that matters. Try to put the rest behind you.' Luna turned to face her grandmother and perched herself on the edge of the sofa next to her dad.

'Mr Porter has gone now. Aurora took him away...' Luna hung her head down, unsure if she should tell her dad about seeing her mum, realising it was not the right time – it would only upset him. Luna wondered if her dad knew the real identity of Mr Porter, that he was in fact Adam, the witch who years earlier had absorbed her dad's powers, after a hex went amiss. Again, Luna decided it would be better not to share this information with her dad. Worried that it might cause further upset, something she wanted to avoid during her dad's recovery.

'We do have some good news. Ariella is getting better. I've been working on her daily and she has shown improvement already. In the last day or so she has been slipping in and out of consciousness, so it won't be long before she's with us again,' nang said reassuringly.

'Daniel said that you knew what had happened. That you knew about Mr Porter. About everything. How did you...' Luna asked curiously, looking searchingly at her grandmother.

'That really doesn't matter now. All you need to know is that everything is as it should be. We're all okay,' nang explained looking directly into Luna's eyes, urging her not to dwell too much on what had happened, but move forward.

Luna nodded resignedly, realising that her grandmother was not going to reveal how she had come to know about events of the night. She looked back at her dad, then heard a hissing from her hoodie, as Sebastian slithered out of her pocket and onto her lap, lifting his head up towards her face.

'Oh, this is Sebastian, my er...my companion creature.' Luna looked at the snake, who affectionately slithered his long silky body around her hands.

'Only Luna could have a snake as a companion.' Neil shook his head resignedly and grinned.

'Indeed,' nang agreed and chuckled.

It was after midnight by the time Luna and her dad returned home. They were both exhausted following the dramatic events of the evening. Before going up to bed, Luna put Sebastian outside, so he could roam freely and hunt if necessary – she did not worry about the cold weather, as he did not appear to be like other adders. Luna then went straight upstairs, into her bedroom and collapsed on her bed. She didn't even bother to get changed; she was too zapped of energy. Luna closed her eyes, expecting to fall straight asleep, but her mind had other ideas, reliving her encounter with Mr Porter and seeing her mum again. As she replayed those events, Luna clutched the amulet, however, she did not feel the same angst that she had before, now understanding that she had the full protection of the magical object. Luna took a deep breath and closed her eyes, eventually drifting asleep. However, her eyes suddenly opened as she was disturbed by a persistent and loud tapping sound coming from her window. Tap, tap, tap, tap, tap, tap, tap it went. Luna got up quickly and hurried to the window, opened her curtains and looked out.

'Luna...Luna,' she heard Oscar calling up from outside. Luna opened her window and peered down at Oscar.

'Do you ever go to bed,' Luna said, sounding slightly irritated, however, part of her was pleased to see him again.

'Come down. I've got something of yours,' Oscar called up. Luna shut her window, and headed downstairs to the kitchen, and out through the backdoor. Sebastian slithered around near her feet, greeting her as she left the house. She picked him up and walked over to Oscar.

'Leon just tried to eat that snake,' Oscar said gesturing to it with his head.

'He better not! He's, my companion...Sebastian, meet Oscar.' Luna said uneasily, wondering if talking to Oscar was wise.

'Hi Sebastian...never thought a Le Fai would have a snake companion,' he smiled vaguely, then continued, his tone now sounding more serious, 'Luna. I wanted to explain things and apologise. I've been a...' Oscar's voice broke off.

'It's in the past. Let's move on from it,' Luna said sighing, remembering what her nan suggested about the need to move forward. Afterall, everything was okay now. They were all okay.

'What about Annie?' Oscar asked uncomfortably.

'Yeah. Annie. Not sure she's going to forgive you any time soon. Might be difficult, but, I don't see why *we* can't still be friends.'

'I hope so.' Oscar looked down at the grass near his feet and shuffled them around awkwardly.

'You said you had something for me?' Luna asked expectantly, starting to feel the cold air wrap around her.

'Oh, yeah. This.' Oscar reached inside his pocket and pulled out the brass pendulum Luna had lost at some point during the night. Her eyes lit up.

'How did you find it?'

'Leon took it. He saw it fall out of your pocket. But then everything kicked off, so never got a chance to give it to you.'

'Thank god.' Luna took the pendulum and put it back in her pocket.

'Guess I'll be seeing you later then?' Oscar said testing her, wondering if he would see her again.

'Yeah, we'll work something out.' Luna avoided looking at him, not sure how she would work things out. She put Sebastian back down on the grass, then headed back in as Oscar turned and glided up into the air heading in the direction of Lindull woods.

Luna went back into her room, sat on her bed and took the pendulum out of her pocket. She felt relieved to have it back in her possession, and started swinging it gently from side to side, wondering if she should draw Jack out straight away, or wait until the morning. As she continued to swing the magical brass object, she zoned out. Then closed her eyes, still gently swinging the pendulum. Soon, Luna felt as though she had been transported into another dimension, to somewhere unrecognisable, like a place you would visit in a dream. As Luna immersed herself in the scene in front of her, she focused in on a framed picture, which appeared before her, floating in a purple and black haze, forming the backdrop of her vision. The picture began spinning towards her, then slowed down as it got closer until all she could see was the scene inside the frame. She could see three disembodied floating heads - one belonged to Mr Porter, the other to Jack, and the third, to her old friend Alex, from back in Leicester. Whilst they were all together in the same scene, at first, they did not appear to be aware of one another. Then they each spoke in turn.

'Where am I?' Jack said sounding confused and dazed.

'Hello, hello? Can you hear me, I hear you, but I can't see you,' Alex fretted, darting her eyes around, trying to locate Jack's voice, but like the others, her face remained fixed in one direction. Mr Porter heard both voices but did not reply at first. He looked as though he was making fast calculations in his mind. He scowled, conceiving where they were. Suddenly Mr Porter gave a sinister smile and acknowledged Jack and Alex.

'There's nothing to fear. I can help you get out. We can all help each other get back home, where we belong.'

As Luna watched on, she wanted to call out to warn her friends not to trust Mr Porter but found herself unable to make any sound.

Mr Porter narrowed his eyes, and gave a satisfied smile, his malevolent face now filling the entire scene in front of Luna. The image of the dark witch continued to expand until it felt as though he was almost upon her. Then suddenly he disappeared, leaving a dark, empty space, with nothing left but a lingering feeling of dread and terror. Luna quickly opened her eyes and had to steady her breath. She felt sick and panicky. Where were they all; and why was Alex there with Jack and Mr Porter - Luna felt puzzled by the abstract scene. She knew that this was not a dream. This was a vision. A vision that made her realise that life would never be the same again. That this was only the start of things to come. Luna felt the amulet grow hot, and she had a sudden feeling of unease about what the future might hold. Something deep inside her - perhaps that part of her spirit bound to the amulet - told her that this was not the last time she would experience this vision. Luna knew that Mr Porter would return with only one thing on his mind - revenge.

To be continued...

Printed in Dunstable, United Kingdom

65700452R00131